NORFOLK INSTITUTE
ART & DESIGN LIBRARY

Please return this book

GREAT YARMOUTH
College of Art

LIBRARY

762.68

075553

D0266509

THE NATIONAL TRUST BOOK
OF
FURNISHING
TEXTILES

Pamela Clabburn

VIKING
in association with
THE NATIONAL TRUST

VIKING

Penguin Books Ltd, 27 Wrights Lane, London W8 5TZ (Publishing and Editorial)
and Harmondsworth, Middlesex, England (Distribution and Warehouse)
Viking Penguin Inc., 40 West 23rd Street, New York, New York 10010, USA
Penguin Books Australia Ltd, Ringwood, Victoria, Australia
Penguin Books Canada Ltd, 2801 John Street, Markham, Ontario, Canada L3R 1B4
Penguin Books (NZ) Ltd, 182–190 Wairau Road, Auckland 10, New Zealand

First published 1988

Copyright © Pamela Clabburn, 1988

All rights reserved.
Without limiting the rights under copyright
reserved above, no part of this publication may be
reproduced, stored in or introduced into a retrieval system,
or transmitted, in any form or by any means (electronic, mechanical,
photocopying, recording or otherwise), without the prior
written permission of both the copyright owner and
the above publisher of this book.

Typeset in 11/13 Monophoto Palatino
Printed in Great Britain by
Butler & Tanner Ltd, Frome and London
Designed by Judith Gordon

British Library Cataloguing in Publication Data

Clabburn, Pamela
    The National Trust book of furnishing textiles.
    1. Textile fabrics—England—History
    2. House furnishings—England—History
    I. Title
    746   NK8843

ISBN 0–670–80560–2

Library of Congress Catalog Card Number 87–51347

CONTENTS

CONTENTS

To Rachel,
who taught me that objects only have meaning
when related to people.

PREFACE

No work of non-fiction can be written without help from others, especially those scholars of the past who painstakingly annotated and transcribed old accounts and inventories and published them in various journals for our benefit. To them and to those of the present, in record offices, universities and learned societies up and down the country, who sort and catalogue the thousands of scraps of paper mercifully preserved in old houses, I owe most of the information in this book.

Many individuals have willingly given me their time, interest and expertise in various fields, notably Dr Hassell Smith, who allowed me to use the computer analysis of the Bacon Archives, and Elizabeth Stern, who taught me to read it accurately. Everyone at Blickling, especially Jacinth Rogers and Liz Adler, read many books for me and did all they could to help, while Rachel Young, Lesley Parker and Derek Bickford-Smith said, 'Why haven't you discussed — ?' Shiela Betterton, James Gilchrist, John Madison, Anne Buck, Margaret Swain, Jenifer Frost and Elizabeth Griffiths fed me with useful pieces of information. There are also those historic Building Representatives and their secretaries in the National Trust who took pains to get me the illustrations I needed, and last, but by no means least, I must thank Ann den Engelse who, in spite of every setback, was determined to produce the best typescript a publisher ever received.

All inventories, accounts, diaries, journals and letters as well as most general works used have been listed in the bibliography. The superior numbers in the text refer directly to the relevant work.

ACKNOWLEDGEMENTS

For the Plates
By kind permission of Gonville and Caius College, Cambridge: 113
Norfolk Museums Service: 3, 62
Private Collections: 72, 107
All other plates, The National Trust, London

For the Figures
The drawings on pp. 100 and 135 are by Anthony and June Dalton

INTRODUCTORY NOTE

Upholstery is the sum of all the textile furnishings of a house; this includes most wall coverings, carpets and rugs, curtains and bed hangings, as well as seat furniture and all the myriad odds and ends made from fabric which turn a house into a home. Plaster-work, carving, graining, panelling, along with sculpture and paintings, can all be admired as works of art, but a house with all this beauty and no textiles would be a most depressing place in which to live.

Until at least the middle of the nineteenth century it was the upholsterer who provided the essential comfort. He organized the carvers, gilders and cabinet-makers, bought his fabrics from weavers, mercers and linen drapers, his braids and trimmings from the braid-makers and *passementiers*, and saw to the stuffing of the chair seats, down pillows and feather-beds, as well as making the mattresses. He provided pulleys and hooks, rings and cloak-pins for the curtains, bars for the shutters and sometimes needlework for the chairs, and in general made the house fit for the family to live in, rather than for the visitor to admire.

This book is an attempt to explain what fabrics the upholsterer had at his disposal from the late middle ages onwards, and how he used them in the service of his clients.

PART ONE

A HISTORY OF FURNISHINGS

One

PRE-1600

The possibilities for the furnishings of a house at any time in history have depended on technical ability, fashion and the practicalities of trade with foreign countries, and these three things are interlocked. The fabrics for

1. Miss Chichester's bedroom at Arlington Court, which would have no character without its textiles.
Late nineteenth century

furnishings cannot be produced without the craftsmen and engineers to make the equipment, whether this is worked by hand or power, and then skilled artisans are needed, as well as a host of those less skilled, to use the equipment to the best advantage. At different periods, different countries have had both the basic requirements and the skill to exploit them and have been in a position to sell to less favoured places. In reverse, the goods produced have been coveted by those without basic skills and natural resources. Many instances of this can be cited: the Chinese skill in silk weaving and their knowledge of silk production; rug- and carpet-making, first by the nomadic tribes of Central Asia and then by the Persians, Indians and Turks; and the production of cotton and related goods in India.

These and many more developments in different parts of the world led to the trading of textiles between nations and, more particularly, have led to a breed of merchants who were willing to risk money and gamble on the safe arrival of goods over appallingly difficult sea and land routes. The availability of specific fabrics for use in thousands of homes did and still does depend on trade between nations. Even today, with all the technology available, Britain would have a much narrower range of fabrics if it were not for her imports.

As far as technical ability went in the years up to and around 1600, China and the Middle East produced both silk fabrics and silk thread; India grew cotton, wove cotton goods and learnt how to print those goods in a wide variety of colours; the Low Countries in Europe specialized in the growing and weaving of flax and hemp.

It was the Chinese who first produced silk from the larvae of the Bombyx moth. Not until the sixth century A D was the science of sericulture brought to Europe: to the Mediterranean countries of Italy, Spain and France, all countries where the mulberry trees would grow, on the leaves of which the larvae feed. The earliest and some of the finest silk fabrics were Chinese, but by the sixteenth century wonderful silks were exported from the Middle and Near East as well as Italy. Italy was famed for her silk velvets, especially those from Genoa, while damasks and brocades came from all the silk-weaving countries, particularly the Near East. Later France was pre-eminent and silk fabrics from Lyons became world-famous.

There was little cotton used in England until the Indian sub-continent was opened up to trade by the West, first by the Portuguese and Dutch, then by the French and British in the sixteenth and seventeenth centuries. A few fabrics used in England appear to have had some cotton in them, but they were virtually all imported. Even in the Caister Castle inventory of a magnate such as Sir John Fastolf, taken in 1459, there is no cotton among all the clothes, furnishings and bed-linen listed, and he was a much travelled man.[108] The first fabrics made from cotton probably came directly from the East, or via Portugal as part of a cargo brought back by one of the early voyagers.

Linen woven from flax was the mainstay for household use and for underclothes and all forms of linings. Flax was grown extensively in northern France and the Low Countries, as well as in Ireland and, to some extent, in England. The best linen was imported from Flanders, with holland being the finest and the most expensive. Different types and grades of linen were often denoted by the town or district in which they were made; cambric from Cambrai, dowlas from Dourlaus in Picardy, darnix from Tournai (Dorneck in Dutch) and Holland.

Hemp produced the same type of fabric as flax, but was much coarser, and it was from hemp that hessian, scrim, coarse canvas and sackings were made (the use of jute is comparatively modern). Hemp was extensively cultivated in Russia, and Russia scrim and Russia canvas – found in many inventories – were always of good quality, even if coarse.

In the production of wool, and cloth made from wool, England was pre-eminent. English hills and pastures could carry a great number of sheep, ranging from the very hardy breeds which produced short, thick fleeces, to those which flourished in the warmer and kinder districts and produced longer, finer wool. This meant that the sheep farmers, often in those early days monks from the big monasteries, could produce wool for both woollen and worsted cloths. The difference between these two types of cloth depends on the breed of sheep which produces the wool. Woollen cloth needs a short-staple fleece, as here the wool, after scouring and cleaning, is carded. Carding means working the wool between two wooden bats set with wires. This, while it separates the threads, leaves them lying higgledy-piggledy, and so when spun they tend to stick out at all angles. When this type of wool is woven it becomes dense, and has a nap. It is then fulled (shrunk) in water and the cloth becomes very thick: wonderful to wear in cold or wet weather. These cloths are the broadcloths, fearnaughts, everlastings and others of that type. They were chiefly made in the west of England and had a ready sale abroad to cold countries.

Worsted was produced from long-staple wool, and instead of being carded was combed. A comb was an iron implement with long teeth set like a comb, but with the handle at right angles to the teeth. When the bunch of clean wool was passed through the teeth the threads lay parallel and could be spun into a smooth, fine yarn. The cloths produced were lightweight, as there was no fulling, and as there was no nap, the pattern of the cloth could be seen, so there were endless possibilities in design and colouring. Worsteds were made chiefly in Norfolk.

The history of fabrics in medieval England depends entirely on the written word. Textiles are one of the most vulnerable of all manufactures: unless they are kept in strictly controlled conditions with little light, an even temperature and expert handling, they soon deteriorate, eventually wear out and are gone for ever. They have always been subjected to hard wear and often to rough handling, so it can be no surprise that there are so few left, and from before the middle of the sixteenth century virtually none, except a few made for the use of the Church. These were so exquisitely embroidered that they were carefully kept and used infrequently.

Our knowledge of early textiles comes largely from inventories. On the death of anyone with removable goods worth more than £5 an inventory and valuation had to be taken for probate, and a great number of these are still in existence in Record Offices up and down the country. They are very rewarding to examine and many of them have been, and still are being, printed, giving a wide range of information. Many inventories list the contents of a house and these show what types of fabric were used in which rooms, the amount of furniture and even the fashionable colours. Others, possibly of more interest, list the goods in a shop or work-place, sometimes with the prices, giving an excellent picture of what was obtainable in either an urban or rural district. It was not only on death that inventories were taken, though these are the ones which are more obviously accessible in Record Offices. The contents of a house might be listed on marriage or change of ownership, or for no better reason than that someone needed to know exactly what was there. These, though they may have been deposited in Record Offices, are often to be found in the house itself, or perhaps in some diary or account-book.

The inventories of medieval kings and princes are of prime interest, especially those of John of Gaunt, Thomas, Duke of Gloucester, and their nephew, Richard II. All give fascinating details of the fabrics and furnishing of the time, as well as the chattels used in a great house. The inventory of Thomas of Gloucester, for example, taken in 1397, gives a wonderful account of the many fabrics available for the rich at that date.[110] It describes many pieces of arras, and beds of gold and silk: one of fine blue satin, the

2. Tapestry woven in Tournai, c. 1480. Montacute House

coverlet, tester and celure embroidered with gold Garters, and three curtains of beaten gold tartaryn. All the many beds mentioned were embroidered, even those of worsted: blue worsted embroidered with a yellow stag, red worsted embroidered with griffins, blue worsted embroidered with a white eagle, and so on. Entries such as these indicate that in the wealthiest homes at this date most of the fabrics were of English make (worsteds), that good, basic dyes were available (blue, red, yellow), and that as well as homemade articles, silk fabrics were imported, as were gold and silver thread. It also makes it quite clear that there was considerable skill in embroidery, using gold threads as well as silk and probably crewel, and that there must have been a fair number of embroiderers and embroidery workshops.

The medieval palace or castle had little furniture: beds, trestle tables, stools, benches and possibly a chair, but these few articles were generally covered with fabrics, often of high quality. Beds were used for receiving courtiers, ambassadors and friends, as well as for sleeping, and so were ornate and handsome; tables were covered with carpets or cloths of pile, tapestry or plain or embroidered fabric; benches were covered with bankers, which were embroidered cloths, and stools and window-seats had cushions. All these furnishings were taken from one house and put up in another as the king or lord moved from palace to castle to manor on the rounds of his estates.

Where did these fabrics come from? The only looms in England at this time capable of weaving material of this quality were producing woollen cloth. But many English of the twelfth and thirteenth centuries were well-travelled. The first Crusade, which reached the Holy Land, was in 1096, the second in 1144. Richard I went to Acre in 1190 and Louis IX of France led one Crusade in 1248 and another in 1270. As well as the aristocratic leaders, many knights, esquires and ordinary soldiers went and saw for themselves what the East was producing at that date. When Jerusalem, Antioch, Aleppo and Acre were besieged and captured there was much looting and few of those who returned did not bring back some souvenir of that momentous journey, often a piece of silk, which was easily transportable. These fabrics gave England its first taste of luxury. Later there was the Hundred Years War against France where, again, the ordinary Briton saw and in many cases acquired luxurious fabrics of which they would not otherwise have known. Wars have always had a large part to play in the widening of men's knowledge and interests.

Gifts from ruler to ruler consisted of objects of the finest quality each country could produce, and textiles figured prominently. Ambassadorial gifts, too, came into the same category, and here the gifts frequently consisted of things which each country hoped would lead to trade. The gifts, for example, which Sir Thomas Roe took to India in the early seventeenth century were those things, including textiles, which it was hoped the Indians would buy. It was a sad fact that they liked so few of them.[77]

With dynastic marriages, the bride's dowry generally included superb objects from her own country as well as money or land, and she often took with her workmen and the knowledge of various crafts which might start a fashion in her new country. Philippa of Hainault, the wife of Edward III, encouraged weavers to come from her own country to England and thereby gave the weaving trade in England an injection of new methods and styles. Although blackwork had been known in England before Katharine of Aragon came to marry Prince Arthur and, instead, married Henry VIII, her interest in this typically Spanish-Moorish technique led to its becoming far more widely practised than would otherwise have happened at that time. A later marriage dowry which had far-reaching effects was that of Catharine of Braganza, who brought Charles II the Portuguese-owned city of Bombay, and thereby gave the East India Company one of the best harbours in the world.

The life of a monarch or lord in medieval and Tudor times had little privacy, the result being that every courtier and hanger-on would see and know about all the new and exotic articles which were produced abroad. This knowledge filtered through the country as the monarch went on progress, or the nobleman went back to his country estates, taking with him some of the sophistication of the capital.

It was the church, however, which brought so many textiles into the country. They came as presents from one prelate to another, and they were acquired and given to the church by rich and poor alike, who both wanted to beautify what was probably the greatest influence in their lives, and also store up riches for themselves in heaven. The church had always been the great patron of the arts, whether in architecture, carving, woodwork, painting or the manufacture of textiles. This is still true today, with Coventry Cathedral as a prime example. Here craftsmen of many nations have combined to produce beautiful and symbolic work.

But in the sixteenth century the church influenced furnishings in a different way. With the Dissolution of the Monasteries in 1538 and the redistribution of their lands, buildings and goods, many superb fabrics, both woven and embroidered, came into secular hands. These fabrics were generally cut up and used in the houses of those who had acquired the lands. Mary, Queen of Scots, Roman Catholic though she was, indulged in this practice. In 1562 she used a cope, chasuble and four tunicles to make a bed for Darnley. These were 'broken and cuttit in her awin presence'.

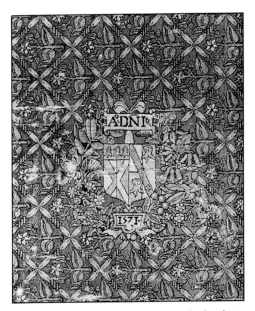

3. *Detail of a table carpet in turkey work, dated 1571.*
Norfolk Museums Service, Stranger's Hall Museum, Norwich

Three years later, in 1565, three copes, two tunicles and a chasuble, probably from Aberdeen Cathedral, were 'employit by the Queen's command' and used in her palace. The embroidery was removed to decorate a bed and the green velvet was used for a high chair, two stools and a *chaise percée*.[185] This pattern was followed all over the country, with church embroideries and fabrics made into many things from beds to cushions.

None of this would have advanced the story of furnishings unless men of every race had had the instinct and the urge for trading. Advances in technology came about because of man's natural desire to make more money by making a better product more cheaply and easily; his desire to explore, to push further, with hope of gain at the end was a further stimulus.

Today it is difficult to conceive how the early traders in their cockleshell boats could come all the way from Phoenicia to buy Cornish tin, and then later adventure round the foot of Africa, eventually to reach India and then

China and Japan, and bring back spices, silks and cottons. The Silk Road from China to the west, via Samarkand, took months to cover and yet was worked for hundreds of years. The amount of goods and lives which were lost by thieving, guerrilla warfare, storms and sickness is untold, but the gain was sufficient and the demand great enough for men to risk their lives in this fashion.

One of the main hazards in the transport of textiles by sea was mildew, which spotted and rotted cloth, however well packed. The records of the East India Company are full of complaints about goods arriving in an unsaleable condition,[77] as are the letters between the merchant, John Norton, in England and his customers in Virginia in the eighteenth century.[56] The wonder is that any fabric at all arrived in good condition, rather than that so much did not. The losses on goods must have been enormous.

The journey from Turkey and Asia Minor to Britain was comparatively simple, and merely involved crossing the Adriatic and landing goods at Venice. They were then brought overland to France and up the Rhine and across the Channel to London. This was the route which brought Turkey carpets, Byzantine silks and Genoese velvets to England, among other things. These were the most prized textiles of the early sixteenth century.

While the rich were having their appetites whetted by these fine imported textiles, the humbler people were virtually self-sufficient. Flax and wool, with some hemp, were the staple yarns, and spinning and weaving were usual domestic occupations. Spinning was done with a distaff and spindle. The wheel, although it was known in India at a very early date indeed, and in Europe by the thirteenth century, did not oust the older method in Britain until the mechanization of most of the processes involved about 1800. Spinning was a vital occupation at all levels of the community. Without it there was no yarn for the weavers to use and therefore no cloth for clothing or furnishings.

There is an attractive but probably untrue picture that in the fifteenth and sixteenth centuries the ladies of the house, their gentlewomen and maids, spent all their free time spinning for the needs of the family. Certainly spinning was an almost universal occupation, but much of it was put out from the big house to the estate and surrounding villages. This was largely because up till the late seventeenth and eighteenth centuries there were few female domestics. Most of the work of the house was done by men who had neither the time, inclination nor suitable hands for spinning. But the needs of the weavers had to be met and it took many spinsters to keep one loom working. Spinning with a distaff and spindle was slow and the making of cloth, whether from flax or from wool, took a great deal of thread. In his book, *Master Weaver*, Richard Early tells how in the seventeenth century his ancestor, Thomas Early, who made blankets at Witney in Oxfordshire, had to spend a large proportion of his time travelling the country around Witney, persuading and cajoling the spinsters into providing the amount of yarn he needed.[68]

The Steward's Account of the Bacon Archives gives a picture of life in a very rural area of north Norfolk at the end of the sixteenth century. The spinning included hemp, flax and wool, and was done partly in the house, but far more by the estate workers and the wives of the men servants. Mostly spindles and whorls were used, the price of a whorl varying between 1d. and 2d. Mrs Bacon used a wheel which had to be brought to Stiffkey from Norwich and cost 2s. 4d., with 2d. being paid to the carrier who delivered it, after which there are several payments for wheel bands and also one for an iron spindle. It seems that when the accounts speak of the spinning of 'yarn' they mean wool, as the yarn is generally for the gentlewomen's hose, or for 'making my master a pair of boothose', which needed a quarter of a pound of yarn and cost 3s. The wool came from their own sheep, as they buy a 'payer of cardes to come woll' for 1s. 8d., showing that the wool used was short staple and was combed on cards into the long slivers needed for spinning at home. Flax was bought, possibly from Ireland or even more likely from the Low Countries, as it was brought by sea to Cley and then taken by the merchant to Wiveton, which was a tiny port not far from the manor house at Stiffkey. It was spun there and, though there is no mention of looms, tenter hooks were bought, proving that the cloth was made locally. As looms were strongly made and lasted many years, while the accounts only run for ten years, it would perhaps be even more surprising if they were mentioned; but there is no way of knowing where the cloth was woven.[1]

There are a great many payments referring to hemp, especially for bunching and spinning, to be made into – what? In Tudor times hemp was grown on every farm to be made into cordage for the Navy, so possibly this was the Bacons' contribution, but the Le Fleming accounts show that it was also woven into a form of lawn used for handkerchiefs and night coifs.

Apart from weaving for clothing and household linens, blankets were often made on the estate. The Ancaster accounts for 1562 refer to blankets

4. *Seventeenth-century bed with sixteenth-century hangings.*
Cotehele House

being made locally at Grimsthorpe, with the payment of three women for seven days, and one woman for four, at 2d. the day each, for teasing wool for blankets – that is, twenty-five days' work.[4] Later in the century, in 1593, the Rutland accounts give the payments for blankets to be made for the 'hospitall' (almshouse) at Bottesford. They paid the weaver, for forty-three yards of cloth for blankets, $1\frac{1}{2}$d. a yard. Two hundred and twenty-four days' work was needed in carding wool and spinning for these forty-three yards. They needed twenty-four pounds of linen yarn to make coverlets, and they obviously did not grow their own flax, as a man was paid 10d. for going to Gainsborough to buy it. They then paid three women for thirty-three days each, at 'dressinge, swinglinge, and heckling flaxe for to make sheetes and coverledges for the hospitall at Bottesforte' at 3d. the day for food and wages, and they needed seven other women of Belvoir for two days to wash and wind the yarn.[11] It was not the actual weaving which took the manpower, but the ancillary processes.

The weaving of textiles was, in the sixteenth century, largely an out-working industry, with individual looms in cottages in the country and in tenements in the town, and this pattern went on with variations until the middle of the eighteenth century. There were, however, some factories as early as Henry VIII's reign. Thomas Deloney, himself a weaver, tells the story of John Winchcombe, generally known as Jack of Newbury. Deloney, referred to by Nashe as the 'ballading silk-weaver of Norwich', wrote the story about 1595, but Jack of Newbury was a real person who died in 1519, and allowing for picturesque and slightly exaggerated prose and verse, the story is substantially true. The poem refers to 'one room being large and long', with two hundred looms, clearly weaving narrow cloth, as there were only two hundred men working them, though later there are references to two hundred weavers working only one hundred looms. Broadcloth was more usual in the West Country than narrow, but Jack may have woven both. Children sat by the looms filling quills, and women carded the wool. Girls spun and children from poor homes picked the wool, taking out the burrs. Besides the weaving shed, Jack also had his own shearmen, a dye-house with forty workers and a fulling mill with two hundred workers. This is a very early reference to a factory, and it does not seem likely that there were many of them.[37]

The 1637 will of Richard Elsdon of Bury St Edmunds in Suffolk gives what must have been a far more general picture even earlier in the sixteenth century. He states that at Fornham he has eight pieces of coarse cloth. Goodman Goslinn at Icklingham has 'six twoe dussen pieces', and Goodman Crosse of Luckford has two pieces. Goodman Lowes is weaving four pieces and Goodman Parker 'foure dussens', and Goodman Kendall has two 'dussen' pieces weaving. 'And there is at my sister six pieces and at goodwife Boldero's twoe pieces. And there is in the house drest and raw thirty pieces, and there is twoe broad clothes and as much yarn as will make another broadcloth....'[138] These men in the villages would go to Richard Elsdon in the town and he would hand out the yarn and say what he wanted made. When it was finished the weaver would take the piece in and get more yarn.

Owing to the use of machinery, this system became outdated; more and more weavers worked in factories, although there were still, even in the late nineteenth and early twentieth centuries, men who worked in the old way. There are people alive today who can remember handloom weavers carrying the beams from their looms from their cottages through the streets of Norwich to the factory, where the web was cut off and more yarn given out and taken back home. The weaver in general has been a very independent man who much preferred to work at his own pace in his own surroundings than in any form of factory.

The emergence of the prosperous middle classes in Tudor England, and the national feeling that a man must show his wealth in his home and on his person, led to the use of more and more exotic and expensive fabrics. Most of these still came from abroad, cloth and linen being the national products of England, but the number of immigrant Huguenot and Flemish weavers, who brought their knowledge of silk weaving from France and the Low Countries, had a great impact on the trade in Britain.

The religious wars in France which continued intermittently from 1562 to 1629 caused a mass exodus of the 'heretical' Protestants from the country. The greatest number fled after the massacre of the Huguenots in Paris on the eve of St Bartholomew in 1572, and among them were many weavers.

They settled chiefly in Exeter, Spitalfields in east London, and Norwich, and brought much-needed new ideas and techniques to the English industry. There was a period when they were not accepted by the local weavers and strict regulations were made defining what the 'Strangers' might or might not do, but gradually they became integrated into the community and Huguenot names, many anglicized, can still be found in the areas where they settled. In 1598 the Edict of Nantes, signed by Henry IV of France, gave the Huguenots liberty of conscience and civil rights in France, but few of those in England seem to have taken advantage of this and returned to France. France's loss was distinctly England's gain, and the New Draperies brought by these immigrants, mostly silks and half-silks, started a new chapter in the story of English textiles.

Two

THE SEVENTEENTH CENTURY

During the seventeenth century householders, rich and poor alike, were wanting, and getting, more comfort in their homes. For a lot of people the century was a disaster, with the Civil War as the nadir. Heads of houses were killed, estates were sequestered and it needed a tightrope such as that on which the Vicar of Bray walked to come unscathed through the labyrinths of religious turmoil. But for all the difficulties many people, especially those of the middle class; merchants, civil servants or seamen, who either kept out of politics and religion or else were on the right side at the right time found life easier, and this ease was reflected in their houses.

Comfort became much more important and houses were better built, with tighter-fitting doors and windows, and thus fewer draughts. Chimneys were more efficient and houses warmer, and upholstered furniture became a priority. It has been suggested that the change in men's dress from the well-padded to the new streamlined breeches was one reason for the need for stuffed seats for chairs and stools, but it may have been the normal progression of each generation wanting and getting more than the one before; the fact remains that for most people, from the parish priest to the squire, life and comfort improved.

At the beginning of the century the furniture was much the same as in earlier days – in other words, the bare minimum. Inventories show little beyond the basics: tables, stools and benches, with some chairs and a cupboard or buffet, and with the bedroom even more sparsely furnished – just the bed, possibly a chair and a cupboard. Practically all this furniture would have been oak, with perhaps an occasional piece of walnut. Hangings, table carpets and cushions would have produced colour, but there would have been an almost complete absence of what might be termed decorative trifles; perhaps a silver-gilt cup or salt, but no porcelain and only useful pottery.

During the century, however, this picture gradually changed. Furniture became lighter, both in character and colour, with walnut as a favourite wood. In mid-century a new shape of chair came into fashion, with a tall back and cane seat. These chairs needed squab cushions. The back-stool, with its padded back and seat, was popular all through the century, often having turkey work for the upholstery. The most spectacular change was in the realm of decorative porcelain and textiles, and that was due to the greatest single factor in seventeenth-century textile history, the formation of the East India Company in 1601, which opened up the warehouses of India, China and Japan to Britain.

5. Bed valance in canvas-work, showing 'Europa and the Bull'.
Mid-seventeenth century. Blickling Hall

For many years there had been desultory trading with the east, by both the Portuguese and the Dutch. It was in 1498 that Vasco da Gama had discovered the route to India via the Cape of Good Hope and had founded a trading post at Calicut on the east coast of India. Drake had made his voyage around the world between 1577 and 1580 and the Levant Company, which traded with Turkey, had dealt in eastern goods on the overland route.

The hub of the trading world was the Mediterranean, and for centuries the Phoenicians, Italians and Spanish had voyaged in and from one of the most difficult seas in the world. It is so shallow that gales can whip up fearsome seas and the skill of early sailors must have been considerable. In *The Merchant of Prato*, Iris Origo tells the story of Francesco Datieri, a merchant in a small town in Tuscany. In the late fourteenth century Francesco was trading with all the Mediterranean countries as well as with England. He was buying cloth and wool mostly from the south and west of England, his ships going to Southampton and London. He bought

Essex cloth, Guildford cloth and unbleached cloth from the Cotswolds and Winchester, as well as Scottish cloth. He also had ships trading with Sicily, Sardinia, Spain, Alexandria, Ibiza and Marseilles, as well as buying hemp from Provence, leather from Tunis and Cordoba, sword blades from Toledo, soap from Valencia, tusks and ostrich feathers from Barbary, ceramics from Valencia and Majorca, maps from Barcelona and slaves from all the accessible Moslem countries and from around the Black Sea.[167]

Large trading ventures, then, were nothing new, but England had not played a great part in them. She had exported her wool and cloth, but mostly through the Staple Towns and the Low Countries. Long sea voyages had not been for her. But the rise of the middle classes and the spirit of sixteenth-century England was personified in the emergence of such buccaneers as Drake, Raleigh, Hawkins and Frobisher. They accustomed English sailors to long sea voyages, and the tales they brought back of the wealth to be found excited the greed of the English merchants who became ready to risk the losses which might be incurred in these ventures. The losses could be, and often were, very great, but the prizes were enormous.

The reason why the London merchants wanted to send ships to the east had, at first, little to do with textiles but everything to do with that necessity for making medieval and Tudor food palatable – spice. There was no way of keeping meat fresh through the winter: as there was little winter feed, most cattle were killed in the autumn and the carcasses salted or, in big houses, put into ice-houses. By February and March, meat was becoming decidedly high and the addition of one or more spices such as pepper, ginger or cinnamon made the taste more acceptable. These spices were very expensive and all came from the east, and it was obvious that they would be very much cheaper if they could be brought by sea in English ships, rather than by the long and arduous overland route, or by Dutch or Portuguese ships.

So in 1599 the Merchant Adventurers of London prepared to 'adventure', or risk, their money (but not themselves) by sending a voyage to the east, and they petitioned Queen Elizabeth for a charter; in 1601 the East India Company was formed.

The early voyages were a three-way venture. The Spice Islands (which are now known as the Moluccas), lie to the west of New Guinea. The islanders did not want to buy English woollens, which were much too heavy for their hot climate, but they did want Indian cottons. So the English traded their woollens in India for light cottons, which they then took to the Moluccas to trade for spice. Some of the cottons were brought back to

6. Bed with crewel-work furniture.
Third quarter of the seventeenth century. Cotehele House

England as a novelty, and eventually the main trade between England and India was in textiles, while the interest in spice decreased as the necessity for it weakened with the provision of more winter feed for stock and, consequently, fresher meat.

The East India Company, known to the Indians as the John Company, flourished for over two hundred years and, while it had interests other than textiles, it was primarily a vehicle for selling the woollen stuffs made in England. This was not always easy as the stuffs were not to the Indian taste, but the main result of the formation of the Company from the point of view of house furnishing in Britain was that it introduced light, cheerful, washable fabrics and encouraged a taste for cotton as a thread to be used for weaving – a taste which still flourishes. It is difficult to visualize a period when the only yarns were silk, wool, linen and hemp, with no cotton, and for that welcome addition to our fabrics we have to thank the intrepid seamen, and the merchants who risked their money in the seventeenth century.

The fabrics which came to Britain along with porcelain and other goods were mostly painted cottons or pintadoes. Although 'painted' is the word generally used it perhaps conjures up the wrong image. These tightly woven, firm cottons had the outline of the design painted on the fabric, but the rest of the process consisted of printing and dyeing using, in the same piece, both the resist method and the use of mordants. The result was much lighter than the word 'painted' conveys. These were the chintz so much valued in Britain.

The first cloths to arrive in any quantity during the first half of the seventeenth century were, naturally, purely Indian in design, but this particular brand of exoticism did not appeal to western taste. By the 1660s Britain was sending designs to India for the native craftsmen to copy or adapt. A comparison between designs in goods made for the export market and those for use in their own country shows clearly how they had been modified, but they were still sufficiently out of the ordinary to appeal strongly to the British.[147]

Chintz were used particularly for bed curtains. Houses, by this time, were better built and there was less need for heavy woollen and tapestry curtains to keep out draughts, so lighter fabrics, especially those as cheerful and pretty as the Indian ones, were welcomed. They had two other advantages: they were washable and, when washed, the colours neither ran nor faded.

The influx of these Indian chintz for both dress and furnishings accelerated enormously during the second half of the century. Although many ships, crews and cargoes were lost, and many fabrics became spoilt during the passage, still more ships and crews were on the route, with better navigation and seamanship, and an astonishing amount of eastern goods reached

7. Chair of State, with applied decoration of strap-work,
1610–20. Knole

Britain. This influx had other, far-reaching consequences which were not resolved until the end of the next century.

As early as 1649 there were disagreements between the Exchequer and the importers over the amount of duty to be paid on chintz. The Company wished to put calicoes in the same category as linens, because linen paid five per cent less duty. Pepys in 1664 tells of the quarrel:

... Sir Martin Noall who told us the dispute between him, as Farmer of the Addicionall Duty, and the East India Coy whether Callico's be Linnen or no; which he says it is having been ever esteemed so; they say it is made of Cotton-woole and grows upon trees, not like Flax or hemp. But it was carried against the Company, though they stand out against the verdict.[58]

In fact, it was many more years before this particular trouble was settled. However, worse was to come. As has happened many times, especially in any trade to do with fashion, the change in taste made for great hardship among the English manufacturers. By 1681 complaints had been made to Parliament: because of the influx of cottons from abroad the demand for silks had fallen off alarmingly. In 1685 the Revocation of the Edict of Nantes meant that more Huguenot weavers fled from France and settled in England, chiefly among the silk weavers of Spitalfields; this at a time of falling-off of trade. Added to which the East India Company, importing silks as well as cotton, was selling them more cheaply than the homemade cloth. By 1696 there was appalling distress among the weavers, leading to riots.[78] It was not only the silk weavers who were upset; the dyers and linen drapers were against the importation of calicoes already stained and printed; the woollen manufacturers were against both silks and cottons being imported; and the Turkey Company were against the East India Company bringing in raw silk for weaving, which they considered their prerogative. None of this, naturally, mattered to the rich — who wanted the new fashion — nor the less rich — who were delighted to be able to buy attractive fabrics from abroad.

In 1696 a Bill was introduced in Parliament to restrain the wearing of imported silks and calicoes; in effect, sumptuary law, and like all sumptuary laws it was ignored and allowed to drop. But a year later, in 1697, 5,000 weavers mobbed the House of Commons, and in 1700 an Act was passed forbidding, from Michaelmas 1701, the use or wearing of 'all wrought silks, Bengalls, and stuffs mixed with herba, of the manufacture of Persia, China or E. India, and all calicoes painted, dyed, printed or stained there, which are or shall be imported into this kingdom shall not be worn or otherwise

8. *Elbow chair covered*
in Genoa velvet with a tassel fringe.
Late seventeenth century. Knole

9. Detail of a settee. One of three panels
of canvas-work set into a frame of pink velvet. Late seventeenth century.
Cotehele House

used in Gt Britain'. However, calicoes were allowed to be imported unstained for re-export only. This drama proceeded all through the eighteenth century and must be continued in the next chapter.

The age-old methods of spinning and weaving did not change in the seventeenth century, but their updating and mechanization, which was so great a feature of the eighteenth century, was led up to by the coming of the 'Strangers' in the last quarter of the sixteenth century. Huguenot weavers settled in various parts of England, as did the Flemings, bringing their skills with them and so enlarging the scope of the fabrics produced in England. The New Draperies were, according to the Letters Patent from Queen Elizabeth, 'bayes, arras, sayes, tapestry, mockadoes, staments, carseys, and such outlandish commodities as hath not bene used to be mayde within our Realme of England'. It is difficult to understand this, as most of the fabrics cited had been made here earlier, but a later list discusses 'bayes, moccadoes, grosgraynes, all sortes of tuftes which were not made there [Norwich] before'.[92]

What is certain is that by 1611 Norwich was producing a wide range of silks and half-silks which were new to this country: bombazines, Spanish satins, striped tobines, damasks etc., all of which were used for furnishings. This opened up another style for those either bringing their old houses up to date or those furnishing new ones; they could buy half-silks locally instead of importing, and they had a far wider choice of fabrics.

While the eleven years of the Commonwealth may have discouraged conspicuous consumption, the Restoration of Charles II gave it a boost. Charles had spent many years in exile in Holland and France; his mother was French and his sister was married to the French king's brother, and he brought back to England a knowledge and love of the French way of living which included the use of beautiful textiles. This, and the importation of Indian calicoes, plus the new home manufacture of silks and half-silks, opened up a new era in textile history.

Three

THE EIGHTEENTH CENTURY

It sometimes seems that in books on architecture, furnishing, costume or fabrics, the eighteenth century is dwelt on to the exclusion of the rest, but there is no doubt that in this century textiles in particular reached a standard and variety never reached before and seldom since. This was partly due to the sheer inventiveness of the period – the use of machinery and the overcoming of technical problems – and partly to the rich flowering of the processes started in the previous century. It was also the time when cotton emerged as a premier furnishing fabric, vying with wool and silk, when the manufacturers in Britain, especially Glasgow and Manchester, challenged the Indian imports and in the long run won the battle.

The saga of the East India Company versus the English manufacturers went on. The passing of the 1701 Act was not the success that was hoped. Plain calicoes were still allowed into England and the woollen merchants complained that 'the allowing calicoes unstained to be brought in has occasioned such an increase in the printing and staining calicoes here, and the printers and painters have brought the art to such perfection that it is more prejudicial to us than it was before the passing of the Act'. They also complained that whereas before the Act only the rich could afford calicoes, and therefore the poor still wore woollen goods, now the plain calicoes could be printed in England so cheaply that even the poor could afford to be in fashion.

Another grumble was that as the India-printed calicoes could be re-exported to the American colonies, there was less demand there for wool, while the Turkey merchants said that their trade was being ruined by the importation of raw silk from India, bought at one-third the cost of theirs from the Near East and Italy, and that consequently the exportation of woollen goods to the Levant was endangered. There are always cries for 'Protection!' when manufacturers feel their markets are undermined.

In 1720 an Act was passed stating that from 1722 no one was to wear any printed or dyed calico, with a penalty of £20 for the seller and £5 for the buyer and also a penalty of £5 for using this fabric 'in Bed, Chair, Cushion, or other Household Furniture'. Only muslins, neckcloths and fustians (at that time a mixture of cotton and linen) were excepted.

10. Soho tapestry: the Continent of Africa, 1733.
Packwood House

Thomas Nash, an upholsterer in London, evidently wanted to get rid of his stock before the Act was ratified and advertised in the *Post Boy* on 15 November 1722:

Whereas by an Act passed the last Session of Parliament Callicoe furniture can be made up, after Christmas, next ... This is to inform those that have Occasion for Beds of the finest Choice Patterns, callicoe Quilts, Carpets to cover, one side of callicoe Gowns to make into Quilts, may be furnished with all sorts by Thomas Nash, upholsterer, at the Royal Bed on Holborn Bridge.[87]

In 1736 yet another Act said that if a fabric had a linen warp, even if it also had cotton in it, it was to be treated as fustian and was therefore exempt. This remained the official stand until 1774, when a further Act permitted the use – as apparel, furniture or otherwise – of printed or dyed stuffs manufactured wholly of cotton in Great Britain. This was to help the Lancashire and Scottish trade and, to make sure there would be no question of mistaking Indian for British, the latter had to have three blue lines running

11. *Detail of canvas-work chair covers*
in the chinoiserie *style. Early eighteenth century.*
Polesden Lacey

through the selvage. Little did the legislators of 1774 think how much easier that would make the task of students two hundred years later, when sorting out foreign calicoes from British.

Manufacturers might grumble and laws were passed, but it all seemed to have had little effect on the use of calicoes in England. Holland became a centre for the distribution of cottons and they were either smuggled or brought openly across the North Sea into Britain. Lady Mary Wortley Montagu, living in Holland, offered to buy 'Indian Goods' for a friend in London,[65] and in 1738 Mrs Purefoy bought chintz for a gown. Three years later she asked her agent to get eighteen yards of chintz for window curtains to match 'workt chairs'. Though the word 'chintz' is used, it is possible that she meant not printed calico but chain-stitched linen, worked either in India or England, with a design copying the Indian patterns, if it was to match 'workt' or embroidered chairs.[60]

The law was not quite a dead letter, however. There were various incidents where women wearing Indian fabrics had their clothes torn off or were heavily fined, and there is a delightful series of letters between David Garrick, the actor, and Sir Gray Cooper of the Customs House. Garrick writes that he has sent plays and scenes to gentlemen in Calcutta, and they in return have sent him and his wife a chintz bed and curtains. She had prepared the room for the chintz when it was seized by the Customs. Could Sir Gray help? Sir Gray says that he would like to, but could not, but would ask the Secretary of the Board. Whether it was owing to Garrick's fame as an actor, a little judicious bribery or kindness of heart on the part of the Secretary, Mrs Garrick got her chintz bed — which is now in the Victoria and Albert Museum.[171]

At the same time as all things Indian were enjoying an enormous vogue, there was another fashion which came from the east. This started soon after the formation of the East India Company in the seventeenth century, with the importation of porcelain into Europe. Until then porcelain was unknown, pottery being the accepted ware for dishes and plates, along with wood, pewter and, for the rich, silver or silver-gilt. Chinese porcelain immediately became much sought after and it was soon copied as well as the workmen were able in Europe, especially in Holland. Furniture from China and Japan followed the porcelain, and the craft of lacquering, also known as japanning in Britain, became popular. The influx of these things, together with the textiles, made the East seem like fairyland to most English people. One says 'the East' advisedly, because it was all so far away, so fabulous and so little known that to the average man one country was much like another, and India, China and the Spice Islands all merged together, even being referred to as Cathay. It was not long before all these imports were being copied in England, but adapted to the English taste while keeping the flavour of 'Cathay'. Known as *chinoiserie*, this can best be defined as the foreigners' exercise in the Chinese style or manner; an exercise which bore very little resemblance to the original.

As far as textiles were concerned, *chinoiserie* was mostly seen in the designs printed on cotton. These, first with block, then with copper plate and later by roller-printing, had designs incorporating figures with a vaguely Chinese look, usually holding sunshades and standing on bridges or rococo-shaped clouds. A Chinese designer might have had difficulty in recognizing

12. *The saloon at Osterley Park arranged in
the eighteenth-century manner.*

the figure and the landscape, but to the European they were exotic and unusual.

This vogue was at its height in the middle of the century, and the fabrics complemented the furniture designs of that time. Perhaps textiles on the whole were less self-consciously oriental than furniture and the new art of porcelain-making, but they certainly kept in step with the trend. One manufactory noted for *chinoiseries* was the Royal Tapestry Factory at Soho in London. During the first half of the eighteenth century it produced many panels with mixed Indian and Chinese themes. Some were designed by John Vanderbank, who was the director until 1727, and others after the designs of François Boucher. French textile *chinoiseries* were more numerous and more delicate in design than the English, with Boucher, Pillement and Huet as the most influential artists, all of whom were imitated in England.

Apart from the tapestries, wall coverings in England were more likely to be of Chinese wallpaper than *chinoiserie* textiles. The wallpaper, in separate hand-drawn and painted sheets, was immensely popular and still decorates many English bedroom walls.

13. Hanging in canvas-work, showing a formal eighteenth-century garden. Formerly at Stoke Edith, now at Montacute House

The most spectacular edifice which might be called a monument to *chinoiserie* was and is the Prince Regent's Brighton Pavilion. It is the epitome of every facet of the cult put together in one building: furniture, decoration, textiles, porcelain and ornaments − it is all there.

The eighteenth century saw a great advance in all the technical aspects of textile production. New machines were eventually accepted, though not without difficulty and unrest all through the century, and these led up to the complete mechanization of the trade in the nineteenth century.

The first invention was the flying shuttle, designed and patented by John Kay in 1733. Up till then one man had only been able to weave cloth thirty-six inches wide, as that was the greatest width it was possible to throw a shuttle from side to side. Broadcloth, that is, any cloth wider than thirty-six inches, had to be woven by two men, one sitting at each side of the loom, throwing the shuttle from one to the other. The specification for Kay's shuttle is so clear and so important that it is worth quoting in full:

This invention relates to weaving and consists in a new invented shuttle for the better and more exact weaving of broad cloths, broad bays, sail cloths or any other broad goods woollen or linen, which shuttle is much lighter than the former, and by running on four wheels moves over the lower side of the web or spring on a board about 9 inches long, put under the same and fastened to the layer, which new contrived shuttle by two wooden tenters, invented for the purpose and hung

14. Chinoiserie *chair covered in*
cut velvet. Tatton Park

to the layer, and a small cord commanded by the hand of the weaver, the weaver sitting in the middle of the loom, with great ease and expedition by a small pull at the cord casts and moves the said new invented shuttle by his pulling it in the middle uniformly over the piece making it unavoidably even and much truer and better than by any method heretofore used.[91]

And so it was, but this, like almost all eighteenth-century textile inventions, aroused great hostility in the weavers, who felt that its use would

*15. Detail of printed fabric in the chinoiserie style,
mid-eighteenth century. East Anglian Collection,
Blickling Hall*

lead to loss of jobs. Even twenty years after the first use of the flying shuttle a mob attacked Kay's house and nearly killed him, and eventually he died a pauper in France.

The speeding up of the weaving process meant that there were not nearly enough spinners to supply the looms, or carders to prepare the wool, and so it became vital to produce yarn faster. The distaff-and-spindle method of spinning was slow, and so was the cottage wheel, as only four to five feet could be spun at a time before the thread had to be wound on. This hold-up had long been recognized, and as early as 1519 Leonardo da Vinci had designed and made the first flyer attached to a wheel, which allowed continuous spinning as twisting and winding could be done at the same time. But nothing had come of this and two hundred years later the same slow methods were in use. With Kay's flying shuttle it was obvious that the next step was to invent a machine which would twist and wind several threads at once. In the same year Kay invented his shuttle, John Wyatt was able to spin cotton 'without the intervention of human fingers', using a succession of pairs of rollers, each pair running faster than the preceding pair. In 1741 Wyatt and Lewis Paul built the first mill at Birmingham. The patent stated 'As the prepared mass, rope, thread or sliver passes regularly through or betwixt these rollers ... a succession of other rollers ... moving proportionately faster than the first draws the rope, thread or sliver in any degrees of fineness that may be required.' A new mill, water-driven, at Northampton contained five frames, each of fifty spindles – a great advance in speed and output. This method was improved by Richard Arkwright who, from the time he patented his water frame in 1769, built new mills in Derbyshire, Lancashire and Scotland and, with those who built mills under licence, employed more than 35,000 hands.[31]

Drafting, or the use of pairs of rollers, as practised by Wyatt and Arkwright and copied by a host of other manufacturers, was not the only new method tried. There were many inventions brought to the Society for the Encouragement of Arts between 1761 and 1767, but the only one to have lasting results was the spinning jenny of James Hargreaves.

Hargreaves was himself a weaver, one of the thousands working for a master who provided the yarn for the weaver to make into cloth, and again like so many more, he was often held up for want of yarn. To minimize the waiting time and speed up yarn production he developed the spinning jenny or engine. This at first allowed eight spindles to be wound evenly at one time, and later 120, and it worked on the principle of the great wheel, i.e., drawing out the rovings or threads and at the same time introducing twist by the rotating of many spindles driven by a wheel. Again, there was much opposition to the jenny by the weavers around Blackburn where Hargreaves worked, till eventually he moved to Nottingham, patenting the design in 1770.

The next influential name on the spinning scene is that of Samuel Crompton. He, like Hargreaves, was both a spinner and weaver, and by the time he was sixteen was using one of Hargreaves' jennies with eight spindles. He realized there were difficulties with its use, and after several years' struggle he evolved a method of spinning which combined Arkwright's rollers with the spinning action of Hargreaves' jenny. As Arkwright's first rollers had been worked by two asses, Crompton, in combining the two methods, called his engine the mule, and this mule pioneered the way for all advances in spinning after 1779. At last it was possible to produce enough yarn to satisfy the weavers, and not just yarn, but yarn of a fineness not seen in Britain before.

At the same time as the spinning and weaving trades were increasing production and improving the quality of their cloths, the printing trade was improving its wares. At the start of the century the printing of both paper and fabric was in its infancy. In both cases the work was done slowly and laboriously with wooden blocks – block printing. This method had been in use since the middle ages and was to continue for a long while. The design was cut into the blocks, which were generally of pear wood or sycamore and not bigger than a man could comfortably hold. Each colour needed a separate block, so the more colours used, the longer the work would take. The block was dipped into a colour, placed on the exact spot on the cloth and struck with a mallet to distribute the colour evenly. It was then lifted from the cloth and put down on the next section of the design. In order to make sure that the block was put down at exactly the right place, there were four metal pins driven into the four corners of the block, and these, which made tiny dots into the fabric, acted as guides for the next block. Often, close examination of old printed fabrics will show these dots, indicating that it was block printed. The blocks gave an outline of the design only, and solid colour was added by other work-people, called pencillers, whose job it was to fill in the colours, being paid at so much a thousand strokes. Again, examination of block-printed fabrics will show how some pencillers were extremely accurate and others careless in their work.[176]

In 1752 Mrs Delany, the wife of the Dean of Down in Ireland, went to see a new manufactory at Drumcondra. She writes: 'Bushe made me go with her to Drumcondra half a mile off to see a new manufactory that is set up there of printed linens done by copper-plate; they are excessively pretty ...'[46] This was the start of a new method, with the design engraved on copper plates instead of on blocks. Francis Nixon, who discovered the process, sold the description of the method to a Surrey printer, George Amyand, and after selling his Irish works, joined him. Copper-plate printing worked on the same principle as block printing, i.e., colour was applied to the plate, which was then pressed onto the fabric, but there were wide differences in speed and end-product.[33]

Each copper plate could be up to about thirty-six inches square, which meant that a yard could now be printed in one movement. This also meant that a larger design could be used and that a very much finer and more varied line could be drawn. On the other hand, only one colour was possible, though this could range from light to dark according to the thickness of the line. The colours used were either red, blue, purple or sepia.

For many years it was thought that this method of printing was a French invention and that the famous *toiles de Jouy* produced by Oberkampf pioneered the technique, but later research has shown that many English firms were involved earlier than the French, notably Robert Jones of Old Ford in London; Hale, Peel, Yates and Tipping of Lancashire; Bromley Hall in Kent; Munns of Crayford in Kent and others.

In spite of the monotony of the one-colour process, these prints were very popular indeed for curtains, bed furniture and chair coverings. They went well with the national feeling for lighter fabrics and colours, which reached its height at the turn of the eighteenth century when white muslins and cottons were fashionable wear.

While one speaks of a fabric 'by' Francis Nixon, Bromley Hall and so on, it is important to remember that before going on sale the fabric had been through many hands and processes. Plain white calico would have been woven in Scotland or Lancashire, then a designer would draw the pattern – he might either have worked for a firm or be a freelance. His designs, if for wood-blocks, might have been taken from a fashionable silk of the day or even from the new wallpapers. For copper-plate patterns the designer might have used adaptations of *chinoiserie*, birds in exotic foliage, classical or rural subjects. After the design was chosen the block or plate had to be engraved, then the fabric and design went to the printers, and later still the fabric had to be finished.

The last invention in fabric printing, which was used until the arrival of screen-printing in the present century, was roller-printing. The original inventor is unknown, but about 1785 a Scotsman, Bell, sold a machine to the firm of Livesay, Hargreaves, Hall and Co. It consisted of a cylinder which was engraved with the design; this cylinder revolved through a bath of dye onto the cloth, printing the design. Originally only one colour at a time could be used and the cloth had to be passed through a succession of rollers, each engraved with a different part of the design, above a different colour. Much later, however, a machine was invented which would print all the colours at once.

Although printing has been discussed with particular reference to cotton, woollen fabrics went through the same process and were used for some

*16. Panel of wool damask, late eighteenth century, made in Norwich.
East Anglian Collection, Blickling Hall*

furnishings, especially the less fashionable ones. At any one time the fashion of the moment only applied to about one-tenth of the population, if that – the rest lagged behind, keeping to their well-tried ways.

There were two other inventions at the end of the century which completed the change from hand-work to factory. One was patented by an American, Eli Whitney, who in 1793 invented the cotton gin. When cotton is picked from the bushes the seeds of the plant are entangled in it, and it takes much painstaking labour to remove them by hand. This work in the cotton states of America was done by slaves, and it took approximately fifty slaves to pick the same amount as one of the new horse-driven gins. As a result, there was much more cotton available for the looms of Lancashire and Scotland.

The other invention was the first power loom, created by the Rev. Edmund Cartwright. He knew nothing about weaving and so did not base his invention on a handloom. His loom was a failure but in the next century other men worked on his principles and built the first successful power looms.

Four

THE NINETEENTH CENTURY

In the main, the history of textiles in the nineteenth century consists of the consolidation and refining of the principles invented by Kay, Arkwright, Crompton and Cartwright, with the gradual turnover from cottage and outworking to factory working, and from hand-work to power.

17. Typical country-house style, second half of the nineteenth century:
The Rose Bedroom at Felbrigg Hall

There were also several inventions in different branches of the industry which made for a great acceleration of these processes. The first was that of a Frenchman, Joseph-Marie Jacquard, in 1802. He designed an attachment to a drawloom which could automatically weave a design without the use of a drawboy, and drawboys had always been the bane of drawloom weavers. When a piece of patterned cloth was woven a series of cords were arranged, attached to the warp threads, which represented the different colours and shapes in the design. A boy stood by the side of the loom and pulled the cords which lifted the appropriate warps, as instructed by the weaver. Boys can work hard or be inattentive, tired, stupid or just plain lazy at a repetitive job going on all day, and often they would make mistakes and pull the wrong cords, which spoilt the pattern in the cloth. However, they had always been a necessary evil in this branch of weaving until the invention of M. Jacquard.

The Jacquard attachment consisted of a number of cards, each punched with a series of holes representing one pick of the weave. The cards, which on a complicated design could run into thousands, were strung together and moved in rotation over an attachment above the loom. As the cards rolled, needles attached by cords to every warp thread rose, and where they went through a hole in the card, so that warp rose; where they hit a blank, the warp stayed down. In other words, the needles and cords acted together as a drawboy, but with far more accuracy.

One of the difficulties of the Jacquard attachment was its height, which meant that it was unsuitable for use in the majority of cottages; so even handloom weavers moved to some sort of factory, however small. This in turn meant that as looms were starting to be grouped together, they were in position for the eventual use of power.

Like virtually all inventions in the textile industry from Kay and before, the Jacquard encountered great hostility from the weavers, who smashed looms and refused to work with this new threat to their livelihood and, like most inventors, Jacquard died a pauper. The machine only began to be used in Britain in the late 1820s and it was 1840 before it was finally accepted.

The beginning of the nineteenth century was a bad time for weaving. While weavers had, in the eighteenth century, enjoyed a hard but well-regulated life, with the introduction of machinery things began to change. The spinning jenny had been invented, so there was now enough yarn for everyone and, as a result, out-of-work and untrained men took to the loom producing too much cloth of poor quality and willing to work for wages far lower than those accepted by qualified weavers in order to keep body and soul together. At the end of the Napoleonic Wars in 1815, returning soldiers with no work also took to weaving, making matters worse. Naturally, there was much unrest, leading to riots. The men in various branches of the wool trade formed unions, which were outlawed by the government, and in 1809 all Acts which had regulated the trade generally, and apprenticeship and the use of machines in particular, were repealed, leaving the manufacturers in a very strong position, of which most took advantage. In 1811–12, Luddites organized attacks on mills and machines, and up to 1832 there were riots which were all mercilessly repressed by the government, leaving the trade in a sorry, embittered state from which it took many years to recover.

In the 1860s, when the American Civil War stopped the export of raw cotton from the southern states, many thousands of British weavers were thrown out of work from lack of basic materials, and starvation was rife, particularly in the cotton mills of Lancashire. The nineteenth century was full of ups and down for the weaving trade, mostly downs.

With the introduction of machinery worked by steam rather than water it became unnecessary for factories to be built near a water supply, and from then on they were built wherever there were good communications, canals or roads, and later, railways being of paramount importance. They were built ever closer and closer together, in towns given over completely to the textile industry, with cotton in Lancashire and south-west Scotland, and wool in Yorkshire. The unlovely towns which resulted inspired Blake to write of the 'dark Satanic mills', and so they must have seemed to those who worked in them.

The nineteenth century saw great advances in dyeing, a branch of the industry which had altered very little from early times. Madder was perhaps the most useful dye. It was a climbing herb and the roots, when pulverized and mixed with minerals or mordants, produced a range of reds, from orangey-brown through to purple. Next in importance was woad, whose pulped leaves when dried and fermented gave a fine blue. Unfortunately, the smell of fermenting woad was so obnoxious that Queen Elizabeth enacted a statute forbidding the planting of woad within three miles of a royal residence, adding that 'she prayeth thus much, that when she cometh on Progress to see you in your Countries she be not driven out of your Towns by suffering it to infect the Air too near them.'[156] The yellows were mostly covered by saffron or weld, both plants grown in England. The colour green had always been a problem, as dyers were unable to fix it, and so greens were made from covering blue with yellow; this can be recognized in eighteenth- and early nineteenth-century printed cottons. The yellow was more fugitive than the blue and reacted to light, with the result that a number of crewel-work bed hangings and curtains of the seventeenth

and early eighteenth centuries now appear to be of a dull blue rather than their original bright green. There had been many efforts to produce a fast green, and as early as 1590, in the *Records of the City of Norwich*, there is a notice to the effect that 'one Arthur Rotye, alien, hath good knowledge of dyeing, especially on perfect greens'. He was brought to Norwich by one Gyles Cambye, another alien dyer, to 'teache William Morley, dyer, and his apprentyce and apprentyces the true and perfect mysterye of dyeing

19. Detail of Berlin wool-work, c. 1840. Lanhydrock House

the said greens and other suche coullers...'[92] Arthur Rotye cannot have been any more skilful than any other dyer, as it was not until 1809 that Oberkampf, a Bavarian dyer working in France, perfected a solid green.

Many experiments with dye-stuffs and allied work went on; Turkey red was discovered or rather rediscovered by Charles Taylor in 1785, and by the beginning of the nineteenth century the bleaching properties of chlorine

18. Chair covered in Berlin wool-work.
c. 1840. Lanhydrock House

had been discovered, which did away with the necessity of bleaching cloth in the open air. Bleaching was always done before dyeing so that dyes appeared as bright as possible on the white cloth.[33]

The real breakthrough in the history of dyeing came in 1856 when an eighteen-year-old apprentice, William Henry Perkin, discovered the first completely artificial dye, mauve, while doing some experiments. This was the start of a whole new industry: the producing of dyes from coal tar, which was then a waste-product from gas-works. To start with, coal-tar dyes only worked well on silk or wool, and with cotton a mordant had to be used, but in 1884 Botiiger discovered the azo dye, Congo red, which could dye cotton without a mordant. From these, harsh as many of them were at the beginning, came all the modern synthetic dyes.

The textile industry became more and more mechanized as the century progressed, and more and more inhuman in the treatment of its workers. Hours were long, work was hard and tedious and wages were low. Children worked in the mills from a very early age and had no chance to grow strong before their working life started. The genuine artist and craftsman felt shackled by the mechanical repetitiveness of the machine and, generally, good craftsmanship was at a low ebb.

The Great Exhibition of 1851 showed a vast conglomerate of every kind of machine-made article from Britain, the Empire and most of the rest of the world. Marvellous though the Exhibition was, it was surveyed with a critical eye by some writers, among them Ralph Wornum, who wrote an article on textiles entitled 'The Exhibition as a Lesson in Taste' for the catalogue of the Exhibition published by the *Art Journal* as a special issue.[35] He had many comparisons and criticisms to make, together with some words of praise. He thought Spitalfields silks were equal to those of Lyons, and Coventry ribbons could not be surpassed, but he considered that, as usual, Britain fell below other countries in the design of chintz, printed muslins and shawls. He felt that much design was too angular: 'they are like the chopping sea of the Nore compared with the waves of the Atlantic.' British carpets he considered to be 'distinguished', 'though the most essential feature, aesthetically, is uniformly disregarded, namely that a carpet is made to be trodden upon'. Ralph Wornum would not have agreed with Robert Adam, who designed carpets to match or complement the ornamentation of ceilings; he says firmly, 'But neither is a pot-pourri from Italian ceilings the kind of thing which is required; what is good for a ceiling cannot be good for a floor.' He disliked the riots of flowers, fruit and foliage in some carpets, also the imitation of parquetry: 'There is something puerile in imitating a floor for a floor', and he concluded: 'some are, of course, less objectionable than others'. Altogether, he castigated the taste of the manufacturers, saying that 'the real cause of the anomaly, is simply and solely want of taste, the utter absence of propriety of design and critical judgement, making no distinction between a ceiling, a wall, or a floor.'

Admittedly, looking through the catalogue, one sees his point; the control and use of machinery might be wonderful but there is ornament piled upon ornament for no apparent purpose other than to show that such things were possible. However, it must be recognized that the objects in the Great Exhibition were definitely show pieces and might equally well be called 'show-off' pieces. They were specifically chosen to illustrate the capabilities of the machine, and it was probably not expected that many of these articles would be used in the ordinary home.

This whole question of design had been exercising artists, craftsmen and manufacturers for many years. It was very much a nineteenth-century problem. In the eighteenth century the patrons who had built superb houses and collected pictures, statuary, silver and ceramics had not only been men of wealth, but were also men of taste and discrimination. On the whole they were travelled and well-educated, could discuss the classics, architecture and art with ease and understanding. The craftsmen and artisans were rigidly and comprehensively trained under the guild system, with long, thorough apprenticeships, and they also benefited from contact with men of taste.

By the nineteenth century changes were creeping in. The patrons might well be *nouveau riche* – possibly clever manufacturers but without a background of taste – and the guild system was breaking down, with a less good, less comprehensive training taking its place. Added to which machines were beginning to take over from hand-work and they were yet far from perfect and not wholly understood. The result was a dearth of competent craftsmen and a decline in taste.

From the early part of the century this decline and the sorry state of design had been recognized by a few men. The first was A. W. N. Pugin (1812–52). He was the son of an aristocratic French émigré who had worked with the architect John Nash in the late eighteenth century. As a Frenchman, the elder Pugin understood the Gothic idiom which was then starting to be fashionable in England. His only son helped with his architectural drawings, but before he was twenty he had designed plate for a firm of goldsmiths, sets for Covent Garden plays and Gothic furniture for George

IV at Windsor. Although he was more than capable in several branches of design, his great love was for the tradition of medieval Gothic church building. He wrote *Ornaments of the XVth and XVIth Centuries*, which was very much praised and, having become a Roman Catholic, he worked for influential Catholics, particularly Lord Shrewsbury and Charles Scarisbrick.[84]

Pugin believed that 'all ornament should consist of enrichment of the essential construction of the building' and he carried out this dictum in everything he designed. Although he died when he was only forty, he had by that time designed not only churches and domestic buildings, but metalwork, stained glass, book bindings and tiles. The branches of his work which are pertinent to this study are those of wallpaper, furniture and fabric. For these J. G. Crace made the articles to Pugin's designs, and also fitted out interiors under his direction. With his writings, buildings and designs Pugin, in a very short life, made a stand for the best of medievalism, which was to be followed by other men through the century.

The problem of poor design worried Pugin as it did many other people, and eventually schools of design were set up in various parts of the country. These had a mixed reception, and were sharply criticized for making the students spend far too much of their time drawing from plaster casts, with far too little emphasis on the needs of the industry. Pugin said:

I do not use too strong language when I say that the School in its present system is worse than useless, for it diffuses bad and paltry taste. I have not seen a single piece of ornament that had anything original or national about it; nor do I see any practical smiths, glass-painters, brass workers, carvers etc. produced. It is in fact a mere drawing school and does not improve the taste or knowledge of the operative in the least.

Pugin was then working on the new Houses of Parliament, and had to get his craftsmen from northern France and the Low Countries.

The same strictures were being made about design in textiles. In 1844 the *Journal of Design* had a lot to say about the public's craving for novelty:

There is a morbid craving in the public mind for novelty as 'mere novelty', without regard to intrinsic goodness; and all manufacturers, in the present mischievous race for competition, are driven to pander to it. It is not sufficient that each manufacturer produces a few patterns of the best sort every season, they must be generated by the score and by the hundreds ... One of the best cotton-printers told us that the creation of new patterns was an endless stream. The very instant his hundred new patterns were out he began to engrave others. His designers were worked like mill-horses. We are most decidedly of the opinion that this course is generally detrimental to the advances of ornamental design, to the growth of public taste, and to the commercial interests of the manufacturer and designer.

The evils of poverty of design and mechanical workmanship were taken up by John Ruskin who was, after Pugin, the most influential thinker and writer on the ethics of arts and crafts. He was born in 1819 and it was through his writings that he inspired those who were foremost in the Arts

20. *Detail of curtain fabric designed by A. W. N. Pugin for Oxburgh Hall, 1830–40*

and Crafts Movement in the second half of the century. Ruskin was an art critic who saw every painting or building not just as the object itself, but always in connection with the lives of those who had painted or built, and the lives of those who would see the results of the work. He hated machines and all mechanical processes and in the *The Seven Lamps of Architecture* he thundered:

For it is not the materials but the absence of human labour, which makes the things worthless, and a piece of terracotta or plaster of paris which had been wrought by the human hand, is worth all the stone in Carrara cut by machinery. It is indeed possible and even usual, for men to sink into machines themselves, so that even handwork has all the character of mechanization.

There speaks the man who obviously never realized just how much drudgery could be involved in hand-work.

In 1851 Ruskin published *The Stones of Venice*, possibly his most influential book, which moulded the careers of William Morris and his friends. In it he elaborates his theories about the superiority of craft-made to machine-made artefacts, saying that a workman should not try for perfection, for that is not a human trait: 'Men were not intended to work with the accuracy of tools, to be precise and perfect in all their actions.' He wanted men to be free to use their initiative and to be happy in their work, and he formulated these rules:

1. Never encourage the manufacture of any article not absolutely necessary, in the production of which INVENTION has no share.
2. Never demand an exact finish for its own sake, but only for some practical or noble end.
3. Never encourage imitation or copying of any kind, except for the sake of preserving records of great works.[164]

The writings of John Ruskin were read with eagerness and comprehension by two men who were up at Oxford in the 1850s – Edward Burne-Jones and William Morris. They were both originally destined for the church, but after Oxford decided to become artists. While Burne-Jones became best known as a painter who also designed stained glass, Morris after his marriage turned his attention to the making of all things needed in the decoration of a house. He might well be called the last of the great upholsterers though the term he used for himself was 'decorator'. The difference between Morris and the upholsterers of the eighteenth century, for whom Chippendale might serve as a model, was that, as well as designing and learning all the processes needed in the making of textiles and other artefacts, Morris was a passionate socialist, imbued with Ruskin's ideas on the dignity of labour. He wanted workmen to be well-paid, work in congenial surroundings and be happy. Unlike Ruskin, he had no objections to machinery as long as it was used as the tool rather than the master. His standards of workmanship were extremely high and no trouble was too great if it helped towards the effect he wanted. He disliked the harsh modern dyes, and so set up his own dye-works and taught himself the art of vegetable dyeing. He did not like the rather slipshod method of roller-printing, so went back to block printing his textiles. He taught himself to weave both cloth and tapestries and, not content with these, to knot carpets. Although he designed wallpapers, many of the houses he decorated had fabric wall hangings, which he felt were more truly medieval, and his interiors in general had a rich, cosy gloom.[74]

21. *Axminster stair carpet supplied by the firm of Morris and Co., c. 1900. Standen*

To enable him to do all this Morris was instrumental in setting up, in 1861, the firm of Morris, Marshall, Faulkner and Company. They called themselves Fine Art Workmen in Painting, Carving, Furniture and the Metals. Morris was the leading spirit, doing much of the designing, particularly of the textiles, and making most of the experiments, but Burne-Jones, Dante Gabriel Rossetti, Philip Webb and Ford Madox Brown all worked for the firm from time to time.[169]

The artefacts, writings and ideals of Morris and his friends made a great impact both at the time and on succeeding generations, never more than today, when there has been a great resurgence of Morris textiles and furnishings, but it is pertinent to inquire how much impact the ideas and artefacts had on the ordinary houses of the late nineteenth century. This period was not short of books on household management, house decoration and allied subjects. Many of those were of a rather poor magazine quality, but were obviously read by a number of people. Mrs Panton, for example, who wrote *From Kitchen to Garret*, and in 1889 a companion volume called *Nooks and Corners*,[168] does not seem to have imbibed Morris' principles at all. She was a consultant decorator, who probably got a commission from London shops like Shoolbreds and Whiteleys when she promoted their goods, and she was a great believer in the 'artistic' house. Although it would seem to our eyes that she must be writing for rather humble homes, this was not so, as she said firmly that no one could expect to have an artistic house with an income of less than £1000 a year, and in 1889 that was a high salary.

Many of her illustrations show the current vogue for *japonnerie*, with Japanese fans, tall bamboo plants, Japanese jars and pictures of one trailing spray of blossom. Her curtains were generally of plain fabric edged with a bobble fringe, and there was much drapery. Her rooms look undeniably comfortable. It would be interesting to know how many of the home-owners in England heeded William Morris and how many Mrs Panton.

These were not the only writers on household matters. Between 1808 and 1828 Rudolf Ackermann produced a magazine called the *Repository of the Arts*.[18] This, while it dealt with many facets of artistic life, had in each number illustrations of curtains, beds, furniture and rooms designed by the upholsterers and cabinet-makers of the day in the current mode. Presumably these gentlemen paid handsomely to get their designs put before such a wide public. Be that as it may, the designs are there, both London and provincial, and must have been an inspiration to many.

In 1838 a book was published called the *Workwoman's Guide* by 'A Lady'.[196] This was intended to be a manual for those who made their own household necessities, but it seems likely that it was of most use to the village seamstress or anyone making curtains and the like for others. It is invaluable today in showing exactly what was made and how, from bed-linen to bonnets, from smocks to curtains, but it is difficult to tell how much it was used at the time.

In 1833 John Loudon wrote a large and most interesting book called, rather dauntingly, *An Encyclopaedia of Cottage, Farm and Villa Architecture and Furniture.*[157] This gave extremely practical rules and suggestions for the furnishing of a middle-class house. The word 'cottage' does not here imply the home of a peasant, but a small, genteel residence.

Charles Eastlake, who was born in 1836, was trained as an architect but never practised. He designed furniture and furnishings, and what is probably more important, he wrote articles for the *Queen* and the *London Review* on various aspects of the home. These articles were put together and published in 1868 as *Hints on Household Taste,*[69] which ran into several editions over the next ten years. It was practical, full of common sense and advocated

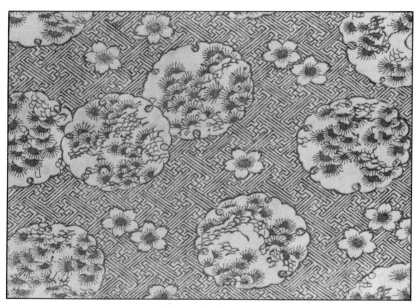

22. *Fabric in the Japanese style.*
Late nineteenth century. Smallhythe Place

simplicity in furnishings, light (if any) bed curtains, iron bedsteads and a return to medieval ways of thought. He said 'I recommend the adoption of no specific type of ancient furniture which is unsuited, whether in detail or general design, to the habit of modern life. It is the spirit and principles of early manufacture which I desire to see revived, and not the absolute forms in which they found embodiment.' These were very much the ideas of William Morris, on whom Eastlake's writings had a great effect.

Possibly the most influential of the late-nineteenth-century writers on matters pertaining to the home was Mrs Haweis, whose book, *The Art of*

Decoration, was published in 1881.[86] Mrs Haweis was a very articulate, artistic woman who hated following the crowd, and who had to earn money to keep her clergyman husband and children. She wrote many articles, and was well-known for *The Art of Beauty*, which was only surpassed by *The*

23. *Late-nineteenth-century room with a carpet designed by William Morris, hand-knotted at the Merton Abbey workshops. Standen*

Art of Decoration. In it she hoped that in future all architects would (like Morris, Burne-Jones, Owen Jones and others) design all parts of a house — wallpaper, furniture and textiles. Her plea was that every household should care for beauty, think for themselves and 'avoid the hated sheep walk'.

Silk as a fabric for both dress and upholstery had always been greatly esteemed but, because of the labour involved in its production, which could only take place during short periods of the year, was always extremely expensive. It was left to the chemists to try and produce a fibre which would take dye well and weave and look like silk.

The first thoughts on alternative fibres seem to have been those of Robert Hooke, an English scientist. In his book, *Micrographia*, he discussed, as early as 1665, the possibility of making an artificial fibre which could be spun like silk. At that date, silk was still the prerogative of the wealthy but was beginning to be wanted by more people. However, nothing came of Hooke's ideas, and it was not until the nineteenth century that the concept gathered momentum. By then there was more knowledge of chemistry, more machinery and a far wider background against which a scientist could work.

In 1842 Louis Schwabe, an English weaver, exhibited a machine for making artificial threads, and in 1855 George Andemans discovered a method of preparing fibres from the inner bark of mulberry and some other trees. These were not strong enough to spin, so he treated them with a rubber solution to form a mixture which could be spun. Again, this was not a commercial success.

In 1883 Sir Joseph Swan, the inventor of the electric lamp, unwittingly came into the picture. He was trying to make a fine filament for his bulbs, and he succeeded and patented the process, but either he did not realize or was not interested in the practical application for the textile industry.

It was left to a Frenchman, Comte Hilaire de Chardonnet, to make the first successful artificial fibre. He started experiments in 1878 and in 1884 produced his first fibre from a nitrocellulose pulp made from mulberry leaves. In 1891 he built a factory at Besançon, and there the first commercial production of artificial silk started.

It was not until 1924 that the trade name rayon was coined, and it was a long while before the term art silk ceased to be used. From this small beginning came the entire manmade-fibre industry, which in many ways completely changed and greatly enlarged the possibilities open to the upholsterer.

PART TWO

THE FURNISHINGS

Five

THE UPHOLSTERER

I have just finished my House, and must now think of furnishing it with fashionable Furniture. The Upholder is chief Agent in this Case: He is the Man upon whose Judgment I rely in the Choice of Goods; and I suppose he has not only Judgment in the Materials, but Taste in the Fashions, and Skill in the Workmanship. This Tradesman's Genius must be universal in every Branch of Furniture; though his proper Craft is to fit up Beds, Window-Curtains, Hangings, and to cover Chairs that have stuffed Bottoms...[30]

So said R. Campbell Esq. in 1747, in what might be called the first parents' guide to careers for their children, *The London Tradesman*. He goes on to say that the upholsterer acts (as an interior decorator would today) by employing 'Cabinet-Makers, Glass-Grinders, Looking-Glass Frame-Carvers, Carvers for Chairs, Testers and Posts of Bed, the Woolen-Draper, the Mercer, the Linen-Draper, and Several Species of Smiths', 'a vast many Tradesmen of the other mechanic Branches'.

R. Campbell goes on to explain the job of the Upholder, or upholsterer, who is not employing other tradesmen but is just working with fabrics.

However, a young Man who has a mind only to be a mere Upholder and has no Prospect of setting up in the Undertaking Way, does not require such a universal Genius as I have been speaking of: He must handle the Needle so alertly as to sew a plain Seam, and sew on the Lace without Puckers; and he must use his Sheers so dextrously as to cut a Valence or Counterpain with a genteel Sweep according to a Pattern he has before him. All this part of the Work is performed by Women, who never served an Apprenticeship to the Mystery, as well as Men. The stuffing and covering a Chair or Settee-Bed is indeed the nicest Part of this Branch; but it may be acquired without any remarkable Genius.

A hundred or so years later, in 1850, Mayhew, in an article in the *Morning Post*, said much the same thing:

The upholsterers who confine themselves to their own proper branch, are the fitterup of curtains and their hangings, either for beds or windows; they are also the stuffers of the chair and sofa cushions and the makers of carpets and of beds; that is to say they are the tradesmen who, in the language of the craft, 'do the soft work' – or in other words, all connected with the cabinet-makers art in which woven fabrics are the staple.[39]

24. *Chair upholstered in the seventeenth century. Knole*

The *Oxford English Dictionary* defines an upholder as a maker and repairer of small wares or second-hand articles of clothing, furniture etc., an upholsterer and undertaker; while 'upholster' is used with reference to the making and selling of beds and bedding, and an upholsterer is a tradesman or shopkeeper whose business is the making, finishing and repairing of articles of furniture and other house furnishing in which woven or similar fabrics, or materials used for stuffing these, are employed.

Another name for the upholsterer, often seen, is the French word *tapissier*. This comes from *tapis*, a carpet, but a carpet in its early sense of a wall hanging or covering for a table or cupboard. The *tapissier* supplied or made these carpets as well as the other textile furnishings for a house and even today a *tapissier* is employed in the Queen's household to look after the upholstery.

The upholsterer's work was increased because in general he was also an appraiser and an undertaker. These two additional jobs fell into line quite naturally as he, because of his interest in and knowledge of all articles of furniture as well as textiles, was in the best possible position to act as an appraiser or valuer. It would be interesting to know whether the men who valued, as distinct from listed, the inventories on the death of a rich man were professional upholsterers or whether they were the executors or stewards of the household. Certainly if the upholsterer furnished the funeral he would be about the place and in a position to do the valuation.

Funerals, prior to the twentieth century, were very elaborate affairs, involving not only the making and lining of the coffin, but also the transformation of the house into a black cave. In 1711, on the death of the 2nd Duke of Bedford, bills were paid for furnishing two staircases and the hall with broad and narrow baize; the Great Parlour with black cloth hangings, curtains, chairs, stools etc.; a downstairs bedchamber with a black cloth bed complete, hangings, window curtains, stools etc.; and an upstairs bedchamber the same.[187] These many yards of fabric would all be supplied and put up by the upholsterer, which shows clearly why he was also an undertaker. Although in many cases the fabric could be, and often was, put away ready for the next funeral, in a number of cases it was up for a considerable time – twelve months or even two years – and so would most likely be worn out. In fact, in the inventory of Worcester House taken in 1643, there were '8 peeces of black Cotton hangings Containeing 125 yards at 9d.', as well as 'A p'rcell of old black Cotton'. Obviously this was mourning fabric put carefully away until it was next needed.[144]

In Hogarth's series, *A Rake's Progress*, the first plate, showing Tom Rakewell on the death of his father, the miser, also shows the upholsterer on a ladder, nailing black cloth all round the room. Tom had no affection for his father but did not dare omit what was common practice in every home to a greater or lesser degree.

Mourning cloths are seldom mentioned in inventories, but in that of the Earl of Shrewsbury for his manor of Sheffield, taken in 1582, there is an entry for twelve mourning cushions covered in black cloth,[130] and on the death of Thomas, Earl of Rutland, in 1543, the value of the black cloth, black cotton and broad 'ruggis' is put at the very large sum of £158 19s. 10d.[11]

It was not only the house which was draped in black: the coach which carried the male members of the family to the funeral also needed fabric, and in 1618 the Rutland accounts show: 'Paid for 40 yardes of black baize to cover a coche for mourning at 2/6 the yarde, 5 li; and for covringe the said coche and taking it of 20s; being all 6 li.'[11]

The funeral accounts of Sir Nicholas Bacon, Lord Keeper of the Seal, who died in 1579, are itemized down to the last penny, and show how the clothiers and weavers must have welcomed the death of a great man. They also show how neatly the cost of the fabric bought by the estate for the gowns of the mourners was geared to the status of the wearer. The principal mourner, the Lord Treasurer of England, had twelve yards of cloth at £1 10s. a yard, while his two attendant gentlemen had seven and a half yards each at 16s. a yard and the three yeomen had one and a half yards each at 12s. a yard. Cloth at these prices applied to the officers of state and their attendants, but the eldest son and the Master of the Rolls, and other members of the family only merited fabric at £1 6s. 8d. the yard. The Dean of St Paul's, the physicians and sundry gentlemen, were valued at £1 a yard and less fabric as well, only five or six yards instead of twelve. Chaplains and 'gentlemen Offycers' were given five and a half yards at 18s., 'gentlemen wayters' at 16s.; heralds, except for Clarenceux, 10s. or 12s. 4d., 'Yomenne Ordynarye' a mere one and a half yards at 12s.; 'Groomes Ordynarye' one and a half yards at 10s., down to the 204 yards at 6s. 8d. for 'gownes of 68 poore menne accordinge to the yeares of hys Lordships age at 3 yeardes apece'. In all, 831 yards of cloth for mourners.

As well as this there was the provision of baize for hangings. In St Paul's forty-six yards of baize hangings in the 'upper quire from the lower parte of the Duke of Lancasters tombe upwards' was given to the vergers in lieu of fees. Incidentally, the Duke of Lancaster's tomb was boarded up 'to save yt from hurte'. York House, where the Lord Keeper had died, had railings put up in the courtyard 'to hang blacke on' and needed two men on guard to watch that it was not stolen; in the house, needles, 500 pins and tenter hooks were bought and three men hired to sew the hangings together and put them up. It sounds as though some of the hangings in St Paul's belonged to the church, as vergers had to be paid and given their dinners 'in givinge attendaunce in the churche when the same was hanged', and poor men were also paid 'for taking down the bayes and mending the same after the funeral'. In all a feat of organization and certainly a fillip to trade.

Another and possibly more difficult task which the upholsterer had to undertake from time to time was the refurbishing of seat furniture with fabrics which had already been used for some other purpose. At the time of the Reformation there must have been a great deal of this sort of work, turning the spoils from cathedrals, abbeys and churches into such furniture as bed hangings and cushions. There is very little documentation, but the diary of Lady Anne Clifford, in conjunction with the inventory taken in 1619 of the 'rich wearing Apparrell of the Right Honourable Richard Earle of Dorset' (her husband), gives an idea of something that was probably fairly commonplace.

In 1617 Lady Anne wrote: 'about this time my Lord made the Steward alter most of the rooms in the house [Knole], and dress them up as fine as he could, and determined to make all his old clothes in purple stuff for the Gallery and Drawing Chamber.' Whether this was done or not is uncertain, but with regard to a later entry there can be no doubt. In October 1619 Lady Anne wrote: 'About this time the Gallery was hung with all my Lord's caparisone which Edwards the upholsterer made up.' On the face of it this is a very enigmatic statement, for why should horse-cloths be hung in a gallery at Knole? However, in the inventory are two items with a note endorsed by the earl himself. The items read: 'one paire of bases of blewe veluett embroadered all over with globes hartes and flames of golde, lyned with blewe Taffetie,' and 'Two Caparisons conteyninge Fourteene peeces of blew veluett embroidered all over with globed hartes and flames of gold.' The note between the two items reads: '(Theis Bases and two Caparysons ware dl vppe 27 Marclj1618: To make a Canapie a Chaire Stooles & Cushyons for Knolle gallarie. Ri: Dorset)'. Later in the same inventory there is a larger set of tawny satin embroidered with silver which was used for the same purpose. This set consisted of a pair of bases, a 'feild furniture with seaven peeces belonging to it', presumably a field bed, one caparison of seven pieces, one trumpeter's coat, and one page's coat. All of these, made from the same fabric, were endorsed as 'furnyture for Knolle' by the earl. This is the make-do-and-mend attitude which one would expect to find in smaller houses, but it would come as a surprise to find it in a great house like Knole, if it were not known that the earl was always short of money, and frequently in debt.

The upholsterer continued to do these three jobs until the age of specialists started in the nineteenth century, when they were split off and the undertaker became a funeral director and the appraiser became a valuer.

The trades of upholders and upholsterers are very old – references go back to the fourteenth century – and over the centuries they have dealt with most things to do with the furnishings of a house: Stow refers to 'Fripperers or upholders' who in the fifteenth century sold old clothes and household stuff; the accounts of Sir Henry Sydney in 1567 refer to 'Hangings and other upholster stuff and work'. They were formed into a small guild, so small that they had no particular livery, and only the warden and two others attended the Lord Mayor of London's feast day in the Guildhall in 1532, the same number as other humble guilds. By the seventeenth century they were becoming more important and in his diary Pepys refers to two upholsterers who were of sufficient importance to be aldermen of the City of London – Alderman Reeves and Alderman Crow – and it is from Crow that he buys his 'camlott' bed, and who sends his men to set up the bed and the hangings of the room.

The eighteenth century saw the upholsterer at the height of his power and influence, acting as an interior decorator would today, but also organizing and directing the schemes of interior furnishings, making the furniture in his workshop and supplying all the necessary fabrics. The best-known name in this category is that of Thomas Chippendale, whose cabinet-making was a secondary concern to his primary work as upholsterer. He had craftsmen in all the different branches working for him, and in *Harewood House* Mary Mauchline has given a picture of what an upholsterer in a large house would do. During the 1770s Reid, one of Chippendale's best workmen, spent most of his time at Harewood in Yorkshire, living in the house for many months together. He unpacked and fixed the furniture sent up from the workshop,

hung walls with damask or paper, made up bed furniture, upholstered the covered seat furniture, laid carpets and put up blinds (including those called Venetian), and made covers for every possible article, 'petty-cotes' for the toilet tables, leather cases to encase the posts of the family bed, and oil-cloths for the sideboard of the celebrated Chippendale suite.

This list of duties shows that as well as being an expert in the use of hammer and nails, and all the heavy work of carpet laying, etc., Reid was also an accomplished needleman. It was he who made the hangings for the State Bed – a considerable task when every stitch was put in by hand. For this he used green silk damask supplied not by Chippendale but by Edwin Lascelles, the owner of the house, and in addition he needed green lustring for the valance, 120 yards of silk 'line', ninety-two yards of green and yellow fringe, eight yards of brown linen, twelve large silk tassels and ten smaller ones and eight brass pulleys in frames and pins. He also had to make up and fringe the quilt and counterpane to the bed, and then make a paper and canvas cover for it when not in use. Reid then made the window curtains, lining them and trimming them, and put up the cornices, curtain pulleys, cloak-pins, etc. It would certainly need a competent and versatile workman to accomplish all these varied tasks satisfactorily.

Chippendale was the best known upholsterer of the period, but he was by no means the only one. Sophie von la Roche tells of a visit in 1786 to Seddons who, she says, employed 400 apprentices, joiners, carvers, gilders, mirror-workers, upholsterers and locksmiths. Among all the chairs, tables, footstools and dressing-tables she saw: 'chintz, silk and wool materials for curtains and bedcovers; hangings in every possible material, carpets and stair-carpets to order; in short anything one might desire to furnish a house; and all the workmen besides and a great many seamstresses; their own saw-house too where many blocks and fine foreign wood lie piled.'[177]

When the younger Thomas Chippendale went bankrupt in 1804 the *Morning Chronicle* advertised his upholstery stock, which comprised: 'fine seasoned feathers Flocks, wool curled hair, blankets, counterpanes, printed and plain calicoes, dimities, tickens, serges, morines, Manchesters, sattin hair cloths, white and brown Holland, a quantity of crimson and various coloured silk damasks, tabinet, lutestring, silk fringe, Brussels carpeting...' A fairly comprehensive collection of the upholsterer's stock.

As well as the famous names catering for the rich there were many small provincial upholsterers supplying middle-class homes, and in some cases needing or at least being given help by those who employed them. Pepys' wife, for example, 'works all day at home like a horse at the making of her hanging for our chamber and the bed', and also: 'Found my wife busy about making her hangings for her chamber with the Upholsterer.' Blundell, in 1717, had 'Mr Crumpton of Liverpool ye Upholsterer' to dine. Times must have been hard for 'he came to see what work I had for him'. Blundell found him work: 'Curtains and Vallance for ye Windows in ye Gallery and the two best Rooms', 'covering 10 Cushions and one Squab-face etc.', 'Reparing ye Beds in ye Garden and Parlour Chambers'. Blundell goes on to say, 'I was busy most of ye day helping them and putting things in order.' Five years later his daughters were coming home after six years at school in Flanders and preparations had to be made: 'The Appolstaror finished new vamping up the Green Bed in ye Parlour Chamber', and, 'I helped Mr. Marsh, Mr. Crumptons man, to fix up the Blew Bed in my Daughters Room.'[43] It is not easy to tell whether the upholsterer really needed Blundell's help, or whether Blundell just could not see anything going on in which he did not have a hand. He could well have been nothing but a nuisance.

Not only did the upholsterer produce and fix all the textiles in a house, he sometimes did, or at least organized, the embroideries of a room. In the seventeenth, eighteenth and nineteenth centuries, many of the furnishings

such as bed curtains, firescreens, chair seats and cushions were embroidered. These were often worked by the ladies of the house, but they could also be produced by the upholsterer.

At Canons Ashby in Northamptonshire there is a set of chairs and a settee, and the bill has been found which states that Thomas Phill, an upholsterer, in 1714 supplied: '6 wallnuttree back chairs, frames of ye newest fashion, Stufft up in Lynnen', and also itemizes, 'ffor making ye needlework covers, and fixing yon on ye chairs'. An additional role.[75]

But many upholsterers, especially in the provinces, must have had more than the one role, and the whole question of who produced what is, as yet, vague. One man over whose activities hangs a large question mark was P. J. Knights of Norwich. Apart from the fact that he won the silver medal of the Royal Society of Arts in 1792 for producing the first shawl counterpane, his career is shrouded in ambiguity. Basically he was a shawl manufacturer and in 1792 was appointed 'Shawl man to her Majesty' (Queen Charlotte), producing shawl fabric to be used in both upholstery and costume: 'On Saturday last Her Majesty and all the Princesses appeared in Norwich Shawl Dresses of Mr Knights Manufactory.' But as well as his activities in the shawl trade Knights appears to have been an upholsterer, in its widest sense, as well. The *Norfolk Chronicle* reported that the Duke of Norfolk visited the manufactory and 'assured Mr Knights that he should furnish three new rooms in Arundel Castle with shawl manufacture and expressed it as his particular wish that every part of the furniture should be executed in Norfolk desiring Mr Knights to find every part of it complete, viz. cabinet works, carving, gilding, upholstery etc.' As far as is known Knights himself only produced fabric, and so would have had to sub-contract among Norfolk craftsmen for the rest. Sadly Arundel Castle was redecorated in the nineteenth century and the archivist there has been unable to find any reference in the records to the work.

Luckily, the National Trust at Blickling possesses one of the only two known shawl counterpanes of Knights Manufacture, although they are in a mutilated state. The counterpane is mentioned in the 1793 inventory, even then put away in a chest, but itemized as from the Norwich Shawl Manufactory. It is now cut up to provide the headboard and valance of the bed in the Chinese bedroom. However, enough remains, together with the prototype of the counterpane given to Queen Charlotte in 1792, and now in Stranger's Hall Museum, Norwich, to be able to describe shawling as used in both upholstery and dress. It could be woven twelve feet wide without a seam, with a silk warp and fine, worsted weft. The design was

25. Chair with canvas-work cover produced by the upholsterer.
Early eighteenth century, Canons Ashby

26. *Centre of a Norwich shawl counterpane (1792)
made into the headboard of a bed in the 1930s. Blickling Hall*

27. *Border of a Norwich shawl counterpane (1792) made
into the valance of a bed in the 1930s. Blickling Hall*

added afterwards by darning. The darning is random, but so close that from a short distance away it looks like weaving. In view of the fame of this fabric in the late eighteenth century it seems possible that there is some more of it somewhere which may still come to light.

The beginning of the nineteenth century saw the upholsterer as busy as ever. There were now few state beds and less ornate hangings, but on the other hand curtains were intricately draped and textiles were still very important. By the middle of the century, however, furnishings were becoming much simpler, even if still rich and heavy. Beds were more often of metal, which did not harbour bugs, and bed curtains were frowned upon as being unhygienic. So, gradually, with the rise of the department store, the ancient craft became split into different sections. The store sold fabrics by the yard in one department, carpets in another and furniture in yet another, and in the workrooms the anonymous 'mere upholsterer' put them together as required.

Six

WALL HANGINGS

Today we are so used to the majority of inside walls being covered with either paper or paint that the sheer diversity of the coverings of the past comes as a surprise. The medieval and sixteenth-century wall inside a house could be stone, brick, plaster, wood or, in some cases, rubble. All these

28. Felletin tapestry, late seventeenth century. Anglesey Abbey

surfaces were cold, dull to look at and dirty, so they were, as often as possible, covered. The coverings were not attached to the wall, but were always hung, and the phrase 'hangings' continued into the eighteenth and nineteenth centuries when the coverings did not hang loose, but were fastened to the wall itself, which by then was generally covered with plaster. Early wallpaper was often glued to canvas which was then either pasted to the wall or else tacked onto battens, while fabric was stretched onto battens attached to the wall. James Ayres[24] has pointed out that in the eighteenth century some houses were built with completely plain panelling which was designed to be hidden by the hangings stretched over it, though by no means all houses at this time had hangings, especially in the towns. Saussure, visiting London in 1725, says, 'hangings are little used in London houses on account of the coal smoke which would ruin them, besides which woodwork is considered to be cleaner and prevents damp on the wall.'[61]

So, while hangings were essential to comfort in the sixteenth century, as building standards improved they became optional, and in the seventeenth century vied with panelling, and in the eighteenth vied with both panelling and the new wallpaper. During most of the nineteenth century, wallpaper was the chosen covering, though at the end of the century quite ordinary houses might have fabric panels in the drawing room while other rooms were hung with wallpaper.

TAPESTRIES

The earliest wall covering was tapestry and it stayed in fashion for a very long while. Medieval tapestries were woven in Europe in what would now be Holland, Belgium and northern France, but was then Flanders and Burgundy. The weaving of these very large pieces became a fine art and was a supreme example of the skill of the craftsman – the weaver – in interpreting the design and intention of the artist, and translating the design into his own medium.

Tapestries originated with the nomadic tent-dwellers of the East. They were ideal for a wandering life, as they were flexible, kept out wind and could be taken down, rolled up and moved on to the next stopping place. A nobleman in fourteenth- or fifteenth-century England also led a nomadic life as he travelled from manor to manor or castle to castle, taking his household and his comforts with him. So when the technique of tapestry weaving had been learnt by the West, the products immediately became popular.

The technique of tapestry weaving is different from ordinary weaving, and this difference explains why many are in such bad repair. They are woven sideways; that is, the warp, when the tapestry is hung, runs horizontally and the weft, which is of weaker threads than the warp, takes the full weight of the hanging, running vertically. Not only is a tapestry hung the opposite way to a length of cloth, it is also woven by a different method. In cloth-making a shuttle is sent from side to side, or selvage to selvage, but in tapestry weaving each colour has its own shuttle which only

29. Detail of a Felletin tapestry showing the technique. Late seventeenth century. Anglesey Abbey

travels as far as the design indicates and returns, so that many shuttles can be in play in one width of the fabric. It is this turning back of the shuttle where a colour ends which makes the small slits which are an integral part of the fabric.

This technique, having been learnt in the west, was used to make the hangings which both decorated and warmed castles and eventually large and even small houses. Castles all over Europe were beginning to be less concerned with fortification and more with domestic comfort, and for that, colour and warmth figured prominently. The hangings were bright and gay, told a story when few could read and helped to keep hall or solar warm. They were generally hung on rods a little distance from the wall, leaving a passage for servants to use behind them. They were easy to take down, could be put onto a baggage cart and taken to the next house to be visited by the monarch or noble on a progress. They were also borrowed from time to time to decorate a house for festivities. A delightful entry occurs in the Steward's Account of the Bacon family. In 1597 the youngest daughter of the house was to be married at Stiffkey and tapestries were borrowed from her brother-in-law at Ashwellthorpe, some thirty-five miles away. They were fetched, but obviously the rooms at Stiffkey were not the same size as those at Ashwellthorpe, so thread was bought 'to tuck the hangings in the Great Chamber'.[1]

With all the wear and tear, moving about, smoke, and the fact that tapestries were hung from their weakest side, it is remarkable that any early ones still exist, and there are few, if any, which have not been repaired many times; the standard of repairs varying from the excellent to the abysmal. Wendy Hefford has calculated from a study of the royal accounts that tapestries belonging to the Crown have been repaired on an average every thirty to fifty years.[88] The standard of conservation has improved significantly in the past thirty years or so, with the result that, it is hoped, repairs may not have to be so frequent in the future. Tapestry conservation and repair is, however, very expensive now, as indeed it always has been; Horace Walpole noted after a visit to Chatsworth that the Duke of Devonshire had paid £180 for the repair of a suit of six pieces. Not a small sum of money in the first half of the eighteenth century.

Because of the size of the medieval hall or church, tapestries were woven in sets, or suits as they were called, with each panel showing one incident in a story. The stories were either biblical, with far more taken from the Old than the New Testament, or mythological. There were also verdure tapestries which consisted of pictures of trees, flowers and wild-life generally. They were such an important item of furnishing that when new houses were being built a room could be made a specific size to take the set, rather than the other way round. In the Great High Chamber at Hardwick Hall there are eight pieces of Brussels tapestry illustrating the story of Ulysses. They were bought in 1587 and the room was then planned especially to take them. Much later, in the 1770s, when the 2nd Earl of Buckinghamshire was remodelling part of Blickling Hall, the size of what was then the New Drawing Room, later called the Peter the Great Room, was determined by the dimensions of the tapestry given to the earl by Catherine the Great of Russia.

The sheer yardage required in a large house was enormous. The 1603 inventory of Hengrave Hall,[113] for example, shows that in the Great

Chamber there were 'Eight large pieces of fine arras hanging', measuring 160 yards. There was also another piece hung between the chimney and the window; two pieces 'somewhat finer' hung each side 'up on the posts of the great window'; two pieces hung over the chimney, 'whereof one hath Sir Thomas Kytson's and the Cornwallis ther armes in ye border of it; ye other wrought with greate beasts'. All this for just one room in a substantial but not enormous house, and the other rooms had tapestries in proportion.

There were no tapestries woven in medieval England, as far as is known. The first documented workshop is that of William Sheldon of Warwickshire, in the middle of the sixteenth century. Sheldon's tapestries are beautifully and finely woven and his works produced small articles as well as detailed maps of English counties, one of which is on loan to Oxburgh Hall. The

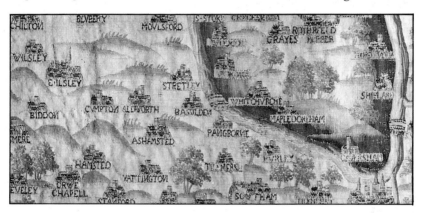

31. *Detail of a Sheldon map tapestry showing Berkshire.*
Late sixteenth century, Oxburgh Hall

Sheldon output was never large and was eclipsed by the factory at Mortlake which was started in 1618 under the direction of Sir Francis Crane and the patronage of James I. This factory was always both encouraged and subsidized by the Crown and produced some excellent work, the best and most famous set being the Acts of the Apostles from the cartoons by Raphael. So well known was the work of this factory that in 1690 Mary Evelyn wrote, in *Mundus Muliebris*:[73]

> Besides all these, 'tis always meant
> You firnish her Appartiment
> With *Moreclack* Tapestry, Damask Bed,
> Or Velvet richly embroidered.

30. *Chair with the Beauvais tapestry cover conserved.*
Second half of the eighteenth century. Polesden Lacey

32. *One of a series of four tapestries, 'Naked Boys Playing',*
designed by Francis Poyntz, c. 1680
for the Mortlake workshops then at Hatton Garden
in central London. Hardwick Hall

Blickling Hall has a suit from Mortlake which tells the story of Abraham. These are at present undergoing their 'twice a century' restoration, one by one.

Soho tapestries made under the direction of John Vanderbank were famous for their *chinoiserie* and Indian subjects, the dates of the factory, 1685–1727, coinciding with the fashion for anything from the east – especially the never-never land of Cathay – in dress, furnishings and architecture. By this date the size of the sets was diminishing, making them more suitable for smaller houses, and at Beauvais and Aubusson they wove seats and backs for chairs and sofas as well as wall hangings, so that a whole room could be furnished *en suite*. The Tapestry Room at Osterley is an excellent example of this lighter, all-over treatment (see illus. 70).

There were virtually no new developments in the nineteenth century until William Morris started to weave at Merton Abbey in Surrey. He tried to get back to the original idea of a weaver interpreting a design rather than copying a painting. In the Beauvais factory in particular, Oudry and Boucher, as painters, had insisted on an exact reproduction of the painters' intentions and colouring, allowing for no interpretation by the weaver, and Morris set out to reverse this trend. He succeeded with the help of Burne-Jones, but he surely spread himself too thin in too many directions to bring tapestries back to the forefront of furnishing.

PAINTED OR STAINED CLOTHS

In his *Description of England*, written in 1577, William Harrison said that 'The walls of our houses in the inner sides in like sort be either hanged with tapestry, arras work, or painted cloths, wherein either diverse histories, or herbs, beasts, knots and suchlike are stained...'[85] The painted cloths he is referring to have been in fashion in one way or another from medieval times until today. In the fifteenth, sixteenth and seventeenth centuries these cloths were used as cheap substitutes for tapestries. Then came the influx of pintadoes and palampores from India, which developed into the European printed textiles of the eighteenth century.

Stained cloths were decorated by members of the Painters and Stainers Guild; the painters painting wood, plaster and other surfaces, and the stainers working on cloth. The designs were painted on either brown hempen cloth or else brown osnaburg,[182] but there are few left and it is not always clear what they were like, though at Belton in the Queen's Room there are painted canvas wall hangings, and there is also a painted cloth in the chapel at Hardwick.

Early inventories are not always helpful about these cloths and it is difficult to know whether the article, often referred to as the 'hanging', is, in fact, tapestry or stained cloth, but generally, tapestries being more expensive, are called that, and 'hangings' mean painted cloths. The L'Estrange accounts[13] for 1533 show that three cloths hang in the parlour, as well as a hanging of red and green lined with canvas. The first three are likely to be stained cloths, while the last probably consists of joined panels of lined fabric in alternate red and green. Red and green must have been fashionable, as Thomas Leman, a Norfolk parson had, in nearly the same year, two red and green cloths with painted borders in his hall, and a 'parcel of hangings painted with vines' in the parlour.[122]

The King's Closet at Knole has wall hangings of a mixed wool and linen, printed. This, though block printed rather than freely painted, imitates Italian velvets and possibly resembles early stained cloth.

*33. Detail of a printed fabric on the wall
of the King's Closet at Knole*

LEATHER

Another type of hanging, found chiefly in the houses of the well-to-do or the aspiring civil-service class that Samuel Pepys belonged to, was gilt leather. Some of this came from Holland, but most from Spain, which was always famous for its leather workers, and indeed the hangings in Rainthorpe Hall near Norwich are said to have come from the cabin of a wrecked Spanish galleon.

These hangings were most popular between about 1600 and 1740 though they were put up both before and after these dates. Kenilworth Castle, the home of Robert Dudley, Earl of Leicester, must have had some of the most

34. Detail of leather hangings, seventeenth century. Dyrham Park

sumptuous pieces, rivalling and probably surpassing the tapestries of the time. The 1583 inventory includes sixteen pieces, 'having everie one in the topp the picture of a man and a woman', three and a half ells deep and two and a half ells in length. There were also three pieces of the story of Susanna, 'paned gilt and blue', three pieces of the prodigal son, also 'paned gilt and blewe', and many more.[119]

In the 1654 inventory of Ham House the room which was the family parlour and is now the chapel had 'a suite of red and gold leather hangings'[111] lining the walls, while at Dyrham Park the present drawing room was originally called the Gilt Leather Parlour (1692–4). Southampton House in

35. Leather panel from the staircase at Oxburgh Hall

London was hung with both tapestries and gilt leather and Sarah, Duchess of Marlborough, writing to her granddaughter in 1732 says 'In this room at Southampton House there is a set of blue and gold leather hangings which I bespoke, and which is now as fresh as when it was put up. And I like it so extremely I have bespoke the same to hang one of my rooms at Wimbledon.'[55]

These were all houses of wealthy people but up-and-coming gentry such as Pepys were not behindhand in following fashion. In 1660 he says, 'This morning my dining-room was finished with grene serge hangings and gilt leather which is very handsome.'[58] It is not clear from this where the leather had been put. It might have been as a fillet round the panels of serge or it could have been paned in alternate panels of leather and serge, but it is likely that he meant that the curtains were of green serge and the panelling was of leather.

36. *Leather wall hanging, 'The Meeting of Anthony and Cleopatra'.*
Dunster Castle

These hangings took a great number of skins, and at Gosfield Hall in Essex, which had many leather hangings, there was in the closet next to the 'workinge roome', '2 sutes of leather hangings for closets containing neere 60 skins a sute'. In the same closet, obviously used as a storeroom, was '1 sute of gilt leather and grene cloth hangings for my Ladies closett...'[101]

The technique of gilding leather varied. Diderot in his encyclopedia cites two different methods, but the wall hangings at Dunster Castle were worked with yet another, earlier technique. Here the leather was prepared by cutting to shape and joined, then sheets of silver foil were stuck on, the design drawn on from a cartoon and the highlights hand-tooled. Finally the hangings were coloured with oil paint and glazes through which the burnished metal gleamed. All hangings were not prepared as carefully as these. At Oxburgh, for example, where the leather is along a narrow passage and up the staircase, with admittedly very awkwardly-shaped panels, the leather has been cut from large pieces and stuck onto the panelling with a fine disregard for design.

While a number of houses still have rooms with leather hangings, panels which depict whole stories are less common and the Antony and Cleopatra series at Dunster Castle is unique in England.

FABRIC HANGINGS

While tapestries, stained cloths and gilt leather were the most generally used hangings at the beginning of the period, and wallpaper at the end, in between by far the most usual wall covering was fabric. Tapestries were needed in cold, dark houses, but they were complete in themselves and nothing could be hung on them. As houses got lighter with more and larger windows and there were more professional artists, so a background on which pictures could be hung was needed, and fabric was used. Pepys in 1667 put it clearly: he spent an afternoon with his wife discussing alterations to his furnishing, 'which will cost money – that is, furnish our best room with tapestry and other rooms with pictures'.[58]

These different forms of wall covering all overlapped to a great extent, so that tapestries remained in some rooms, and indeed in whole houses where the owners could not afford or did not wish to change. Wallpaper was available by the middle of the seventeenth century, though not in common use until the eighteenth.

Very few houses, even those with the richest owners, had the same type of wall coverings in each room at any one time. Tapestry, panelling, wainscot, fabric and wallpaper could be and frequently were seen together. The state or best rooms might well be done up in the latest style, but the lesser rooms were often left as they had originally been decorated, often many years before. Tapestry was sometimes taken down and put into a smaller room, having to be cut about in the process, which is one reason why so many are mutilated. In the 1970s a room in an old house in Norwich was being redecorated. The walls were covered with 1930s-style wallpaper. The architect was curious and started picking the paper away. No fewer than seven layers of wallpaper were discovered glued onto a very pleasant tapestry which was stretched on battens fastened to the wall. The reason the tapestry had been left when it went out of fashion soon become obvious, as behind it was an unplastered rubble wall. It had been cheaper and easier in the late eighteenth century to use the tapestry as a base for the paper rather than plaster the wall.

Fabric as a wall covering in one form or another was in fashion all through the period we are dealing with, though it was at its most popular in the eighteenth century. At that time it was an integral part of the room, fastened to the wall and immovable; it ceased to be a 'hanging' in the early sense of the word. It is sometimes difficult in inventories to distinguish between bed curtains, window curtains or wall coverings, as all three can be referred to as 'hangings', but there are many clear enough to tell us which fabric was used and in what colours.

As far back as 1459 a very detailed inventory was taken on the death of Sir John Fastolf of Caister Castle in Norfolk.[108] Sir John is supposed to be the prototype of Shakespeare's Sir John Falstaff and was a very rich man. As well as many tapestries he had a hanging of blue worsted thirteen feet long, one of deep green eleven yards long and yet another with 'men drawen in darke grene worstet'. The last was presumably embroidered, and this suggests that the first two were of plain fabric, unnapped and smooth, in a single colour. Worsted was not such a common fabric as say, though that too was woven from long, staple wool, in a twill pattern. Say was used for all types of hangings: bed, window and wall as well as being made into clothes. In 1511 John Borel of Yarmouth[97] had hangings of say in the hall (colour unspecified), parlour (green) and red chamber (red). On the death of Dame Agnes Hungerford, who was executed at Tyburn in 1523 for the murder of her husband, a very detailed inventory was taken as her goods were forfeit to the Crown.[116] Among them were three pieces of say, striped in red and green for hanging in the hall, and a 'hanging of red say with hundret of pyn apples imbroidered with golde to put on the same hanging' was in the Queen's Chamber. This suggests that the pineapples were embroidered ready to apply onto the say, and one cannot help wondering what the king's embroiderers then used them for. Did they later adorn one of the royal hangings?

There are many references to say being either red or green and they must have been the most popular colours, but other colours were used. The 1603 inventory of Hengrave Hall says that blue and yellow say hangings were in the 'chamber where yet musicyons playe'.[113]

Gradually the fabrics used for wall coverings altered, with, as always, the great houses changing first, while the more humble remained in the older fashions. Hardwick Hall had a complete inventory taken in 1601[112] which lists all the hangings, showing that the Hall had a considerable number of very large ones, as well as tapestries. These were of applied work, allegorical in the Elizabethan tradition, and showed Heroines accompanied by the five Virtues; the Virtues and their seven Contraries; and the Liberal Arts. The art of domestic embroidery had reached a peak and Bess, the chatelaine, was a skilled needlewoman who would certainly have directed the work as well as doing much of it herself. Hardwick did not only have embroidered hangings; there were others of 'clothe of golde, velvette, and other like stuff'.

At about the same date Hengrave had, in the Tower Gallery, 'hangings of greene flannelle complete, with a valance indented and fringed with lace and bells'. Although this sounds as though it might refer to curtains, bed or window, in this case it certainly can only refer to wall hangings, as there is no bed in the gallery and the 'curtyon' is separately listed as of 'green carsye'.

Darnix was used for lesser rooms and Worcester House had, in 1643, 'Darnix hangings about a Closset', which must have been either very old or very cheap, as they were only valued at 6s.[144]

Some houses had different sets of hangings for summer and winter. The 1641 inventory of Arundel House[115] was presumably taken in summer, as the Great Chamber was hung with paned red and yellow damask, but 'Also for the Roome there is a suite of Freeze hanging in the Wardrobe'. This pattern continues through all the main rooms, with the winter hangings being always of frieze.

As the tacks fastening the fabric to the battens would have shown, fillets were used to cover the edges and these fillets were an integral part of the design. They could be metal, gilded, composition or braid, either plain or ornate. In some cases the fillets went around the architraves of the doors and the fireplaces, which might mean that they had to be specially designed to adapt to the shaping. Their colour was important to the decorative scheme. Gilt metal or gilded rope complements rich crimson damask at Felbrigg, but one of the most subtle schemes is that of the State Bedroom at Blickling Hall. Here the colour is ivory and gold; ivory moiré wall panels, ivory paint, ivory chair covers, with the ivory columns which form the bed alcove picked out with gold, and the chairs gilded. The bed behind the pillars, however, has crimson silk furniture with the royal arms and emblems applied in gold. The whole decorative scheme is held together by the ivory wall panels having fillets of narrow crimson braid.

From an inventory taken at Stow Hall in 1709[135] it seems that before the use of fillets the mouldings of the panels were used to hide the edges of the fabric. Stow Hall was a house which belonged to a 'Turky merchant' and was furnished in the fashionable eastern style even to the extent of

37. *Metal fillet around the marble mantelpiece*
in the saloon at Felbrigg

having 'India' paintings on the ceilings, while there were India or japanned pictures, screens, bed furniture, wainscot and curtains. In one room, the 'Dyneing Room to the Drawing Room', which had japan wainscot, there were '10 black japan mouldings for the hangings', while in a room used as a storeroom were '12 mouldings for the hangings in the best bedroom'.

During the eighteenth century damask was by far the most generally used wall fabric – sometimes of silk, sometimes of wool stretched tight on battens. It was handsome, a good background for pictures and very long lasting. There is still damask on walls which has been there for well over

150 years. Damask was not outrageously expensive, and a good flock paper which often copied damask design was nearly as dear. Lady Mary Wortley Montagu, in writing to her daughter, Lady Bute, in 1749 says, 'I have heard the fame of paper hangings and had some thoughts of sending for a suite,

38. *Gilded rope fillet covering the fastenings of wool damask hangings in the cabinet at Felbrigg Hall.*

but was informed that they are as dear as damask, which put an end to my curiosity.'[65] Mrs Delany, however, felt that if she was going to cover her walls with pictures it was much more sensible to use paper.[46]

From the middle of the seventeenth century there was a great vogue for the exotic, and unusual goods were being brought into the country by the East India Company from India and China, particularly wallpaper and fabrics. The paper, hand-painted onto separate sheets, was used sparingly in small rooms, while the chintz were mostly seen as bed hangings and curtains. But in 1663 Pepys, in the forefront of fashion, writes that 'after many tryells bought my wife a Chinke; that is a paynted India callico for to line her new Study. which is very pretty.'[58] This trend went on through the next century, with Indian fabrics being used as well as the more usual worsted and silk.

The use of fabrics for wall hangings continued in the nineteenth century, especially in the great country houses, but middle-class homes generally settled for the often prettier wallpaper, which was much more suitable for their smaller rooms and, being cheaper, could be renewed more frequently.

39. *Detail of Chinese wallpaper, Saltram*

This did not always meet with approval and Loudon, writing in 1833 in his *Beau Ideal of an English Villa*, suggests that in the drawing room at least the walls should be 'hung with watered silk or satin and watered stripes alternately or panels of silk with gilt moulding. Where silk or velvet is used for furniture a papered wall has a poor effect except perhaps a plain flock paper which has the appearance of cloth or a paper printed in imitation of striped or watered silk.' Mrs Lybbe Powys comes right to the point when she writes in 1803 about an engaged couple, saying that 'after he returned from Paris, finding paper hangings were there call'd vulgar, immediately took all down and hung all with sattins'.[59]

Seven

BEDS

A bed is the one article of furniture which no house is without, and it has always been considered the most important item in any dwelling. In times when it was unlikely that people would be able to sleep without others – often several others – in the same room, a bed, snugly curtained, represented warmth, comfort and privacy.

It could be expensive and, once purchased or made, became a family heirloom to be handed down from generation to generation. The best bed in a house was generally willed to whoever inherited the house, so that it need not be moved, with the others being left in descending order through the family.

Because of its importance in the household, early wills and inventories give an excellent idea of the variety and types which were current, and as they were often solidly made of oak there are quite a few Elizabethan and Stuart beds still to be seen.

It is not always easy to interpret the wording relating to different types and different parts of a bed in the fifteenth and sixteenth centuries, and indeed even the *Oxford English Dictionary* admits to the ambiguity. The frame or bedstead was the least important part and could be in use for many years; it was the hangings on which skill and money were lavished. It is difficult, however, to be certain of the shape of these hangings if the meaning of the parts is unclear.

Basically, an early bed had a wooden frame, often with posts (though the phrase 'four-poster' had not yet come into being), a covering over the top, either suspended from the ceiling or else slotted into the top of the posts, and a board behind the pillows of variable height. In the fifteenth and sixteenth centuries the board behind was known as the tester, while the flat top was called the celure or seler (or any other variation on the spelling). During the sixteenth century the meaning changed and the top was called the tester and the back of the bed the headboard, though the old names ran parallel.

Some beds were referred to as 'canopy' beds and these had covered frames which jutted out from the wall, usually suspended from the ceiling, while a 'sparver' bed, from medieval times to the end of the sixteenth century, had a round canopy from the ceiling very like the alcove bed or the French canopy bed of the late eighteenth century.

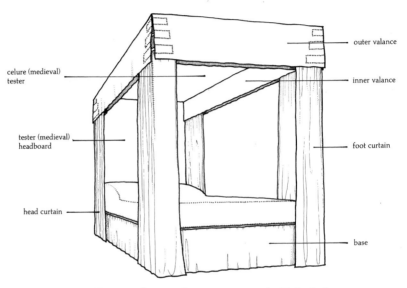

40. *Diagram showing the various parts of a Tudor bed*

There were generally two sets of valances round the celure, an inner and an outer, with the curtains running between them, their rings or pulleys invisible. There were also valances on two sides of the bed hanging from the frame to the floor, known as bases or pantes. And most important were the curtains, sometimes three, more often five, hanging from celure to the floor.

Early beds had their rectangular frames 'corded', and payments for cords, lines and ropes appear in many household accounts. The frames had holes bored through them, horizontally, and through these holes thick cord or rope was passed, making a hammock which became the base for the mats, quilts, mattresses or feather-beds on which the sleeper lay. The Rutland accounts for 1611 show that mats to lay under feather-beds, 'being rough and shaggie', cost 18d. and 7s. the mat.[11]

According to William Harrison in his *Description of England*,[85] there was a great increase in the comfort of beds and of the quality of life generally about that time. He says, 'there are old men yet dwelling in the village where I remain which have noted three things to be marvellously altered in England within their sound remembrance ...' The first was the greatly increased number of chimneys,

the second is the great (though not general) amendment of lodging, for (said they) our fathers, yea, and we ourselves also, have lien full oft upon straw pallets, on rough mats covered only with a sheet, under covers made of dagswain or hapharlots [coarse shaggy materials] (I use their own terms), and a good round log under their heads instead of a bolster or pillow. If it were not so that our fathers or the goodman of the house had within seven years after his marriage purchased a mattress or flock-bed, and thereto a sack of chaff to rest his head upon, he thought himself to be as well lodged as the lord in the town ...

He went on to say that pillows 'were thought meet only for women in childbed. As for servants, if they had any sheet above them it was well, for seldom had they any under their bodies to keep them from the pricking straws that ran oft through the canvas of the pallet and rased their hardened sides.'

This description is certainly borne out by inventories and wills, although even at this date there is evidence that the comfort of servants was not always ignored. In the Bacon Archives, '2 coverletes for serveing mens beds' were bought in 1589 at a not inconsiderable cost of 12s.[1] Later, in 1715, Lady Grisell Baillie bought '2 beds green and blue' for servants. This refers to the curtains, but she also bought '2 fether beds, 2 bolsters, 2 pillows, 2 twilts, 4 blankets' and '2 folding beds for the above sd beding for servants'.[2] The fact that these beds folded away by day indicates that they were for the use of upper servants, possibly ladies' maids or valets who would sleep near their masters or mistresses in a corridor or closet.

And in all our notions of early discomfort for servants it is worth noting that at Caister Castle in 1459 even the porter slept on a feather-bed, and it is not until the 'grete stabull', the 'Sumer Stabull', and the 'Gardinares Chambre' are reached that the beds only have mattresses rather than feathers; even they have sheets and coverlets.[108]

The frame of the bed was usually made by a carpenter, joiner or, for the more ornate beds, a cabinet-maker, but in outlying districts or in not very well-off families it might be made on the estate. This last kind of homemade bed is very well documented in the Bacon Archives where, in 1591, a bed was made for 'Mistress Ann', who was about to be married. The basic frame is not mentioned but it would appear to have been made on the estate. Crumlin, who was the horse keeper, but also did much of the shopping, was paid 10d. for 'nayles and gyrthes webbe for Mistress Ann Frame', and 6d. for '200 of garnysheninge nayles for the bed'. So the frame had a webbing rather than a corded base and was decorated with large studs, possibly brass. Then the tailor was paid 2d. 'for eyes to hange the vallance of a bed' and Crumlin again was paid 1s. 3d. for 'a dussen curtayin ringes 2 and 70 curtaiyne ringes', presumably of two different sizes, the seventy-two for the drawing curtains around the bed, and possibly the dozen to hang the tester. Finally 'to the embroiders sonne for 24 weeks 3 days at 3s. the weeke ...' It is sad that the fabric he embroidered for the curtains is not specified, though in twenty-four weeks he should have been able to embroider all the bed curtains. At the same date, his father, John Roofe, the embroiderer, was also working at Stiffkey, but for another member of the family. He was paid 5s. a week for thirty-four weeks and it would be interesting to be able to compare their work and see whether the son was really 2s. a week less skilful than his father.[1]

There is another glimpse of a bedstead being homemade in the accounts to Sarah Fell of Furness in Lancashire.[3] In 1673 she pays 'Thos. Wilson wright for his men 15 dayes in sowinge a tree into bedsteads' 5s. 10d., and in 1675 she pays the same Thos. Wilson 1s. 1d. for 'workeinge and makeinge a trundle bedstede' and 'for a bedd coard'. It may be coincidence but both these smallish estates were in very isolated parts of the country, and it was probably considerably cheaper to make furniture on the spot rather than deal with transport difficulties.

Lady Grisell Baillie also had a bed made in 1697 and paid the turner for making the frame, and then for curtain rods, ropes and tacks; a feather-bed, bolster and two pillows; scarlet crape for the curtains and calico for lining them; sewing silk and thread, and payment to the upholsterer for fitting the furniture – amounting in all to £114 Scots money.[2]

Bedsteads were made of oak, walnut or beech, and though generally of considerably lesser value than the furniture, were often enriched with gilding and even precious stones. Many of them were taken wherever the nobleman went, and in the Rutland accounts for 1537 a trussed bed (which could be taken to pieces easily) with gilded posts was bought by my lord to carry to the court. In 1599, in the same accounts, bedsteads are painted and gilded green and gold, and a purple bed is silvered.

The L'Estranges of Hunstanton pay a painter in 1522 for 'painting my Masters arms on the fanes of the bed',[13] and at Cannons in 1733 John

Loveday saw 'a gold and velvet bed, Coronet at the Bed's head, with precious stones, pearls, emerald and garnet' – very opulent.[158]

On the frame, corded, webbed or with stretched sacking or rush mats, came the mattresses, and again from account books it becomes obvious that whereas the wealthy went straight to an upholsterer and bought what they needed, the less well-to-do often bought the components and then had them made up, either in the house or by a local man. In the Bacon Archives there are payments for 'cloths to make mattresses' and to Simon Bright the payment of 3s. 8d. for 'makeings fower matresses and fower flockbedes'. He charged 1s. 4d. for making a feather-bed. To stop the feathers working through the cloth, '9 pennyworth of turpentyne and Rosin to make gomme for the same bedes' was bought.[1] The turpentine would dry out, leaving the rosin hard on the ticking. While the turpentine still smelt it would have the added advantage of inhibiting the many bedbugs which lurked in the framework of all wooden beds.

Feather-beds tended to become lumpy after a while, especially if they were not turned and pummelled frequently. The same Simon Bright was also employed to remake the beds, and this he did by 'dryveing'. Driving is a method of separating down from feathers by blowing a current of air through the beds. This also breaks up any lumps. Simon probably used bellows for this, and anyone who has ever broken up feather-beds and pillows will know why an outside man was employed for the job rather than one of the indoor servants: it is an extremely messy performance. The Ancaster accounts also mention 'dryvers' in 1560 and 1562.[4] John Bee of Lincoln was a 'fetherbedd dryver' who drove beds and bolsters at 2d. the piece and, like Simon Bright, he also made new beds and bolsters.

These feather-beds would be put onto another mattress which could be straw or hair or even both, while the poorer people would make do with chaff, 'dust' (which was also chaff) or straw. Feather, down or hair were the usual fillings for top mattresses, or were until the days of the interior spring, and as late as 1838 the *Workwoman's Guide*[196] was advocating three layers per bed, the first mattress to be 'made of straw, it is very thick, and as hard as a board; these are never made at home ...' 'The second mattress is made of horsehair or wool for large beds; and for children, of chaff, sea-weed, beech leaves, cocoa nut fibre, paper, and many other things of that sort ...' It was suggested that this second mattress could or should be made at home. The top layer, known as the bed as distinct from the mattresses, should be filled with 'chicken, turkey, goose feathers and down for the higher classes, and mill-puff which is a kind of cotton, for the lower classes'.

While the lower classes had to make do with millpuff, flock or chaff, the upper classes had greater comfort. One of the most expensive and presumably the most comfortable bed fillings was feathers from the geese raised outside Bordeaux, and in the Rutland accounts for 1610 there is an item for four hundredweight of best Bordeaux feathers, costing £26; two pieces of Milan fustian for pillow cases costing £5, with an added 12d. for the portage to Belvoir.[11] Four hundredweight of feathers must have made a very large package.

Hamden Reeve, an upholsterer working at St Martin-in-the-Fields, supplied the bedding for Queen Anne's bed at Kensington in 1705, which consisted of a 'large fine Dimity Bed tick and Bolster covered with White Satin and filled with Seasoned Swans Down containing ninety pounds of Downe in them', at a cost of £18 10s.[87] There is not a great deal of down on one swan so the ninety pounds represents a lot of birds. Earlier, in 1573, when the new Bacon home at Stiffkey was being furnished, Nathaniel bought nine yards of ticking for a feather-bed which took eight stone of feathers to fill it; the total cost, with the making, was £3 18s. 6d., and for other beds he needed thirty-six stone, three pounds of feathers, carefully itemized as being at fourteen pounds to the stone.[1] These feather-beds represented a considerable item in the household budget, especially when the driving, extra feathers and new ticks were taken into account.

Swansdown and Bordeaux feathers obviously came from far away, but it appears that few of the ordinary feathers came from the home poultry yard. Probably their sale was a profitable sideline for the game and poultry dealers, but some came from Antwerp where, in the sixteenth century, the best beds were made. There was a tremendous trade between England and the Low Countries, with merchants spending as much time on the other side of the North Sea as in England, and in *Tudor Family Portrait*[194] we find John Cave buying beds and feathers in Antwerp for Sabine Johnson; in 1573 John Mountford writes to Nathaniel Bacon asking how many stone of feathers he wants and how many feather-beds, saying that he hopes to buy it all at Antwerp and thinks it will be well worth the money.[41] This may well be the thirty-six stone, three pounds of feathers paid for in that year. Other places abroad where feathers were bought included Burgos and Denmark, which are both mentioned in Sir Henry Sydney's accounts in 1576.[7]

From the point of view of the status symbol, if not necessarily of comfort, the curtains were the most important part of the bed, generally referred to as the 'furniture'. They were always as good in quality, and as showy, as the owner could afford. In large houses the main bedroom, at least until the end of the eighteenth century, was used as a reception room and the bed often resembled a throne, placed on a dais, sometimes in an alcove, behind pillars and a balustrade. The higher the edifice and the more elaborate the cornices, posts and curtains, with tassels, fringes and embroideries adorning expensive and beautiful fabric, the more the owner was seen to be rich and a man of importance. These beds, from the sixteenth, seventeenth and eighteenth centuries, were so well made, of such good material, that many of them can still be seen today, some in the houses for which they were built.

Everyone has their own favourite, whether it is the embroidery on the Daniel Marot bed at Clandon, the green velvet bed or the State Bed, with its original appliqué motifs, at Hardwick, the seventeenth-century crewel-work hangings in the White Room at Cotehele or the eye-filling crimson bed at Beningborough. Three of the best known are at Knole; that in the Venetian Ambassador's Room, made for James II and furnished with sumptuous cut green velvet; the Spangle Bed of the early seventeenth century, crimson satin, with a strap-work pattern applied in white satin, sewn with an uncountable number of sequins, the valance edged with a fringe of woven silver thread; and the King's Bed of gold and silver tissue lined with salmon-pink satin, embroidered with black and silver thread. This last, which is now being conserved and brought back as nearly as possible to its original state, became very dirty and tarnished. Maria Edgeworth was extremely unimpressed when she visited Knole in 1831, and wrote rather crossly, 'In the silver room a bed as the show woman trumpetted forth of gold tissue which cost 8 thousand guineas now in tarnished tatters not worth with Christie's best puffing 8 thousand pence this day.'[47]

However, not all bed curtains were of this quality, and very many different fabrics were used, ranging from the very cheap to the extremely expensive. The most common, and probably the cheapest, fabric used in the sixteenth century was say, a worsted stuff of variable price and quality which could be dyed all manner of colours. Sometimes the say was embroidered, as 'Yellow say bed, sewed with black crewel';[12] it could be plain, as in 1488 when Robert Morton had a bed with celure and tester, three curtains, three hangings and a riddle of green say.[125] Sometimes two colours of say were joined together, making stripes of red and yellow, and again the say was versatile enough to be painted, as Thomas Leman had done in 1534: 'Bed hangings of green say with painted border, the sparver of dornix, paned [striped]'.[122]

In 1668, after much thought, Pepys decided on a camblet bed,[58] and in the seventeenth century, serge, flannel and linen were all used, embroidered or plain, as well as damasks and velvets.

But for sheer richness and eye-catching ostentation nothing could exceed the Tudor beds. A bald description given in inventories aided by imagination

42. *Detail of an ornate bedhead. Late seventeenth century.*
Beningborough Hall

gives a vivid picture. This description of a bed in Kenilworth Castle in 1583[119] will serve for the many hundreds in the homes of the wealthy:

A faire, riche, new, standing, square bedstedd of walnuttree, all painted over with crymson and silvered with roses, fowre beares and ragged staves all sylvered, standing upon the corners. The tester, ceeler, dooble vallance and cases of crymson velvet richly embrothered in the cinquefoiles of cloth of sylver with my Lorde's armes very richly embrothered in the middest of the ceeler and tester, supported with the white lyon and bears, sylver, lyned through with redd buckerome. Three bases and dooble vallance fringed with a deepe fringe of crymson silke and sylver. Five curtians of crymson satten of xiij breadthes, stripped downe with a bone lace of sylver with iiij[xx] long buttons and loopes of silver, and a lyttle small freinge of crymson silke and sylver rounds about the curtaines, lyned through with white taffeta sarcenett.

41. *State Bed with embroidered silk furniture.*
Eighteenth century, Erddig

*43. Small four-poster bed with furniture
embroidered by Lady Betty Germain. Late seventeenth-century.
Knole*

Whether or not this magnificence would aid sleep is another matter.

While there were talented embroideresses working on their own beds, very many more were made and worked professionally, and the Purefoy letters give a very revealing description of how this was undertaken.[60] Henry Purefoy, a bachelor, lived at Shalstone just outside Buckingham with his mother, a lady of great character. In 1735 she decided she wanted a new bed with quilted furniture, and so on 11 January she writes to Anthony Baxter in London, who acted as their agent: 'I desire you will send me ... some patterns of Quilting you mention together wth the lowest price of each pattern. I shall want enough to make one of the new-fashioned low-beds without a cornice, if I like the Quliting & the price I will let you know the exact quantity ...' On 1 February her son writes to London:

I res^d your letter in due time but had not the 4 patterns of the Quilting till yesterday ... My Mother would have one of the new-fashioned low beds with 4 posts to them & a quilt to the same, she will endeavour to learn how many yards will do. If you have any friend an upholsterer let me know between this and next Saturday what quantity he thinks it requires in a post letter and also what is the price of such a bedstead that takes to pieces & goes on 4 swivell whealls to draw about. My Mother sais she will be unwilling to give above 10s a yard for the Quilting.

He adds a postscript: 'Upon further consideration I have returned your 4 patterns of quilting ... There are none of the Quilting will do but that whereon H Purefoy is wrote on the Edge. That will not do neither unlesse the same holds like ye pattern both in cloath & work ... If it was finer stitched & as good a cloath I should like it better.' On 10 February he writes again:

... since you warrent ye quilting as good as the pattern & if it so proves my Mother will have five & forty yards of it at ten shillings and sixpence a yard. But if it is not so good you must expect to have it returned for she would not have any of the others if she might have it for nothing. Therefore pray see that the two cloaths of each side of the Quilting be as good as the pattern & the work as good ... My Mother intends to have the bed made up in the house by reason [if] the work must be cut it will require great care to have it fastened right again. We thank you however for your kind proffer to get it made in Town.

By 10 March the quilting had been made and delivered: 'Have rece^d ye Quilting ... The Quilting was very bare measure.' Despite the last, one hopes Mrs Purefoy was pleased with her bed.

These letters show that the upholsterer or the embroiderer of the eighteenth century had many yards of various designs, probably in many different techniques, made up ready for sale, as, though it would have been possible to have quilted forty-five yards in under a month in a very large workroom, it was unlikely. In fact the speed of the whole transaction from the original suggestion on 11 January to the completed order on 10 March which included the to-ing and fro-ing of the agent, and the slowness of the Buckinghamshire carrier, is extraordinary. Trade cards show that this sort of transaction was common. Elizabeth Watson, for example, embroideress at the Sign of the Wrought Bed, states in 1706 that she sells: 'Wrought Beds from £7 to £40 packed, with all sorts of fine chain stitch work,' and in 1710 she advertises: 'Wrought beds, curtains and quilts.'[87]

44. Light, printed-cotton hangings on a bed at Dunham Massey

During the eighteenth century the hangings of a bed gradually became lighter both in look and fact, except for the unrepresentative State Beds in great houses. Cottons and linens were more accessible, especially chintz from India and printed cottons from France as well as England. All these were washable, which was a great advantage as, splendid as the velvet, damask and woollen beds must have looked when new, candle-grease and smoke from bedroom fires would have tarnished and dirtied them very quickly.

— 110 —

It might be thought that the simpler fabrics would have led to simpler hangings, but on the whole this was not the case. The fabrics themselves might be and often were less ornate, but due to their comparative lightness and draping qualities, and in tune with the emergence of the great cabinet-makers and upholsterers, bed hangings became more and more intricately draped with swags, bows, knots, tails and complicated arrangements of rings and pulleys, making the bed into a whirl of drapery, as eye-catching as it was dust-catching.

The question was always whether the outside or the lining of the bed hanging was the most important, whether it was to be viewed from the point of view of the visitor or the sleeper. Generally it seems that in the most important beds, used for display, the outside was the most ornate, but that in the beds of rather lesser establishments the linings were the most beautiful, but this does not always hold true. Celia Fiennes[48] refers to one at Lowther Castle of 'flower'd damask lined with fine Indian embroiery', and another at Burghley, a 'blew velvet bed with gold fringe and very richly embroidered all the inside with ovals on the head piece and tester where the figures are so finely wrought in satten stitch it looks like painting ...' but at Mr Routh's house at Epsom it is the other way around – the bed is of cross-stitch 'lined with yellow and white strip'd sattin ...'

From the middle of the eighteenth century for nearly a hundred years French beds were in fashion. The difference between them and the traditional four-poster was that they had no posts – generally a bracket came from the wall above the bed over which fabric was draped in various ways. Sheraton's *The Cabinet Maker and Upholsterer's Drawing-Book* (1793–1802)[180] and Ackermann's *Repository of the Arts* (1808–1828)[18] show these beds with the draperies depending sometimes from a crown or coronet and sometimes from a bar. Frequently with this type of bed, the bed itself was turned the other way; that is, parallel to the wall instead of at right angles to it. The draperies here are simpler and the fabrics lighter but no less rich.

A very good summing up of the fabrics fashionable for beds in the late eighteenth century is found in the trade card of William Clarkson, 'Upholder, Appraiser, Cabinet Maker and Undertaker', who made and sold 'Four Post and other Bedsteads with Damask, Mohair, Moreen, Harrateen, Cheney, Cotton and Check Furniture'.[87] It is noticeable that none of these fabrics, with the possible exception of damask, was made of silk; they were all worsted or cotton.

In 1838 the *Workwoman's Guide*[196] gave instructions for the making of

many household objects, from children's dresses to beds, specifically for those who could not afford to go and buy them. In it there are eleven different kinds of bed illustrated: the Four-Poster, Tent, Camp, Half-Tester, French Pole, French Arrow, Canopy, French Block, Turn-up, Stump and Trestle. All except the last two have some form of drapery, and although the title page suggests that the descriptions are to help the inexperienced, it is surprising just how much drapery the author considers essential for the middle and lower classes.

It was about this time that metal frame beds began to take over from wooden. This was partly due to the Industrial Revolution and the rise of mass production in the iron industry, and partly to the fact that metal bedsteads did not harbour the ubiquitous bedbug as the wooden had done. For most of the nineteenth century wooden and metal frames were equally popular, with draperies becoming less prevalent largely on health and sanitary grounds.

Charles Eastlake in *Hints on Household Taste*[69] approved of the change.

Time was when a huge 'four-poster' was considered indispensable to every sleeping appartment, and night-capped gentlemen drew around their drowsy heads ponderous curtains, which bade fair to stifle them before morning. Let us consider the gloom, the unwholesomeness, the absurdity of such a custom, viewed by our modern notions of health and comfort, and remember whatever the upholsterers tell us, that the fashion of *our* furniture, too, includes many follies at which posterity will smile.

He went on to say:

Many people nowadays prefer, on sanitary grounds to sleep, through the winter as well as the summer, in beds without hangings of any kind. It is difficult to conceive, however, that in a well-ventilated apartment, a canopy and head curtains can be at all prejudicial to health, and it is certain that they may be made to contribute not a little to the picturesqueness of a modern bedroom.

The design Eastlake shows is of an iron bedstead with a canopy or half-tester using a wide-striped fabric cut on the cross for the plain curtains and pelmet, and on the straight for the plain headboard and box-pleated lower valance.

He did not advocate any but the simplest and least pretentious hangings, of dimity where there was not too much dirt, possibly cretonne, chintz or printed cotton in London, the curtains to hang straight and be tied back simply when not in use. In his advocacy of simple fabrics he echoed John Loudon,[157] who in 1833 wrote that in what he called 'company rooms', bed

45. Tent bed with matching window curtains.
Early nineteenth century. Castle Coole

and window curtains could be of silk, woollen stuff, chintz, dimity or printed calico, 'according to the fortune or taste of the owner', but that for the family printed calico or dimity was best, as they were washable. An interesting sidelight is his suggestion that for servants' rooms there should not be more than two beds per room, and the curtains should be of woollen stuff to prevent accidents from fire. Did he think that they would go to bed drunk and so be careless with their candle, or that they would smoke in bed, or is he generalizing about the lack of care found in servants?

In the late nineteenth century there were many books written on various aspects of home management – including the provision of beds – and one, called *Ward and Lock's Home Book*[89] (a companion volume to Mrs Beeton's *Book of Household Management*), is firm in the belief 'That every lady COULD do the work herself if she would but try,' the 'work' being every aspect of bed hangings and bed-linen. The book is not dated, but appears to have been written somewhere in the 1880s, and the bed shown and discussed bears a striking resemblance to that of Eastlake in 1878, only here it is called 'The Arabian'. The writer makes one point about hanging the bed curtains which might help to identify sets of bed hangings put away in big houses, saying that 'the curtains after hemming may be hung into the rings upon the bedstead ready to receive them. The safety curtain pin is excellent for this purpose.' The last remark applied only to wooden bedsteads. The iron ones, having no rings, when the curtains had six or more short strings of the same colour, these were tied round the little side bars indicated by their position on the top of the bedstead. In other words, rings were for wooden beds and tapes or ties for iron.

46. Handsome furniture on a bed at Basildon Park.
Probably 1829

46a. Quilt, professionally worked in metal thread and coloured silks;
c. 1730. Blickling Hall

Eight

HOUSEHOLD LINEN

Linen, whether for the bed or table, has always formed a very important branch of household furnishings, as is shown in inventories and accounts. Illuminations in medieval manuscripts give a good idea of the prominent part both bed- and table-linen took in the decoration of a house. Often the quantities required seem to be very great, even allowing for the possible influx of visitors and the less frequent opportunities for washing linen. Very little research has been done in either of these matters and the interpretation of entries often leaves areas of doubt.

SHEETS

Most inventories, from those of the very rich to those who had enough belongings, however few, to warrant an inventory, list sheets of some kind, though there is great variety both in quantity and quality. One thing soon becomes clear: however wealthy the householder might be, sheets were not thrown away, or even used for another purpose, until they were quite useless as sheets. In a large household there must have been many accidents and illnesses but, judging by the number of sheets listed as 'sore worne' or 'olde and torn', they were not put aside to be used as bandages or kitchen cloths, but were kept in use even if only as spares.

Originally the fabric for sheets was woven from flax or hemp, and it is difficult to discover when cotton was first used – probably not until the nineteenth century. Good-quality linen came from the Low Countries or northern France, and later from Ireland. Katharine of Aragon had sheets of fine holland, and of 'Camerycke' cloth.[118] This was cambric, made in Cambrai, woven from linen until the eighteenth century, after which cotton was used, but by then cambric was not often used for sheets. Dame Agnes Hungerford in 1523 had thirty-four pairs of 'fyne Normandy canvas' as well as some made from 'fine Holland and Rennes'.[116] Lesser households had sheets made from harden which was woven from the poorest part of hemp, only a little better than the 'towen' sheets used by the poorest, which would have been very coarse and rough.

In 1638 the sheets which belonged to Anne, Viscountess Dorchester, are listed as fine holland, flaxen, middling and 'old thinne'; but she also had one best sheet which was 'Holland wrought in blacke worsteed of a running worke'.[101] This would be a top sheet with the embroidery in Holbein or double running-stitch worked as a border, to show when the counterpane was removed.

Two hundred years later the *Workwoman's Guide* advocated three different qualities of sheeting for a gentleman's household.[196] Linen for the spare or best bed, second quality for the family and a 'commoner sort' for servants. If the family went to the seaside in the summer they were to take calico sheets as they took up less room in packing, they would not suffer as much from the 'very indifferent washerwomen' to be found at watering or sea-bathing places and if lost on the journey it would not be a disaster.

In the sixteenth and seventeenth centuries most sheets were made in the household from cloth either bought or spun at home and locally woven. Lord Howard of Naworth paid Margey Willson 3s. 4d. for 'sewing sheetes and other woorke'; in this household the flax was spun at home, sent out to the estate to be woven and bleached and then brought back into the house to be made up. Tenter hooks are bought for 'James' for stretching the linen and 12d. is paid for mending all the old sheets.[12]

It is not easy to tell how much of the spinning and weaving was done at home and how much put out. The poor spun when they could and certainly were not able to put out, but it becomes more difficult to assess in the well-to-do households and small and large estates. In most households there seems to have been a combination of both. In the Bacon family in the late sixteenth century[1] the wives of the men servants and the estate workers spun both flax and hemp, and prepared the hemp by twisting, bunching and scouring. Bunching involved beating the retted fibres with mallets or beatles and was very heavy work, unsuited to any but the strongest women.[72] Spindles and whorls were bought for 'my mistress' and a 'whele' and wheel bands, but these may have been for use in the house or for her to give to someone on the estate to use.[1]

Nearly a hundred years later, Sarah Fell was paying for much the same work. In 1673 she paid for spinning both linen and hemp tow, and

'Dodgsons wife with the lame hand' is paid for spinning tear of hemp and hemp tow: tear was the best and finest part of hemp. All this spinning then went to Geoffrey Fell the weaver to be woven for linen sheets, underwear and other necessities.[3]

Sometimes cloth was bought unbleached or grey and then whited on the estate. In 1527 the L'Estranges bought thirteen and a half ells of grey canvas for sheets for the modest sum of 5s. 6d., while linen for sheets 'ready whyted' was 4d. a yard.[13] In the same way, in 1596 Nathaniel Bacon bought '24 yards of gray cloth at 16d. a yard to make 3 pairs of sheets'.[1] Sadly, it is impossible to compare prices, as neither the width nor the quality is known.

Sixteenth-century inventories often mention the width of a sheet – so many breadths of fabric – but seldom the length. The Bacon entry of twenty-four yards for three pairs seems very little – only four yards per sheet and, if of only two breadths (which seems very narrow unless it were for children), gives a length of six feet per sheet. If this is so it is in very strong contrast to an earlier inventory, that of the Willoughbys at Wollaton.[9] The lengths of sheets there are specifically mentioned and they are either three and three-quarters, four or four and a half yards long. On trying this length out on a bed six feet, three inches long, it appears that if the bottom sheet is well tucked in at the foot, brought up to the head and tucked under as a fold, then brought up and taken round the bolster, the length can be used up. But what was done with that length of top sheet is unclear. It might have been folded in half width-wise and used double, though it would have seemed simpler to have had a long bottom and a shorter top sheet, but as they were always listed in pairs this was obviously not the case. It is noticeable that bolster cases are seldom if ever mentioned and so probably a long bottom sheet was required. Even longer were three pairs of fine sheets 'gyven to my Lady' of four breadths and an unbelievable six yards in length, mentioned in the de Veer inventory of 1513.[146] A very special present, perhaps a marriage gift, but it is difficult to see how the six yards were used up.

Long sheets were still used in 1594 when the inventory of Sir William Fairfax was taken. Here they were all a minimum of five yards long, but 'three fine large sheetes of hollands for a womans chamber in child bed' are ten and a half, seven and a half and five and a half yards long, with a value of £12.[106]

Before the Act of Charles II which forbade bodies to be shrouded in anything but wool, it was the custom to use one of the best linen sheets.

A sad little entry in the 1624 Fairfax inventory remarks on an odd sheet as being 'the fellow to the one which my Lady was wound in'.[106]

Pillowcases are more straightforward. The fabric was seldom mentioned, nor the size, though they are sometimes listed as 'long'. They had different names in different parts of the country, being generally known as pillow beres until the nineteenth century, but in the west called pillow ties. This might indicate that they were bags tied with tapes at the ends. Later they were given their present names, pillowcases or pillowslips. Like all household stuffs, they were carefully kept. In 1629 Mrs Coke of Bramfield in Suffolk had '5 pillowe beeres wrought with black silke with as many lawne ones to weare over them'. This sounds as though the lawn cases were put over the embroidered ones at night and taken off for show in the daytime.

BLANKETS

Early blankets were made from fustian and are often listed as 'fustians', the fabric used giving the name to the article. Nearly every bed had only one pair, which seems very little even allowing for the extra quilts on most beds, until it is realized that, according to the Wollaton inventory of 1594,[9] they were three and a half, four or five yards long, and so were easily doubled, making a cosy four thicknesses. The fustian used for blankets may have been woven from wool, or from a mixture of wool and linen. In the Stow Hall inventory of 1620, one bed had a blanket of holmes fustian (from Ulm) as might be expected, but it also had two new ones made from broadcloth, which was a very unusual fabric for blankets; another bed had two 'blew' blankets. Ruggs were often coloured, but blankets seldom.

Rather later, blankets were made from blanket cloth, which was all wool and could be bought or woven on the estate. In 1674 Sarah Fell, in her very rural part of Lancashire, bought oil to grease the wool for blankets, and she paid Isabell Atkinson 2s. 5d. for spinning eighteen and a half pounds of wool for blankets. It would be nice to know why 'little Coops wife' only received 2s. 4½d. for spinning her eighteen and a half pounds of woollen yarn. However, all the wool yarn then went to Geoffrey Fell, the local weaver, to make into blankets.[3]

Specifically mentioned in many inventories are Spanish blankets. These were expensive and highly prized. Nathaniel Bacon paid 10s. for one in 1590[1] and most large houses had one or two, though at Kenilworth there were six.[119] These blankets were made from the wool of Spanish merino sheep which gave what was considered to be the best wool obtainable. It is difficult to say whether they were made in Spain or made in England from Spanish wool. The blanket bought by Nathaniel Bacon was brought by sea to Wiveton, but whether the merchant, John Braddock, had bought it in Spain or in London is not known.

By the seventeenth century blankets could be made from many different fabrics. The Standen inventory of 1623[133] lists fustian, cotton, 'fine', white cloth, linsey woolsey, russett and an 'old French blanket', but by the end of the century they were generally white, of woven and napped wool.

In the eighteenth century blankets were woven by blanket manufacturers and among the foremost in the country were the Earlys of Witney in Oxfordshire. The district around Witney had always been known for

47. Rosed corner on a blanket. Blickling Hall

blanket-making and as early as 1584 thirty were bought for Kenilworth from 'Colier of Whytney'. The Early blanket dynasty started in the late seventeenth century and was flourishing in the eighteenth. Between about 1711 and 1860 they made what became known as the 'rose' blanket. These, of excellent quality, had motifs embroidered in the four corners. The embroidery was rough, hand-spun crewel wool being used, with long, straight stitches. The sizes of the motifs vary between nine and twenty-one inches in diameter. According to Professor Alfred Plummer and Richard Early in *The Blanket Makers*,[172] this decoration was known as 'cornering'. Blankets were woven in one long length weighing a hundred pounds, which was a suitable weight for a man to carry and the size bale which fitted into the fulling stocks. The decoration was put on to show where the length should be cut up into individual blankets after fulling. Arthur Young says the workers were paid $\frac{1}{2}$d. for each design. If the twenty-one-inch device on a blanket at Blickling Hall was worked for $\frac{1}{2}$d. that was sweated labour at its worst.

In 1788 John Early presented a pair of blankets to George III and Queen Charlotte, 'beautifully rosed at each corner'. Rose blankets were popular in America, and John Norton, an American merchant in England, had to send some to customers in America.[56] In 1768 he sent R. Nicholas, among many other sundries, '3 pr best and finest double mill'd rose large Bed Blankets', and Florence Montgomery notes five rose blankets in the 1797 inventory of Aaron Burr's home.[161]

They were still used when the *Workwoman's Guide* was published; Richard Early says that the embroidery only stopped when blankets were woven by machine after the 1850s.

RUGGS

It is not known exactly what is meant by the word rugg, found in so many sixteenth- and seventeenth-century inventories, clearly referring to some kind of blanket or coverlet. It is sometimes used by itself, sometimes with the addition of a colour, as 'blew' rugg, red rugg, occasionally with the addition of the word Irish or, less frequently, Spanish. Rugg was a fabric generally made from Irish wool which was rough and hairy and thus warm, even if coarse. It has been suggested that when used on beds ruggs were only found in humble homes and in servants' quarters, and certainly many inventories bear this out. The Ancaster accounts for 1561 has, 'For 54 yards of Irish rugge for coverlettes for servantes at 7d. the yards',[4] and in only one of many entries in *Farm and Cottage Inventories* which contain ruggs is there, in 1743, 'A sacking bottom bedstead with stuff curtains, 3 old blankets, one blew rugg'.[107] Both these entries suggest a coarse, unattractive and cheap article.

But there are other entries which show rugg to have been used in the best rooms in most aristocratic houses. At Kenilworth, for example, in 1583, there were thirty-five white Spanish ruggs, one 'blew' rugg, two green ruggs and two white Irish ruggs.[119] In 1597 Nathaniel Bacon bought '2 Ruggs whight' for the large sum of £4 10s.[1] At 45s. each, they were four times as expensive as the Spanish blanket, for which he paid only 10s.

These entries are corroborated by those in the Stow Hall inventory of 1620, where a very elegant bed with white damask curtains had a white poland rugg of a breadth and a quarter. Ruggs made in Poland are not often found, but Stow had three, the other two being crimson and murry, once again matching the bed furniture.

Ruggs were sometimes dyed to match the bed furniture; the 1594 inventory of Sir William Fairfax has in most bedchambers, listed immediately after the bed, a matching rugg as the next most important item, valued from 20s. to 30s. each.[106] At Standen in 1623, in the King's Chamber, was 'One pair fine blancketts, whereof the one White Rugg and the other white cotton'.[133]

In her article, 'Jane Lambarde's Mantle',[19] Janet Arnold discusses the large, rich, oblong mantles worn by high-born ladies in the last part of the sixteenth and the first part of the seventeenth centuries, and suggests that these mantles were also used as an extra bed covering when required. They were often of velvet, lined with shag and embroidered or laced, and they were known also as 'bernias', a word deriving from Hibernian or Irish. The original bernias were rough woollen cloaks worn by Spanish soldiers, which were made from Irish cloth exported to Spain; various dictionaries of the period make it clear that a bernia could be a rough wool cloak, a bed covering or a fashionable garment. These mantles may well have been used as ruggs.

One of the most interesting allusions to ruggs comes from the 1595 *Book of Household Rules*, drawn up by Lord Montague at Cowdray. It states that it is the duty of Yeoman of the Wardrobe to look after the lodgings of any visitors, to see that their rooms are clean, decorated with herbs, flowers and greenery, and to make sure that the beds are made up on the arrival of the visitors 'and the better sortes of quiltes of beddes of any tyme of nighte taken off, and Yrish Rugges layd in their places'.[197]

In the eighteenth century ruggs are seldom listed except in the inventories of poorer folk, but that they were used in wealthier homes is evident from the number of upholsterers who advertised them on their trade cards. For example, Nathaniel Hewitt, a London upholsterer, between 1768 and 1777 made and sold '... Blankets, Quilts, Ruggs, Coverlets'.[87] It seems unlikely that those would be rough and hairy.

On this evidence it appears that a rugg was an extra covering for a bed, thicker and not as ornate as a counterpane but more attractive than a blanket, which could vary in quality from the poor and coarse to the good and expensive, generally made in Ireland, or from Irish wool. It could be that Spanish ruggs were made up from fabric sent from Ireland to Spain and then exported from there to England. On the other hand, they could simply be a better-quality article made from Spanish merino wool, possibly indistinguishable from a Spanish blanket.

BED COVERINGS

What are the differences between a quilt, coverlid, counterpane, counterpoint, bed mantle and bedclothes of tapestry work? That there were differences is plain, as in many long, and clear, inventories several of the words are used in the description of one bed, making it obvious that to the writer, if not to us, there were considerable variations. In 1624, in Sir Thomas Fairfax's house, a bed had both a 'counterpointe' and a coverlet,[106] and in 1743 in the Striped Bedroom of Theophilus Lingard there was a coverlid and a counterpane on the bed. It would seem that the coverlid or coverlet was a plainer and simpler piece of fabric, used almost as a case cover, which was thrown over the more elaborate counterpoint or counterpane to protect it from dust and damage. The *New Dictionary of French and English* by Miège, published in 1679, defines a counterpoint as the same as a counterpane and says that they are both quilted. Equally, a *contrepointeur* is a quilter or counterpoint-maker. This may have been the accurate definition, but the word was not always used in that sense. In 1638 Anne, Viscountess Dorchester, had '1 large counterpointe for a bed, of Holland wrought in collours of needle worke of weaving worke of wostead'.[101] This sounds much more like an early piece of crewel-work than a quilted cover.

The word quilt, or twilt as it was often written, implies several thicknesses of fabric joined together. They were not necessarily patchwork, or even elaborately quilted, but were certainly used for added warmth, and in some cases, softness. Beds often had five or six quilts, which seems excessive in an English climate until it is realized that some went under and some over the sleeper. The inventory of Sir John Jernagham in 1737[117] specifically lists upper and under quilts in 'my Lady's Room', which appears to have had twin beds – very unusual at this date: 'Two Bedsteads with Blew Stuff Curtins, Two Beds, Two Boulsters, Two Pillows, Two Under Quilts, Six Blankets, and two Upper Quilts'. As there was also a quilting frame in the lumber room, these quilts were likely to have been homemade. It is also likely that upper quilts had more decoration than under quilts.

When two or more top coverings of equal merit are listed for a bed, is it that these are for alternate use, or best and second-best, rather than both being used together? The bed in the 'Cheife Chamber' at Hengrave in 1603, which was of black velvet, yellow taffeta and gold embroidery had 'one large twilt of yellow satin embroidered, one large twilt of crimson taffetye sarcenet of the one side and tawny sarcenet of the other, twilted very finely on both sides, and perfumed'.[113] It seems improbable that two such beautiful quilts should lie one over the other.

Not all bed coverings were elaborate. On the contrary, in the many houses where the bed was in a room used by everyone in the daytime, the bedclothes were often covered by a plain piece of fabric, generally green, red or blue. These coverings were often made of darnix, a fabric woven with a linen warp and wool weft, durable and rather coarse, which had many uses. Some of these plain fabrics were embroidered, and there appear to have been local specialities: there are many references in East Anglia to Pulham-work. The Pulhams are villages in south Norfolk which in the sixteenth century had a thriving industry making coverlets, but in what this particular 'Pulham-work' consisted has never been discovered. There are also references in the de Veer inventory of 1513 to coverlets made in Bury St Edmunds — 'a coverlett of bery makyng' — and to coverlets made in Norwich.[146] These techniques remain unidentified. It seems likely that there were specialized workshops in various towns which all had their own particular styles of embroidery.

A change in bed coverings came with the introduction of Indian fabrics in the seventeenth century. As the East India Company only started importing in a rather tentative way in 1601, it is surprising to find how quickly quite ordinary houses had India cotton in them. In 1620 the inventory of Henry Clarke,[127] a West Country vicar, shows as part of a bed 'a pintado and one yellow Coverlidd', the plain coverlid probably covering the new and exotic pintado. He also had an old pair of pintado curtains. To have old pintadoes in 1620 suggests friends or relatives in the young East India Company or perhaps their acquisition from a Portuguese trader in Bristol. By the next century most people with any pretensions to fashion would have some Indian coverings in their homes, in spite of any Acts of Prohibition. Mrs Lybbe Powys in 1771 said that Lady Blount of Mawley in Shropshire had 'more chintz counterpanes than in one house I ever saw; not one bed without very fine ones'.[59]

The eighteenth century produced an enormous amount of embroidery, both professional and domestic, and bed covers were favourite vehicles for the work, with the advantage that all the work showed equally well. There were a number of techniques used; quilting and crewel-work continued, using lighter designs to follow the fashion, and patchwork, once there were both Indian and English cottons to use. Heavy gold and silk embroidery

48. *Quilt, professionally worked in metal thread and coloured silks;*
c. 1730. Blickling Hall

was seen on State Beds, as well as Chinese silk embroidery. In fact a collection of eighteenth-century bed coverings could be made which included all known methods of work. Felbrigg Hall in Norfolk housed a representative collection, the 1771 inventory listing the following: '1 large bed quilt, crimson silk lined with green; 1 Counterpane, Marcella quilting, scarlet silk lined with green; 1 China quilt lined with white; Coloured linen quilt lined with white; 2 white counterpanes; Manchester; 1 India Counterpane without a lining; 1 old green silk Quilt; 1 Flowered Linen, lined with green stuff new; 1 coloured Worsted Counterpane, New.'[109] These were all counterpanes that had been put away; the list does not include those on the beds.

By the late eighteenth and early nineteenth centuries white counterpanes were fashionable. Sophie von la Roche, who travelled to London and stayed at an inn at Ingatestone in Essex, remarks that 'the bedcovers are of a white

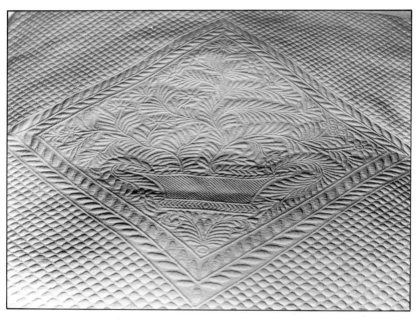

49. Detail of a quilt in trapunto, corded and wadded quilting.
Cotehele House

cotton material with fringe decorations woven in'.[177] This was probably candlewicking, where the thick cotton yarn which was used to make the wicks of candles was also used to decorate fabrics in little tufts. It was the same sort of counterpane which was mentioned by Robert Southey[63] in *Letters from England*. In 1807 he says that 'the counterpane is of all English manufactures the least tasteful; it is of white cotton, ornamented with cotton knots, in shapes as graceless as the cut box in a garden.' These strictures were aimed at the machine-woven variety known as Bolton-work, which were made about 1800. They soon lost their popularity and were relegated to the servants' bedrooms. Hence the remarks made by Charles Eastlake later in the century (1878).[69] He says:

50. *Detail of a machine-made quilt. Bolton work,*
c. 1800. Cotehele House

51. *Detail of a patchwork quilt worked by Beatrix Potter's mother, 1863.*
East Anglian Collection, Blickling Hall

Our English notions of cleanliness would scarcely permit us to tolerate any kind of coverlet which could not be periodically washed. Hence the modern counterpane, in some form or other is likely to remain in permanent use for our beds though it must be confessed that in design and material it has greatly degenerated from the quality of those made some five and twenty years ago. From an artistic point of view the counterpanes now manufactured for servants bedrooms, in which coloured thread is introduced for the knotted pattern on a grey or white ground are very suggestive in colour but I fear that any approach to this style of coverlet would be considered objectionable in 'best' bedrooms.

The 'best bedrooms' at this date would have had machine-embroidered silk, hand-embroidered cretonne or rather garish patchwork in silks, velvets and satins, such as the one made by the mother of Beatrix Potter in 1863.

TABLE-LINEN AND TOWELS

From medieval times onwards the greatest attention has always been paid to table-linen. When a table was just a rough board on trestles the cloths which covered it showed the status of the owner, and all through the period, in any inventory or list, the household linen is put in descending order of importance, with damask at the top, followed by diaper and moving down to coarse or servants'. Napkins were an essential part of the linen chest and were numerous, as they were used for a far more vigorous wiping of the fingers and mouth and washing of the hands than is imaginable today.

Linen damasks, woven in a technique borrowed from the weaving of silk damasks, were expensive. The pattern was woven in a twill weave and as the weavers became more accomplished they began to depict not just patterns, but whole scenes commemorating some event or showing some religious scene. Strangely, although there are still many of these tablecloths to be seen, they were seldom listed separately, but in the Erddig inventory of 1726 is a 'tablecloth of King Charles II in the Royal Oak'. By 1726 this must have been a very old tablecloth, as it would have to have been woven after the Restoration. It is not always easy to see these designs and they are even more difficult to photograph well as they only show up when the light catches the pattern at the right angle. That the design shows at all is due to the fact that flax is hard and shiny and so with the twill weave going in different directions the light is reflected off each thread in a different way. Napkins showing a scaled-down version of the cloth could be bought at the same time.

Illustrations of early table settings sometimes show the linen apparently creased. Until the nineteenth century linen was never ironed but always pressed, that is, folded and put into a linen press which was then screwed down so that the folds made exact creases.

Diaper, which came second in importance, was woven on a simpler loom than damask and consisted of small repeat patterns. In 1522 two dozen napkins of coarse diaper were bought for the L'Estrange family for 8s., and sixteen ells of canvas for 'borde cloths' for the hall for 6s.,[13] while in 1573 Nathaniel Bacon bought a damask cloth for 23s. 6d. and a diaper cloth for 10s.; this shows clearly the relative values of the linens.[1] That even diaper was considered expensive is shown by Pepys, who says in 1660: 'From thence walked to my father's, where I found my wife (who hath been with my father to day buying of a tablecloth and a dozen of napkins of Diaper, the first that ever I bought in my life).'[58]

Most diaper came from the continent and each country wove it in a slightly different fashion. Today we do not understand the differences, but they must have been apparent, as the diaper in use at Stow Hall in 1721 is listed as Irish, French, Dutch and Russian, as well as fine, coarse and fringed.

Every inventory which lists household linen has in it many different kinds of towels and often kitchen cloths for various purposes which do not come into this study. However, the 1831 catalogue of sale at Stow Hall has as one lot ten hand towels, two round towels, two toilet covers and twenty-eight doilies. It is not usual to find doilies mentioned at this date. They are now generally considered to be small mats to put under cakes and sandwiches at teatime, but earlier doilies were fringed napkins, generally of a rather coarse linen, which were used at dessert.

Nine

THE FURNISHING OF WINDOWS

Sixteenth-century inventories seldom mention curtains for windows. Practically all references to curtains are for those drawn round a bed. The century was a time when the whole nature of building and required comfort was changing. Windows had been, and still were in many cases, voids, with wooden shutters which were barred across at night and in bad weather and could be fastened back in daytime. These empty spaces could also be filled with fenestrals, which were frames which could be pushed into place. They were sometimes latticed, often fitted with cloth and paper. The next step was to fill the lattice with horn and, by the time of Henry VIII, windows could be fitted frames filled with glass. Glass, however, was rare during most of the century except in the great houses. In 1541 a 'chist of glass' which cost 46s. 8d. was bought at Lincoln for Belvoir Castle.[11] Even at the end of the century glass windows were sometimes taken out and stored when the family was away, as protection against damage.

If glass windows were rare, curtains were certainly unusual. There are none mentioned in the Fastolf inventory of 1459,[108] nor in that of Kenilworth in 1583.[119] The new Bacon house being built at Stiffkey in 1573[1] had no window curtains, and even Hardwick Hall, the superb house built at the end of the century, had very few.[112] The Fairfax inventory of 1594 has none,[106] but that of 1624 shows that by then about half of the rooms had curtains while the rest had shutters only.

This rarity makes it all the more remarkable that the 1509 sequestration inventory of Edmund Dudley's house in Candelwykstrete in London[104] should specifically refer to curtains in three of the rooms: the Great Parlour, Great Chamber and the gallery next to the Great Chamber. Each of these important rooms had identical curtains; the entry in each case reads, 'ij courteyns of grene saye hangyng in the Wynddowys'. The words imply that the curtains were either hanging from a rod or were tacked above the window. This cannot possibly be construed as being any form of fenestral. Even more explicit is the inventory of Thomas Leman of Swaffham in west Norfolk, taken in 1534.[122] He was a parson, well-off but not wealthy, and in his parlour he had a little curtain of darnix 'to draw before the window'. Barbara Winchester has noted that at Canons Ashby in mid-century the windows were hung with yellow say,[194] but these references are not usual and in general the sixteenth century was curtainless.

By the beginning of the seventeenth century curtains were becoming very much more common, though only in the houses of the well-to-do. Families below the status of, say, vicar still did without, relying on wooden shutters inside or out to keep out cold, weather and draughts. Larger houses began to have curtains, even if they were not of rich fabric. The 1603 inventory of Hengrave[113] has, in the Great Chamber, four coverings of green buckrum for the windows as well as four large curtains of green kersey for the great windows and two for the two little windows. The 'coverings' appear to be some sort of blind, and may well have been mounted on a frame and pushed into place in order to keep out the sun. 'Window clothes' of arras, which are also mentioned, were probably for covering window-seats rather than the windows themselves. There must have been great efforts made to keep Hengrave warm, for in the Great Chamber there was also a portiere: 'At ye Greate Chamber Dore One curtyn of Grene Carsye lined wth southage wth a curtyn rod of iron w[h] is to hang afore the dore, wth a great hooke to putt it up when it is not drawn.'

The great house at Ingatestone belonging to Sir John Petre had curtains in all the best rooms in 1600. The majority were of red and green say, joined in strips, lined with blue or green buckrum, and others were of green wadmal, which was a rough woollen cloth, admirable for keeping out draughts.

Anne, Viscountess Dorchester, whose inventory was taken in 1636,[101] had curtains in some of the rooms of 'stripte stuff', possibly calamanco. Curtain rods are listed in most rooms and in the 'Closett next the workinge roome' were '60 peeces of stripte stuff of light collours. some for hangings, others for window curtains ...' which may mean that the curtains had been taken down and put away for the summer. It is noticeable that many early curtains were striped, either striped in the fabric, or else paned, which meant that two narrow widths of contrasting colours were joined together, giving a wider and clearer stripe.

Inventories generally mention the curtain rod as well as the curtain itself and it is clear that in the early part of the seventeenth century, windows generally had only one curtain per rod — looped or pulled to one side — rather than the pair which later became the norm. If the fabric mentioned was thin, for instance sarcenet or taffeta, it is possible that the curtain hung over the window by day as well as night, acting as a sun-blind. So, when in 1623 Lord Howard of Naworth paid 49s. for '4 ells of mingled [shot] taffeta to mak a curtin',[12] it could well have been for a sun curtain. It would seem that ten years later he renewed or added to his curtaining, as he bought '100 courtinge ringes' for 2s. 4d.

It has been said that pairs of curtains on one rod came into fashion in France in the 1660s and then travelled to England, but Peter Thornton has noted that at Ham House there were divided curtains twenty years earlier.[111] At Worcester House, in Lord Harbert's Chamber, there were two window curtains and one rod, and in the Great Chamber there were five curtains of 'stripte stuff' and three rods.[144] In 1624 Sir Thomas Fairfax had, in the Great Chamber, two darnix window curtains 'and an iron rod for them.'[106]

However, earlier still, in 1611, in the chamber over the parlour in a house belonging to a gentleman of Norwich, one John Skelton, there is listed, '2 window curtains of darnix and one curtain rodd', though in the chamber over the kitchen he has '2 window curtains of blew linnen and 2 little curtin rods'.[131] These entries all suggest that the fashion for a pair rather than a single curtain may have started in England, rather than France, and much earlier than has been suspected.

Seventeenth-century curtains were generally of warm but cheap fabric. Sarah Fell used fustian,[3] Pepys used say[58] and James Master, who seldom mentions household expenditure in his account book, bought two lots of calico for curtains at different times at 12d. or 16d. a yard, and also lashed out on one lot of damask at 8s. a yard.[14] Hengrave used several different fabrics, including kersey, both yellow and green, white striped moccadoe, buckrum and 'tawnye tapestrye layed with yellow lace'.[113]

By the middle of the eighteenth century, window curtains were considerably more important in the overall design of a room than they had ever been before, but they were still considered of less interest than the bed curtains. The fabric of the window curtains often matched that of the bed, but if it did not it was often of inferior quality. We read and know of many very elaborate bed curtains, but seldom hear of window curtains being embroidered. It is difficult to say why this should be — bed furniture would take much longer to work and quilted window curtains, for example, would have been both warm and attractive — but, as always, the bed was the chief item in the room and the curtains took second place.

There were three styles for window curtains which prevailed during the 1700s: festoon, drapery and, later, French draw, but in studying them there will always be a problem because there were, even then, no definite rules as to what was meant by the first two names. Various appraisers for inventories, upholsterers and writers used the names interchangeably, and

52. *Festoon curtain pulled up, c. 1760. Uppark*

if they were not sure, it is even more difficult for us, two hundred years on, to be certain.

As far as can be gauged a festoon curtain was one which consisted of a single piece of fabric, possibly gathered, tacked above the window frame.

53. *Festoon curtain carved in wood above a mirror.*
Wimpole Hall

It was the size and shape of the window and was divided into three by two vertical rows of small rings. Cords, fastened at the bottom of the curtain to a small weight, were threaded through the rings and over pulleys at the top, then brought down on one side of the frame. When these cords were pulled the curtain rose, forming three graceful swags at the top of the window. This type of curtain took very little fabric and needed virtually no trimming, and so was economical as well as fashionable. It was sometimes known, quite logically, as a Venetian curtain, because it was of much the same shape and style as a venetian blind.

The other type of curtain which was equally fashionable was what was then usually called 'drapery', for which the modern term is 'reefed'. The word in this context has no eighteenth-century origin but appears to be a name coined by upholsterers and interior decorators in this century. A draped curtain resembles nothing so much as a woman with her hair parted in the middle and looped up with slides at the sides. It is a pair of curtains fastened above the window frame and meeting in the middle at the top. Each curtain had one, two or three rows of rings sewed diagonally at the back, dividing the curtain into three parts. As with festoon curtains cords were threaded through the rings, over pulleys and were fastened to decorative metal pins at the side of the window frame. When the cords were pulled the curtains stayed together at the top and then divided, forming swags, with the ends hanging down to about the height of the chair rail. A letter written by Lady Anson to Lady Grey in 1750 explains the shape. She says: 'The Window-Curtains in the Bow-Window [at Wimpole Hall] I promised an account of, is divided, as I thought, into two parts, and drawn up by three Lines of a Side – comme ça

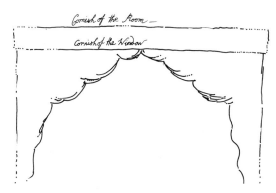

and these points hang down as low as the Sur-base, and the space between the two Cornishes has ornaments and festoons of stucco'. The surbase is a moulding or border immediately above the base or lower panelling of a wainscoted room, or a chair rail if there is no wainscot. If the points only hung to the surbase, they would finish from two to three feet from the floor.

54. Drapery curtains (modern reproduction).
Wimpole Hall

Towards the end of the century both these styles had become less fashionable and again it was a French style which became popular and has dominated curtain making until today: the French draw. Before the Revolution many wealthy English were as at home in France as in England; there was a considerable amount of inter-marrying and a great deal of time was spent there while on the Grand Tour. The English were always ready to cross the Channel to see the latest fashions in decoration of houses as well as in costume, so it is no wonder that so many fashions in upholstery should come from France.

This latest fashion consisted of a pair of curtains, lined – and in the nineteenth century interlined – which could be pulled back from the centre of the window by cords. They then hung down straight, but were drawn

55. Metal cloak-pin in the saloon at Felbrigg

56. Pair of cloak-pins for fastening window cords. State Bedroom, Blickling Hall

into a curve by being looped over large metal pins known as cloak-pins. Contrary to their name, these pins in no way resemble the pins on which cloaks were hung, as they generally have large decorative ends which stop the curtain from slipping off, but their size and design add to the general look of the curtain. When curtains are looped over cloak-pins they make a very definite shape, hanging well forward before folding back over the pin, in contrast to the much straighter look of the nineteenth century, when they were held back by cords and tassels, with no deep loop.

A problem which still bedevils curtains makers is that of the length of the repeat pattern of the fabric when related to the length of the curtain. It is important that each curtain of a pair should have the pattern repeats in exactly the same place, but to achieve this, large amounts of fabric are often wasted in the cutting. At no time was this more true than in the middle of the eighteenth century, when the pattern repeats tended to be very long. Mrs Purefoy, who had difficulties with the quilting for her bed, also had

57. *Curtain held back with cord and tassels.*
Oxburgh Hall

problems with the design of her curtains when she ordered chintz for new ones at Shalstone. She writes to Anthony Baxter, her agent in London, saying that she needs eighteen yards of chintz for her drawing room, 'or something which would suitt workt chairs, workt in shades upon white ...' In her next letter she thinks that only the best chintz will do but 'you say the pattern is 3 yards long and our window curtains must be 3 yards & a quarter long ...' And she adds a housewifely note: 'I suppose you will warrant its standing ye colour when it is washed.' Evidently the chintz design would not do; 'since I cannot have a Chintz the pattern whereof is long enough for the Room I would rather have chuse a white Indian Damask ...', and she eventually takes fifty yards of the damask, but still needed chintz for another room. She ends by saying — strangely, for such a particular lady — 'as to the ffancy of ye patten I leave that to you ...'[60] One feels sorry for Anthony Baxter.

It is extremely unlikely that any house would have had only one style of curtain at any one time and an analysis of the window curtains at Blickling Hall in the 1793 inventory gives a picture of changing styles — which must have been much the same for many houses.[96] In the 'Garretts', where the servants slept, there were no curtains except around the very comfortable beds, though in one room there was a single curtain and rod. The turret rooms had curtains with no rod, presumably tacked to the window frame and draped to one side. On the next floor down, known as Buckingham Row, the rooms had checked or striped curtains, sometimes one and sometimes two, but as rods are not mentioned, they must also have been tacked and draped to one or both sides.

Lower still, in the most important bedrooms, the curtains were drapery in Lady Rose's room and festoon in her dressing room; cotton festoon in the Green Damask Room; a single green satin curtain in Lady Bellmore's room and cotton festoon in her dressing room; festoon in Lady Vallatort's room and cotton festoon in the Copperplate Room. There was chintz drapery in the Blue Room and dressing room and festoon in the Chinese Bedroom with cotton festoon in both the dressing and powdering rooms. As for the reception rooms, the Old Drawing Room had Manchester striped drapery, but the New Drawing Room had festoon curtains of the same fabric as the hangings, as did the State Bedroom. There were festoon curtains in the dining room, drinking room, Lady Buckingham's bedroom and dressing room and the study, which had dimity festoon. In Lady Emilia's bedroom and dressing room were Manchester striped curtains but only one in each room; the same applied to the valet de chambre's room, but the lady's maid's room had a curtain and rod, as did Lady Emilia's keeping room, and the justice room.

This list of curtaining, in a big, but not enormous house, shows that at any one time there might be varied styles, with the larger rooms being more up to date, though Blickling must be considered old-fashioned in having no draw curtains by 1793. The inventory was taken in September,

58. Pelmet board and valance over the window,
matching those on the State Bed, Beningborough Hall

and it is clear that the summer curtains were still up as, with the exception of one harrateen, one moreen and one satin, all the rooms had cotton curtaining.

While curtains were obviously important, pelmets were even more vital to the look of the room, provided it was a modern house with high ceilings. Low-ceilinged Tudor and early-Stuart rooms could not stand the weight or the gloom of deep pelmets under the ceiling, but as rooms became higher, with tall, sash windows, so it became more necessary to have some sort of definition at the top of the curtaining. Apart from its decorative function, a pelmet served to hide the pulleys, boards, lines and rods used in fixing the curtains. In the largest houses these pelmets, together with their valances, were almost overpowering, with patterned fabrics, braids, fringes and bows.

In bedrooms they often echoed the shape of the bed valance and the same draped shape could be used on the matching seat furniture.

Ackermann's *Repository*[18] shows many designs for window draperies. In practically every case the cornice, pelmet and valance are of much greater importance, and often of far richer fabrics, than the curtains themselves. At this period these often had what Ackermann calls 'sub-curtains' of transparent silk or muslin, sometimes hanging straight and sometimes draped behind the main curtains. There was also a tendency for either the poles or the cornices – or both – to have reference to contemporary events. In 1814, for example, he shows a design produced by Morgan and Saunders:

The azure and white, which may be sprinkled with lilies, are the colours of the legitimate dynasty of France... The eagle of Russia surmounts the whole, in allusion to the superiority she has obtained in arms... The doves sporting with laurel, the insignia of victory, are emblematic of confidence... Indeed to the fertile imagination, this design, though not incumbered with ornament, will appear replete with the most delicate conceits and comprehensive allusions...

This design had the pole in the shape of a double-ended spear with the doves, eagles, etc. disporting themselves above; the azure curtain, heavily fringed, was swathed over the pole, the sub-curtains drawn to one side and the main curtains looped over cloak-pins at a different level each side. Probably at no other time has furniture and furnishing been so conscious of what was happening in the world, from the eastern conceits of the Brighton Pavilion to the sphinx-headed Egyptian chairs, and sofas with trophies such as those described on the curtains.

Towards the nineteenth century rods and rings became more important, and pelmets often disappeared completely, but their loss was compensated for by throwing lengths of fabric, generally fringed, over the rods, with the tails hanging down on the outside of the frame. Where there were several windows, either in a bay or in a line down a room, these fabric lengths could go from one window to another, providing a single horizontal line, with the tails hanging at the outermost ends of the end windows. This type of drapery needed meticulous adjustment if it was to look right, and it was a housekeeper's nightmare.

The *Workwoman's Guide*,[196] which contained 'Instructions to the inexperienced in cutting out and completing those articles ... which are usually made at home', shows what seem to be almost fussy draperies, all depending from thick wooden poles, some of them having handsome wooden rings. The *Guide* states that in a bedroom window, curtains 'should always accord with the hanging on the bed, both in colour and material, as also in shape'.

It also points out that, 'It is desirable to have as little window drapery as possible to family or secondary rooms, particularly nurseries or servants' rooms, on account of their liability to catch fire, especially as toilet tables are so often situated within the window.' For the same reason it was advocated that servants' bed furniture should be woollen, not calico.

John Loudon's *An Encyclopaedia of Cottage, Farm and Villa Architecture and Furniture*,[157] which ran through many editions and was extremely influential all through the mid-nineteenth century, advocated simplicity for the smaller house, though the villa of that time was a very substantial five- or six-bedroom house, largely built on the outskirts of London and most industrial towns, for the rising manufacturer. Loudon had no time for swags and swathes:

Hence, all the modern plans of suspending enormous folds of stuff over poles, as if for the purpose of sale or being dried is quite contrary to the use and intention of curtains and, therefore, in abominable taste; and the only object that these endless festoons and bunchy tassels can answer is to swell the bills and profits of upholsterers who are the inventors of these extravagent and ugly draperies, which are not only useless in protecting the chamber from cold, but are the depositories of thick layers of dust, and in London not infrequently become the stronghold of vermin.

He is equally scathing about fringes, and points out that the origin of the fringe was as a method of tying off the warp ends of fabric; therefore, if it had to be used, it should appear to be as much like warp ends as possible. He gives four rules: 1. the fringe should never consist of heavy parts, but simply be threads tied into ornamental patterns; 2. deep fringe should not be suspended from a narrow valance; 3. no valance should be formed entirely of fringe; and 4. the fringe should not be sewn upon stuff but always on the edge of the fabric. It is allowable at the very top, as it may be supposed to be the top turned over. All this gives an excellent idea of how a great number of people were making their curtains and valances.

He goes on to give his idea of what a moderate-sized house or villa should have for curtaining. The gallery should have cloth curtains without drapery, and those of the saloon (to be used as a music room) should be of watered silk without drapery, supported by large rods of gilt brass with handsome knobs. The drawing room could be more elaborate, with fringed curtains, 'the draperies simple in large folds, the cornices massive and gilded. Inner curtains of figured muslin edged with silk ball fringe to match the outer curtains.' The library should have curtains 'of merino damask, lined with glazed stuff (this sort of damask has a poor effect without a lining as it is commonly used)'. Then there should be inner curtains of plain muslin, edged with fringe which was the same colour as the curtains. The dining room was to look handsome and heavy with velvet curtains trimmed with gold lace and fringe, with carved and gilded cornices. Altogether an attractive picture.

However, the taste of the majority of people at the time and in years to come was towards the heavy and ornate. With the rise of wealth it was considered necessary that visitors should be able to assess a man's income by the furniture and fabrics of his house, and so both Loudon and, forty years on, Eastlake, went largely unheeded and ignored. Heavy Nottingham lace took the place of the plain muslin advocated by Loudon, and it was not long before it was considered necessary to have three sets of curtains on all the windows in the main rooms: Nottingham lace covering the whole window to keep out both flies and the gaze of the curious; a light silk pair; and a heavy velvet or plush outer pair. The result was that very little light came into the room – a far cry from the Regency style, in spite of the large cornice draperies of that earlier period.

Eastlake, in 1878,[69] was also scathing:

Now … the useful convenient little rod has grown into a lumbering pole … not only hollow but of metal far too thin in proportion to its diameter. Instead of little finials gigantic fuschias etc. Sometimes this pole being too weak for actual use is fixed up simply for ornament while the curtain slides on an iron rod behind it … Curtains are immoderately long, so that they may be looped up in clumsy folds over two large and eccentric looking metal hooks on either side of the window. Dust gathers thickly in the folds …

These dusty and heavy folds were partly due to the fashion for heavy fabrics – velvets, plush, tapestry – and partly to the linings and interlinings. The eighteenth-century curtain had been lined, with the edges held together with a narrow silk braid, but they had not been interlined. It was this nineteenth-century innovation which gave such a dark, rich look to the curtains.

For the last twenty years or so of the nineteenth century, the fabrics of William Morris, and those architects and designers who followed him, became very influential. These designers were not as a rule so much interested in the way curtains were made as in the fabrics from which they were made, and Morris designs, timeless though intricate, are still popular today. They, together with the eastern fabrics imported by the recently-opened department store, Liberty's, were the fashionable fabrics by the end of the century. Of course, humbler and less pretentious folk were still following the older fashions. Flora Thompson, in *Lark Rise to Candleford*, described the new villas, which were much smaller than the earlier ones: 'As they were built, almost before the paint was dry, the villas were occupied and the new tenants tied back their lace curtains with blue and pink ribbon and painted on the gate the name of their choice "Chatsworth" or "Naples" or "Sunnyside", or "Herne Bay".'

BLINDS

An item of window furnishing which has been in vogue from at least the early seventeenth century until today is the blind, used mainly as a protection against sun, but also for privacy. The first blinds were of fabric, cotton or silk, generally oiled for strength, and also painted. One of the problems was that when painted and rolled the fabric, especially if silk, tended to crack in exactly the same way as trade union and other painted banners do today. In the late seventeenth century Roger North tells of meeting a Mr Weld, a rich philosopher who lived in Bloomsbury, who was 'of a superior order and valued himself upon new inventions of his own ... [He] claimed the invention of painted curtains in varnish upon silk which would not bend and not crack; and his house was furnished with them ...'[166] It has been suggested that Mr Weld must have used some form of thinner for his varnish, which perhaps made the fabric sticky, although not brittle.

Cleaning this painted fabric also posed problems and in 1729 John Brown, an upholsterer, advertised that he 'made and sold Window Blinds of all Sorts, Painted in Wier, Canvas, Cloth and Sassenet [Sarcenet], after the best and most lasting manner so that if ever so dull and dirty they will clean with sope and sand and be like new ...'[87] Soap and sand sounds very drastic and one wonders what his method of painting was that could withstand such treatment.

During the eighteenth century venetian blinds were in general use. These were slats of thin wood joined by tape at the sides which could be adjusted to keep out all light or allow a small amount into the room. Although popular, these were never wholly satisfactory as the tape tended to wear out, or one side stretched more than another so that the blind hung awry. In 1791 Mrs Papendiek noted that 'The Venetian blinds I had new strung at home with silk ferret [tape], and the bars painted to match, – one coat.'[57]

By the middle of the century blinds must have been universal, and virtually every upholsterer advertised that he made all types. George Speer, for example, in the 1770s sold: 'Venetian, Spring and all other Sorts of window Blinds'; William Gwinnall advertised '... Blinds for Windows made and Curiously painted on Canvas, Silk or Wire' in 1741, and there were at least eighteen blind-makers in London alone.[87]

About 1750 spring blinds, which were also called spring curtains, were invented. These were the ordinary spring blinds with which we are familiar today, working (or not) on a spring at the end of the roller, which in theory allowed the blind to stay at any required level. The Duchess of Bedford had, in the dressing room of her London house, 'Two festoon window curtains of red and white Tabary, unlined, and Two spring curtains'.[187] These would appear to be two windows close together with a blind each and one pair of curtains on the outside of the windows.

In 1807 Robert Southey, describing the English house, says: 'Each window has blinds to prevent the by-passers from looking in; the plan is taken from the Venetian blinds, but made more expensive as the bars are fitted into a frame and move in grooves.'[63] This fear of by-passers looking in is understandable in a town but at the turn of the century a form of blind or shutter was fixed to the bottom level of the glass pane in the country as well as the town. These, known as 'snob' or 'draught' screens, were made with thin upright brass rods to which was attached green gathered silk.

59. Draught screen. Early nineteenth century. Peckover House

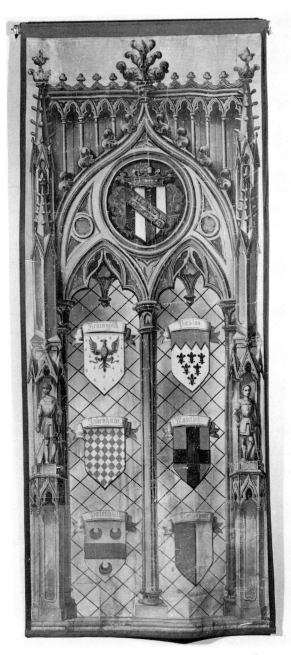

60. *Painted blind, c. 1850. Oxburgh Hall*

There do not appear to be many in existence today, though there is still a pair in the drawing room at Peckover House on the North Brink at Wisbech. They were probably far more common than we now think, as one is shown in a sketch by John Harden (dated 1818),[76] and there is also one in a watercolour painting by Mary Ellen Best of 'Mrs Duffins dining room York', in the early 1830s.[36] Both in Wisbech and York the houses were located where it might have been possible to see into the rooms, but at Brathay Hall in Cumberland it would be unlikely that there would be anyone to look, except perhaps the gardener. In John Harden's sketch, the screen is swung open so that the light falls on those in the room who are reading and sewing.

In 1847 Thomas Webster wrote a very comprehensive book on household management. Referring to blinds he says, as might be expected, that they were for excluding the sun's rays or for preventing anyone looking in, 'at the same time permitting a view from within'.[193] He refers to venetian blinds, still fashionable, and Holland blinds, which could be rolling blinds either with or without springs. He preferred the plain rolling blinds as more economical and less apt to break.

Webster also referred to sun-blinds made of linen painted as transparencies: 'some are extremely beautiful, representing scenes in nature, either landscape, interiors of buildings, or arabesques, and are particularly convenient when it is desirable to exclude the view of disagreeable objects. They are put upon rollers in the same manner as other blinds, being painted in varnish that does not crack in rolling.' This seems to be the same or a variation of the blinds referred to by Roger North. There is, hanging on the wall of the King's Room at Oxburgh, a blind 'painted as a transparency', which was possibly designed and painted by one of the family in the 1850s.

Short blinds were and are those attached to the lower half of the window to prevent anyone looking in. They were first of frilled muslin on a brass rod, later of Nottingham lace in the same style, but Webster stresses that in 'better houses' they generally had venetian blinds of short vertical rather than horizontal laths, or blinds made of woven wire or pierced zinc put into a mahogany frame. These could be painted and were not apt to get out of order. The last remark was obviously true, as even today some old-fashioned shops still have these painted wire blinds in the lower part of their glass doors.

Ten

SEAT FURNITURE

The most general and obvious work for the upholsterer was in the area of seat furniture, in which he complemented and finished the work of the cabinet-maker, joiner and turner. Seating before and during the sixteenth century was uncomfortable, consisting of benches and stools with an occasional chair for the master of the house or important visitor. Some members of the household might have cushions on their stools, but hardness was the rule and any softening the exception.

Towards the end of the sixteenth century, stools and chairs began to be upholstered and the Bacon accounts show what was apparently normal practice. In 1588 six stools were made at Stiffkey and it would seem that the frames were made somewhere else, possibly on the estate, as there are not any payments shown for them. For the actual upholstery, '2 dussen of gyrthwebe' was bought – presumably meaning twenty-four yards – costing 3s., and 700 garnishing nails for 1s. 9d. Then four pounds of deer hair was used for the stuffing, at 1s. 4d; nine skins (it is not clear whether they were of deer or sheep) made the seats, and the stools were finished off with fringe which cost 11s. Although there is no payment shown, the work was probably done by Thomas Crumlin, the horse keeper, who certainly made stools a few years later.[1]

Even at this early date the decoration cost more than all the necessities put together, and later, in 1592, six and three-quarter ounces of long gold fringe for some chairs was bought at the high price of 6s. an ounce. This is a trend which continued and indeed intensified during the seventeenth and eighteenth centuries, where it is found that the fringes, tassels, fabrics and laces of a bed or chair might cost many times more than the framework.

Other accounts show the use of deer hair as stuffing rather than horsehair. Though there were many deer in England at this date, there were also many horses and it seems strange that deer hair should be preferred.

The Bacon accounts also show that sowetage, a coarse fabric used for linings, variously called soultige, sultige or soulwitch, was used for the backs and seats of chairs and the seats of stools in the same way unbleached calico is used today. The accounts show that more stools were made in

61. X-stool covered with a seventeenth-century fabric.
The legs were originally covered with fabric fastened with what
might well be 'garnishing' nails. Knole

1592, or the old ones were refurbished, and apart from the sowetage, deer hair was again bought for 'the corners of the stools'.

At this time, too, various different kinds of nails and what are today called studs were used in the upholstery. Garnishing nails were bought for the stools and beds, and 'embostinge' nails for chairs; there were also 'great chair nayles' and 'skirt nayles', as well as tacks; all in very large quantities. Surprisingly, all the upholstery in this house seems to have been done by Thomas Crumlin, who was clearly a man of many parts. He looked after the horses and stables and for this reason did most of the shopping in the nearby towns and villages, as well as making and upholstering the furniture; for this he was paid in 1597, in addition to his wages, 2s. 4d. for making four buffet stools and two chairs, and 2d. for making six cushions. All the cushions used in the house were lined with sheepskin, bought from the glover at $4\frac{1}{2}$d. each, rather than taken from the farm. No stuffing for cushions is mentioned, so they probably consisted of a fabric top, worked or plain, on a sheepskin with the wool inside. In 1596 two cushion cloths or tops were decorated with twelve yards of bone (bobbin) lace costing 8s., and in 1592 the local tailor was paid for two ounces of Genoese silk for the ladies to work a cushion cover; he also drew the design for them at the additional cost of 1s.

Although cushions have been used from medieval times until the present, often in large quantities, it was in the sixteenth century, with the furniture generally still hard, that they were most welcome. They were used on chairs and stools and also in window-seats, and sheepskin seems to have been the most commonly used lining. As well as the Bacon family, Sir Henry Sydney used them in 1567 when he bought six arras cushions with skins for lining.[7] These were stuffed with feathers and the six cost £3 19s. 3d. As late as 1673 Sarah Fell bought a sheepskin for a 'quishon bottom'.[3]

The covers were varied and helped to give the rooms warmth and colour. They could be embroidered at home, and the many cushions worked by Bess of Hardwick shown in the Hardwick inventory of 1601 must have been some of the most beautiful.[112] Most of these were worked in fine tent-stitch, which wears very well, and this technique has been popular ever since. Dame Agnes Hungerford had in her house in 1523 fifty-four cushions. Some of these were ordinary and some old, but seventeen were of different coloured velvets embroidered in gold, some thirty-six inches, some fifty-four inches long, for benches and window-seats. Others were of russet damask or 'tawny sarcenet imbrodered with branchis'.[116]

Some cushions were covered with the best parts of worn-out tapestries and in 1534 Thomas Leman had four old cushions of tapestry with the Scriptures and three with the Holy Lamb depicted on them.[122] Earlier still, in 1488, Robert Morton had twelve cushions in the hall as well as three bankers (bench covers) of green saye lined: in the 'fysshe chambre' were twelve cushions of white leather and in the chapel chamber nine little cushions of carpet work, six old cushions covered with red saye, ten cushions of tapestry work and three bankers of tapestry work, delightfully described as 'palyd and febyll'.[125]

By the end of the sixteenth and throughout the seventeenth centuries the majority of cushions were worked on canvas, using either tent-stitch, cross-stitch or Irish-stitch. This last was the simplest of all to work and was used by the least accomplished needlewomen. Later the stitch, which was also a pattern, became known as flame-stitch, Hungarian, Florentine, or latterly, Bargello. It consisted of straight stitches worked in an undulating pattern in different shades, giving the effect of flames. Lady Anne Clifford, who worked so hard to have her Cumberland estates returned to her, and who was virtually incarcerated at Knole when she was being more than usually intransigent, often made cushions of Irish-stitch and says, in 1619, 'it being my chief help to pass away the time at work'.[44] She apparently used no other stitch, so was not likely to have been a good or interested needlewoman, just bored.

The fashionable technique of the mid-seventeenth century, stump-work, or raised-work, to give it its original name, was generally used for panels

62. *Cushion in stump-work (raised-work) with original*
passementerie *trimming. Mid-seventeenth century.*
Norfolk Museums Service, Stanger's Hall Museum, Norwich

and caskets, but was also used for cushions. This can only have been for those which were meant to be seen and not used, as the technique made the cushions both fragile and uncomfortable. The designs were a hotch-potch of Old Testament stories, such as Solomon and the Queen of Sheba, David and Bathsheba, or Esther and Ahasuerus, with life-sized flowers and insects scattered indiscriminately over the ground. The technique included small wooden and parchment moulds covered in silk, used for hands and faces; outlines of leaves and flowers were made with wire, filled in with various lace stitches. These were often left loose and were liable to get broken. Sometimes the edging of the cushion was of *passementerie* arranged in loops and swags. It was all charming but impractical.

63. Cushion with framed medallions representing five ladies.
This and the preceding cushion were for decoration rather than comfort.
Seventeenth century. Knole

By 1600 upholstered chairs and stools came into more general use, and therefore there was less emphasis on cushions. One of the techniques found most frequently in seventeenth-century upholstered covers is turkey work, used particularly on stools with short padded backs which were generally known as 'farthingale chairs'. This is a misnomer as, far from being merely feminine chairs, they are found in dining rooms and in other rooms used by both sexes or by men alone. They formed the intermediate stage between a stool and a more comfortable chair. Although turkey-work covers were common, many other types were also current. For example, in 1603 Hengrave had, in the 'Dynung Chamber', two great chairs covered with turkey damask and, in the Winter Parlour, a great chair, a little chair, a little stool and a high joined stool, all covered with red flannel embroidered with lace, which sounds very cheerful for a room used in winter.[113]

The main seventeenth-century fabrics for upholstery and cushions were

64. High backed stool upholstered in velvet.
Seventeenth century. Knole

damask, leather, scarlet, turkey work and tuft and plain mockado, but turkey work and leather were used more than anything else. The high-backed chairs associated with Charles II's reign were not upholstered and would only have needed squab cushions if anything, but towards the end of the century the more comfortably upholstered wing chairs came into being.

By the early eighteenth century stools were out of fashion and upholstered chairs were usual. High-backed wing chairs were often covered in needlework simulating tapestry, or tapestry itself and the wide-seated Georgian chairs for dining tables or sitting rooms were, again, usually covered in needlework. It is often a moot point as to whether the covers seen today are original or not, and this can seldom be decided without taking the covers off to see if there are other rows of nail holes or not. This need not be conclusive, as the seat could have needed re-stuffing, and the original seat might have been put back, but if the seat did need re-stuffing, one would have expected the cover to have been worn out. A case in point is a chair from the Gubbay collection at Clandon Park – a wing chair upholstered in needlework, recently conserved. At first sight, the chair and cover appeared to fit perfectly, though the cover did seem to be a few years older than the frame. However, it was soon seen that the seat had been sprung (not before the 1860s), and on closer examination it was obvious that while the needlework was roughly contemporaneous with the frame they in no way belonged together; the needlework was probably cut from a seventeenth-century bed curtain in this century. Here there was very likely no intention to defraud; just an old frame re-upholstered with suitable needlework in the 1920s or 1930s and sold as a perfectly acceptable marriage.

It was in the eighteenth century that the fashion for using cottons and linens as upholstery fabrics as well as for curtains began. This was due to the Indian and the English printed cottons now obtainable which fitted in with the new feeling for lightness and charm rather than the heavy solidity so prevalent in the seventeenth century. They could also be used as decorative case covers which could be easily washed, and they were a boon to the amateur needlewoman. A great deal of canvas work was still being stitched, and it must be to this that Mrs Delany was referring when she wrote to her sister Ann in 1743: 'I have bought your worsted and silk for my brother's chair that you are to work; I could not meet with any workwoman that would do it under two guineas and a half. The material for working came to 18s.' She goes on to give her sister explicit instructions,

65. *High backed chair covered with tapestry. Probably French. Late seventeenth century. Anglesey Abbey*

'I beg you not to be under any concern for my sky. I would have it clear of clouds, the pink silk must join the hill, and the blue silk next, – about one third silk, the other blue worsted ...'[46] In fact, though Mrs Delany herself was a most accomplished needlewoman and artist, it looks as though her sister took a very large part in the work.

67. *Wing chair being conserved, showing the attractive base of what may have been bed curtains completely covered when the cushion is put in place. Early eighteenth century. Clandon Park*

Both the amateur and the professional were busy in the eighteenth century – the amateur working covers for the professional to apply, and the upholsterer covering furniture with fabrics sometimes supplied by the owners. In the *Shardeloes Papers*, John Linnell's bill dated 27 July 1768 is for 'Making and Carving 8 French Elbow Chairs by Drawing, and Gilding the same in parts in Burnish Gold, the same stuff'd in Canvas with the best of Materials and cover'd with your own Crimson Silk Damask and nail'd with the best Gilt Nails, all compleat 4/18/–. Making and carving 2 Sophas to match the Chairs £24.0.0.'[62]

Horace Walpole, when furnishing the breakfast room at Strawberry Hill, used a blue and white paper in stripes adorned with festoons on the wall, and then had 'a thousand plump chairs, couches and luxurious settees

66. *Wing chair with canvas-work cover. Early eighteenth century. Clandon Park*

covered with linen of the same pattern'. Exactly the same as the big wallpaper and fabric firms are doing today with their co-ordinating ranges.[16]

In the second half of the eighteenth century there was a fashion for covering settees and chairs with specially woven tapestry, generally Beauvais, Aubusson or Soho, made exactly to the size and shape of the chair, settee and sometimes matching screen. One of the most famous of these

69. Seat furniture covered with a Beauvais tapestry
woven to fit the furniture. Late eighteenth century. Osterley Park

sets is in the Tapestry Room at Osterley Park, where the design is after Boucher, woven at Beauvais. Though these covers were often made in France, the furniture could be a mixture of French and English. Mrs Lybbe Powys, describing the drawing room at Heythrop, says she was told by the owner that the chairs were 'of tent stitch-work at Paris, the carved frames made there and gilt in England'.[59]

The 1842 sale catalogue of the contents of Strawberry Hill lists a settee in the Round Room, described as: 'A shaped Front carved and gilt sofa, representing four chairs in appearance with carved arms, covered with the rich Aubusson tapestry, worked in Roses with bands of flowers on a white ground, stuffed with hair 8' long.' In 1771 Horace Walpole had paid £104 12s. 6d. for this settee, four chairs, a screen and the packing of them all.

68. Chair upholstered with canvas-work. French, c. 1735. Waddesdon Manor

70. Settee covered with tapestry from the suite,
'Les Nouvelles Indes'. French, mid-eighteenth century.
Waddesdon Manor

Taste gradually changed, moving towards more comfort in furniture, but
it received a set-back at the end of the eighteenth century and the beginning
of the nineteenth with the comparative austerity of the neo-classical, post-
Revolution period. This austerity matched the plainness and apparent
simplicity of dress, with white muslins hanging straight from a high waist.
It is epitomized in the designs of Thomas Hope. In his furniture hard squab
cushions fit into chairs shaped like those of ancient Greece and Rome,
settees have hard stuffed bolsters, and gone are Horace Walpole's 'plump

71. *Library chair with over-stuffed leather seat.*
Mid-eighteenth century. Montacute House

chairs'. In fact, if one may judge from the designs shown by Hope,[90] and those which Ackermann illustrates in the *Repository*,[18] there can have been no other period after the sixteenth century when furniture was so uncomfortable and unaccommodating to the human form. But as uncomfortable as they may seem to us, Maria Edgeworth did not appear to feel it. In 1821 she writes home to Ireland: 'I am now writing in a delightful armchair – high backed antiquity – modern cushion with moveable side cushions with cushion elbows lying on the lowest of low arms, so that there is just comfortable room to sit down in a place between cushions ...'[47]

The reaction to this hardness was hardness of a different kind. The mid-nineteenth century saw furniture over-stuffed, with much deep buttoning, and all too often woven horsehair was used as a covering. This horsehair seldom wore out, but it became frayed at the arms and edges of chair and sofa seats, and there are many people alive today who can testify to the

72. *Deep buttoning on a mid-Victorian chair shown before re-upholstering. 1860s. Private collection*

extreme discomfort felt by children when this frayed fabric pricked the backs of their bare legs. It was very hard and very slippery.

A look at any of the catalogues and periodicals referring to the Great Exhibition of 1851 and other exhibitions of about that time, shows a plethora of carving and ornamentation of the framework, but in general the upholstery was in the heavy velvets and plushes of the time, plain, with deep buttoning. This style did not lend itself to the use of patterned fabrics. They came a little later: chintz and cretonnes, a riot of overblown roses and unknown flowers made into loose covers for furniture. These covers, which have continued to be used into our own day, could be taken off, not to reveal the splendours of the upholstery fabric, but to wash them. The fact that upholstered furniture was difficult to clean satisfactorily made the use of loose covers an attractive alternative.

Charles Eastlake in *Hints on Household Taste*[69] has much to say about the buying of upholstered furniture. He thought the shopkeeper would always mislead the customer as regards taste, though he understood the need for strength and wearing qualities. He says: 'I strongly advise my readers to refrain from buying any article of art-manufacture which is "handsome", "elegant", or "unique", in commercial slang: it is sure to be bad art.' He was tired of unmeaning curves in furniture and advocated simplicity of outline, pointing to the Knole settee: comfortable, well-upholstered, with the back cushions and sides stuffed with feathers, re-covered in plain velvet with braid decoration. His designs for furniture were all solid, often upholstered in the new, machine-made tapestry, sometimes with a little buttoning and generally with the addition of fringe.

The Arts and Crafts Movement, which included such well-known figures as William Morris, his daughter and partners, the Newberrys in Glasgow, Charles Rennie Mackintosh and his wife Margaret Macdonald, as well as the teachers and students at the Birmingham School of Art and the Royal School of Needlework, made a great difference to textiles in general, especially those used as curtains and wall panels, and to the design and decoration of furniture, but they did not have much impact on upholstery. The influence of the movement on the furnishings of a room was shown particularly in such things as screens and cushions and in the general attitude to the room as a whole. Tall three- or four-fold screens became very popular, often covered with embroidered panels using what are now called 'Art Nouveau' motifs. The teaching of embroidery, especially at Glasgow and South Kensington, became the norm, rather than the executant discovering it for herself from the magazines of the time, and so the standard of workmanship rose considerably. There were, too, some very talented designers and architects who now did not think it beneath their dignity to design for textiles, and so in many new homes, at least, there began a 'Total Look' which took in furniture and textiles together with wall coverings.

Probably the greatest influence on furnishings at the end of the nineteenth and beginning of the twentieth centuries was Liberty's, the shop in Regent Street which specialized in goods brought from the Far East, especially Japan.[17] Unlike India and China, Japan had had virtually no contact with the west since the beginning of the seventeenth century, but in 1853 a US

73. *Chair covered* en suite *with the bedroom furnishings,*
c. 1829. (see illus. 46). Note deep fringe and tassels
covering the legs. Basildon Park

naval squadron had sailed into the Bay of Yeddo, after which trade started
in a sporadic fashion. From then on the fashion for Far Eastern objects had
blossomed. The fabrics were used for the newly popular draped, 'aesthetic'
styles of dress, and draping, rather than any form of stiffness, became the
rage. Bamboo furniture became popular, and screens, mantelpieces, pianos

and anything which could be draped was draped with eastern, or English imitating eastern, fabrics.

The other thing which gave rooms and furnishings their particular flavour during the last half of the nineteenth century was the multitude of small textile objects, mostly worked by the ladies of the house, which made a striking contrast to the rooms of the eighteenth and early nineteenth centuries.

Eleven

CASE COVERS

Case, or slip, covers, also known as loose covers, have been in use since at least early Tudor times. When used on solid furniture such as tables or beds they have been purely for protection, but when used on seat furniture they could be to protect fine fabrics, hide shabby ones or change the look of a room at little cost.

The careful housewife of whatever generation or income has always wanted to preserve her good and expensive furnishings and has also in part wanted to impress the neighbours with her housewifely skills. Mrs Gaskell, in *Cranford*,[79] highlights the lengths to which the 'genteel poor' would go to preserve their furnishings. The Misses Jenkyns had bought a new carpet for the drawing room and,

Oh, the work Miss Matty and I had in chasing the sunbeams as they fell in an afternoon right down on this carpet through the blindless window! We spread newspapers over the places, and sat down to our book or our work; and lo! in a quarter of an hour the sun had moved, and was blazing away on a fresh spot, and down again we went on our knees to alter the position of the newspapers. We were very busy too, in cutting out and stitching together pieces of newspaper so as to form little paths to every chair set for the expected visitors, lest their shoes might dirty or defile the purity of the carpet.

Before the removal vans of the twentieth century the transport of furniture was a lengthy and difficult process. The table or other piece was probably bought in London or some other large city and might have had to be taken to a house in the country, possibly two or three hundred miles away. This journey could be by carrier's cart, which took goods of any shape or size, or it could be by sail around the coast to the nearest, often very small, port, and then taken on by cart. In either case it would be subjected to much movement, banging and handling and might very likely arrive broken, or at best slightly damaged. For this reason, as well as for safety in its new home, each piece of furniture generally had a case made to fit it, often of leather. Before 1535, when the inventory of Baynards Castle in London was taken, Katharine of Aragon had three iron chairs, in leather cases lined with yellow cotton, and also '4 lyttle stoles – each having a yellow case lined with yellow cotton'.[118] In 1599 the Rutland accounts show that two leather cases were made, in which the bedstead, table and stools would travel to Ireland.[11] It is not always easy to distinguish between what we might term packing cases, used for transport, and cases for permanent use in the house, but generally the furniture was put first into its permanent case and then into a packing case.

When big houses had case covers for their chairs and stools, the fabric used was meant to change the whole appearance of the room. It might be expected that the cover would be made of a fabric as near as possible, at least in colour, to the upholstery underneath, but this was not so. In 1603, in the Great Chamber at Hengrave,[113] there were twenty-four high joined stools 'covered with carpet work like the carpets, frynged with crewell' and 'yellow buckrams to cover the stooles with'. In the same chamber were two great chairs covered with crimson figured satin, fringed with crimson silk and silver; they also had yellow buckrum covers. This entry gives two entirely different pictures of the Great Chamber. In one, turkey-work coverings, usually in fairly dull reds and greens, with the two great chairs a focal point of crimson and silver; in the other, when the covers were on, a whole roomful of yellow buckrum. This would have given pleasure at the change, as well as protection for the upholstery.

It was otherwise at Donington House, which belonged to the Earl of Huntingdon. There the couch chair and high stool, both of embroidered red velvet, were covered with red baize, and a note at the end of a list of furnishings states that, 'All the chairs and stools in this chamber have covers upon them.'[6] These would all have been of red baize: so at all times the furniture would appear red, which was evidently the preferred colour for that particular room.

Hengrave must have had a very careful housekeeper, as in the same Great Chamber even the table carpets were covered. The table carpets were probably either beautifully and heavily embroidered, or else of turkey work, and to keep them clean there was 'one large bord clothe, or grene clothe, to laye over yᵉ carpetts of yᵉ long borde', as well as two more green cloths to cover the carpets of the cupboards and square board.

The suggestion that case covers were used to change the look of the room is borne out by the Fairfax inventory of 1624: 'six high stooles covered with leather seates & covers of greene cloth & fringe on them, which may be taken off at pleasure...'[106] As with the Hengrave covers, these served a dual purpose. Pepys spent much time in rearranging his furniture and was very colour conscious, anxious to have his home appear

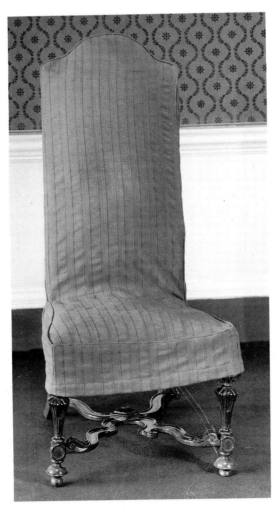

74–75 (opposite). *Embroidered chair, c. 1680, with and without its cover. Clandon Park*

to the best advantage; he found case covers useful to change the look of his rooms. In 1663 he was 'altering my chairs in my chamber, and set them above in the red room, they being Turkey work: and so put their green covers upon those that were above, not so handsome'.[58] The shabby chairs were covered with green; those with turkey-work seats, probably with a lot of red in them, could be put in the best bedroom.

Leather was a material frequently used for what might be called the 'hard'

furniture; for carved and gilt tables, girandoles and stands at Temple Newsom and for cedar tables at Ham House, but it would have to be put on with great care, as the leather could well damage fine carved detail. To guard against this, the cases for the cedar tables were lined with 'clouded lustring'. Serge was also much used, for example on chairs and settees at Canons Ashby, which were upholstered in needlework and cased with gold serge. On the furniture of the ballroom at Bedford House,[187] the serge was green, and at Harewood House it was green for the chairs and crimson for the stools.[159]

The Blickling inventory of 1793[96] lists many different fabrics for covers; leather and green for the pier tables in the New Drawing Room, with striped Manchester on the chairs; cotton on the stools and white fabric on the mahogany stools in the State Bedroom, but here no bed cases are mentioned; cotton covers in Lady B.'s dressing room; dimity in the study; chintz in the Copperplate Room, while in Lady Emilia's keeping room the couch has a 'Flower'd Quilted Cover'. All the other furniture had covers, but the fabric is not mentioned.

In 1786 Haig and Chippendale sent seven cases of furniture to Lord Walsingham at Merton, including striped cotton cases for the mahogany armchairs, sofa squabs and cushions.[52] The firm evidently renewed cases as well, as included were the cases for a sofa 'now at Merton' and the 'old stripe case sent us as a pattern'. The covers were not remade by the village seamstress, as might be expected, but by the illustrious firm of Haig and Chippendale.

Beds were special. They were expensive status symbols and with all their enrichment, very vulnerable to dust, dirt and mishandling. Their owners considered it a waste of money to pay out hundreds of pounds and then let the fabric deteriorate when the family was away. So most elaborate beds had extra curtains made, fastened to separate rods, which completely shrouded and protected the bed. In 1703 Dyrham Park[105] had case curtains of worsted paragon protecting the striped velvet bed lined with silk, and Sir John Smyth's lady had 'a Bedstead and old Green Damask furniture with Case Curtain and Rod...'[132] The State Bed at Harewood House was magnificent, in Chippendale's most elaborate style, with green damask furniture.[159] The upholsterer, one of the firm's senior workmen, made the furniture and then made canvas and paper covers for the bed and, in 1774, coverings of baize, so it was well protected. Sheets pinned to the hangings were also used. Celia Fiennes[48] saw, at Ashstead Park, several damask rooms 'so neatly kept folded up in clean sheets pinn'd about the beds and hangings', and nearly a hundred years later the 1771 inventory at Felbrigg mentions, among the linen, 'Six Birds Eye [diaper] pieces to pin upon Bed Curtains'.[109]

As well as the covers over the pieces of furniture, care was taken that

76. Reconstructed case curtains for the State Bed at Dyrham Park

not too much light should penetrate to fade carpets, curtains and pictures. The expenditure of Lord Roos included 10s. for 'the hire of paper windows last year, 1668, to save the hangings in the dining roome and drawinge roome'[11] – obviously some form of blind. A hundred years earlier in the same household, 10d. was paid for a curtain to draw in front of her ladyship's picture. No wonder furniture and furnishings lasted – they were seldom seen.

So little were they seen that travellers such as Celia Fiennes and many others never expected to see the houses they visited unshrouded. It was accepted etiquette that when the family were away, which was frequently, any visitor of a certain class might be shown round the house by the housekeeper, who would expect a tip or 'vail' for her trouble. In some houses there was bickering between various upper servants as to who should have the right to take visitors round and thus add to their salary. The visitors saw little as they would find the chandeliers tied up in a bag to keep the flies away from the glass drops, the furniture in their cases, the beds with their curtains drawn and probably the window curtains taken down and the shutters closed. Under these conditions it is surprising that so many wanted to see the houses when all they could see would be the actual building. This is a far cry from today, when all visitors expect to see National Trust houses in impeccable condition, and often fail to understand the necessity for protecting the furniture.

Even more interesting than the actual covers used is the owners' attitude to them. From portraits and conversation pieces it becomes apparent that no one was ashamed of their covers. They are seen in countless pictures. Perhaps one might expect to see them in a portrait of Dr Johnson, an untidy man, but not necessarily in a conversation piece of the children of George III, where the chair with a dark red cover, fringed and tied round the legs of the chair, is plain to see. The family when alone always expected the seat furniture to be covered, and would probably have felt uncomfortable sitting on the best fabrics. They did not mind friends finding covers on and they only removed them for parties and special guests. Mrs Delany put it plainly when, while living in Ireland, she 'is honoured with a visit from our Viceroy and Queen; they sent over early in the morning to know if we were disengaged as they would breakfast. To work went all my maids, stripping covers off the chairs, sweeping, dusting etc. and by eleven my house was as spruce as a cabinet of curiosities.' On her birthday, among all her other preparations, Mrs Delany put 'my best covers on my chairs'.[46]

Carpets were by no means immune to all this care. At Harewood House,

Reid, the upholsterer, 'after he had laid the carpet on the great staircase, covered it with oilcloth and serge . . .'[159] The great carpet protector, however, was drugget. By the end of the eighteenth century this fabric had changed from being used mainly for costume to being a much wider, stronger woollen for protecting carpets, as it still is today in most National Trust

77. *Case cover of large cotton checks in the picture of*
'The Revd Charles Everard and two others playing billiards',
by J. H. Mortimer (detail). Upton House

houses, and others open to the public. In the nineteenth century drugget was often kept permanently on the passage-ways so that the carpet did not wear excessively where people generally walked. The *Workwoman's Guide* says that druggets were very wide, sometimes two and sometimes four yards, and 'are chiefly employed to lay over another carpet, to preserve it when the room is in daily use, and only removed for company. Sometimes druggets alone are laid and when of a handsome brown or marone colour, look extremely well.'

78. Fabric of window curtain protected by rows of couching.
Uppark

A painting by Mary Ellen Best dated 1838 shows a large piece of drugget on the floor of the room in which she is painting. One would like to know if that particular piece was taken up when company came or whether it lay there permanently.

Lately there have been many watercolour and pencil sketches discovered showing the interior of rooms, particularly in the first half of the nineteenth century. *The World of Mary Ellen Best*,[36] *John Harden of Brathay Hall*,[76] and *Mrs Hurst Dancing*[181] are three of the best known and in each, particularly *Mary Ellen Best*, case covers are a feature of the rooms portrayed. The fabrics are frequently striped – the stripes about one inch wide – in a single strong colour on white, and the colour seldom bears much, or indeed any, relationship to the colours of the room. The covers in no way sink into the background; on the contrary, they often appear positively aggressive.

Covers continued in the second half of the nineteenth century, but towards its close they were used possibly more for style than for protection, as they multiplied until there was nothing left uncovered, company or not.

Flowered chintz and cretonnes were popular, with deep self-frills round the seat furniture; tables had fitted covers with worked edges, and many a child hid beneath the large chenille cloths which covered tables to the ground, listening to things they were not meant to hear! With so much covering and, often, three sets of curtains, rooms inevitably became very dark, about which Mrs Panton, in *Nooks and Corners* (1889), has a few straight words to say: 'Then too, the dear ladies were so fond of stuffing up their windows and darkening their rooms still more by the drawing down of blinds and the eliminating of every morsel of sunshine for fear their precious carpets would become faded; and I am sorry to say that this affection for half dark rooms yet lingers among many who ought to know better.'[168]

Perhaps the last word on the subject should go to Augustus Hare who, in *The Story of my Life*,[83] tells of his visits to his grandparents in the first half of the nineteenth century. For him – a small child – and his parents, no changes were made to the look of the house, but he had an aunt who was

a very simple person, utterly without pretension, but because she was Lord Derby's daughter Grannie always treated her as the great person of the family. When we went to Stoke, no difference whatever was made in the house, the stair carpets were not laid down, and though the drawing room was constantly lived in, its furniture was all swathed in brown holland after the fashion of an uninhabited London house. When the Stanleys or Leycesters of Toft came to Stoke the stair carpet was put down and the *covers'-covers* were taken off; but on the rare occasion when Aunt Penryhn came to Stoke – why, sublime moment! – the *covers* themselves were taken off!

Snobbishness, frugality or just careful housekeeping?

Twelve

MISCELLANEOUS FURNISHINGS

All through the four hundred years we are covering here, rooms had in greater or lesser degree what could be called minor furniture. This varied from generation to generation, but reached its zenith in the nineteenth century, though each age had its own ideas as to the extras which helped the look or comfort of a room.

79. Casket in raised-work (stump-work).
Mid-seventeenth century. Fenton House

In the sixteenth century there were few additions to the basic necessities, but by the seventeenth the teaching of needlework to girls had raised the level of proficiency to the point where the results could be put on show. The lessons followed a well-tried pattern. First the girl would work a whitework sampler, using plain linen thread and practising various kinds of lacis and filet, as well as working geometrical patterns in satin-stitch. Then she would work another sampler in coloured silks, which could show lines of patterns or rounded motifs scattered over the work. Only when she had proved capable of completing this satisfactorily did she progress to her most ambitious project, which was an embroidered casket, worked in silks on linen, in a wide variety of stitches and motifs. Sometimes the motifs illustrated an Old Testament story, sometimes one taken from mythology. The stitches used were varied and often the work became three-dimensional and was known as raised-work, which in the nineteenth century was called stump-work. These caskets took a long time to work and some were left unfinished; then the pieces which were done were framed and hung as

80. Mirror with surround in raised-work (stump-work).
Mid-seventeenth century. Cotehele House

embroidered panels. Raised-work was also used as a surround for the newly obtainable mirrors, complete with figures, animals, flowers and leaves, houses and insects, all created without regard for scale or perspective.

Screens of all kinds were used by each succeeding generation – large six- or eight-fold screens, firescreens, pole screens, banner screens and hand screens. They served three purposes: they kept the draughts at bay, they preserved delicate complexions and they decorated fireplaces in summer.

Large draught screens could be covered with knotted tapestry, and of this type the superb, early-eighteenth-century example from Waddesdon must be exceptional. The panels were woven at the Savonnerie factory in France,

81. Screen with panels woven at the Savonnerie factory,
after designs by Desportes, 1719. Waddesdon Manor

after designs by Desportes. The technique is the same as in the Savonnerie carpets but the work is finer, with eighty-nine knots to the square inch.

Equally superb, in a different style, is the screen at Wallington worked by Julia Blackett, Lady Calverly, in 1721. This is embroidered in fine tent-

stitch with scenes from Virgil's *Georgics* and *Eclogues* and they, together with the panels now in the Needlework Room, which Lady Calverly also worked, show what a first-class embroideress of the time could accomplish.

Inventories list many screens: in 1785 Merton Hall, for example, had, in the hall – usually a draughty place – two chair screens and one large screen and in the drawing room two mahogany slip screens.[142] Chair screens folded, but were shorter than draught screens, just large enough to give protection to the occupant of the chair. Slip screens were rectangular, stood on the ground and had a centre panel (often filled with silk) which could be raised or lowered. The one in the dining room of Blickling Hall is an example.

Banner screens were in vogue in the middle of the nineteenth century. These were fastened with a decorative clamp to the mantelpiece; a series of arms from the clamp enabled the screen to be adjusted to any angle, and from the end hung the banner, often shield shaped. The banner was embroidered in a variety of techniques but the most general was Berlin wool-work with the addition of beads, and two of the most popular designs were 'Morning' and 'Evening', after pictures by the Danish artist, Thorwaldsen. These were generally worked in *grisaille* (a style which used beads of white, black and grey, both opaque and clear) on a scarlet cross-stitch ground.

Pole screens became more common in the eighteenth and early nineteenth centuries, and were very elegant adjuncts to a room. The frames and stands were designed by such cabinet-makers as Chippendale and Sheraton as well as many others. They consisted of a pole, often on tripod legs, and a frame which could be adjusted to any height required. The panel was generally canvas-work, depicting flowers, birds or animals.

Standing firescreens, while still used as protection from the heat, were also used for placing in front of the fireplace in summer, in order to hide the empty grate. Some of the frames were very beautiful, either carved in mahogany or else gilded, and often the work inside was of comparable quality, in a variety of techniques. As with the pole screens, the firescreen frame became much more solid in mid-nineteenth century, and was often filled with the ubiquitous Berlin-work of the time. In the 1840s there was a great following for the novels of Sir Walter Scott, and many of the designs used were of scenes from his novels, especially those with a Gothic-medieval flavour, such as *Ivanhoe*, worked in a colouring and grouping known as the 'style troubadour'. Implicit in this style were romantic scenes, with draped curtains and mock-medieval clothes. There was nearly always a hectic pink

82. Detail of a screen worked by Julia Blackett,
Lady Calverley, 1721. Wallington

83. Pole screen with
canvas-work panel, c. 1740.
Clandon Park

84. Pole screen with
tapestry panel, possibly from the
Fulham factory, Basildon

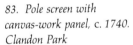

flush on the cheeks of the characters, possibly suggested by the very high incidence of tuberculosis at that time.

A bedroom accessory in use from at least the seventeenth century until today in one form or another was the *toilette*. The only English name this ever acquired was the clumsy 'toilet cover', or, later, dressing-table set, but it was an integral part of all bedrooms. In the seventeenth century a

85. *Firescreen with needlework panel, c. 1840.*
Felbrigg Hall

dressing-table was just an ordinary, small rectangular table, covered with
the usual table carpet which could be plain fabric, embroidered fabric, turkey
work or even an eastern carpet. Any appurtenances were laid on the table,
but because of their nature there was apt to be spillage and dirt in one form
or another: combs with hairs, powder, various cosmetics as well as lotions
and perfumes. To protect the good table carpet from such accidental mess,
another cloth, a washable one, was laid over it, and this was the *toilette*:

always white, of some fine fabric, sometimes embroidered. When table carpets finally became unfashionable, the *toilette* was still retained to protect the wood of the now more elaborate dressing-table. The new purpose-made dressing-tables of the eighteenth century had a mirror incorporated in the design, and this mirror was dressed to match, so that the table could have had a froth of ruffled muslin or other light fabric, which sometimes reached the ground and climbed up to the top of the mirror, to be tied with a ribbon bow. Mrs Delany wrote in one of her letters that the Duchess of Portland was working on twelve *toilettes*, which sounds like one for every guest room at Bulstrode.[46]

Generally the eighteenth-century *toilette* consisted of a table-covering with a four- to six-inch frill or valance hanging down, and a 'petticoat' gathered, reaching to the ground. This was the type described in the Blickling inventory of 1793,[96] where eight of the bedrooms had a 'toilet table and petticoat'. In the nineteenth century the *toilette* ceased to be so elaborate and became a runner, generally hemstitched all round, with embroidered ends, and this in turn developed into three mats, one large and two small, often circular, for the brush, comb and other accessories. The main point about all these *toilettes* was that however elaborately they were worked they could be washed and pressed.

At the end of the eighteenth century, fine stitchery reached a standard of excellence seldom surpassed, and there was a fashion for embroidered pictures. These were sold as kits or else could be drawn onto the silk by the drawing-master of the girls who were to make them; in Stranger's Hall Museum, Norwich, there is one which is said to have been drawn by the artist, John Crome. The usual background was a silk fabric, and skies, hands and faces were generally painted in, with the rest of the picture being finely worked using a single thread of silk. These pictures made very effective room decorations, in tune with the light, turn-of-the-century decor.

The sampler which had been a work of art in the seventeenth and eighteenth centuries became, in the nineteenth, little more than a schoolgirl's exercise. In most cases they were derivative and pedestrian, but doting relatives framed them and they became valued heirlooms, never more than in the present day.

The nineteenth century saw more embroidered articles for the dressing-table and bed, in the shape of pincushions, hair-tidies and watch pockets. It is difficult to decide how necessary these were, but at this date there were numbers of ladies with too much spare time who sewed and embroidered gifts, and also for the everlasting numbers of bazaars. There was a rising

86. Needlework picture, c. 1790. Fenton House

social conscience which coincided with the resurgence of the church, and one of the ways in which this conscience could be placated was by working for many fund-raising efforts, which mostly took the form of bazaars. Many people bought out of good nature, without worrying too much about what they bought; in consequence houses tended to have a great number of decorative objects which were scattered around the rooms. Among these objects were antimacassars, which are still in use in many homes, now known as chair backs. During the second half of the nineteenth century

87. Bamboo Room at Cragside, with a white antimacassar on the sofa. Late nineteenth century

men oiled and pomaded their hair with macassar oil; when they leant back in a chair or sofa, this oil came off onto the upholstery leaving a bad stain which was difficult to remove. To guard against this, the careful housewife made or bought rectangles of linen, generally white and embroidered, which she put over the top of the chair or sofa, to receive the oiled head. Again, the whole point of these was that they were washable. In the same way, she covered the arms of her furniture where dirty or greasy hands could smirch the upholstery, but these were seldom embroidered and were either made of the same fabric as the loose cover, or of plain white linen.

88. Detail of a table cover in striped plush.
Second half of the nineteenth century. Blickling Hall

Fireplaces were also decorated in summer, and in 1837 Mary Ames, writing to her daughter, says, 'Elizabeth has just finished the stove veil. It is made up of roses and leaves and looks exceedingly pretty and much admired. One row pink roses with dark green leaves, one row white do. with light green do. a pretty contrast sewn thick to cover wire. Sewn upon wire tape, five rows cover our stove, all full-blown roses.'[40]

There are few of these to be found today, just as there are few mantel and shelf covers, sometimes called lambrequins. These could be made of undecorated fabrics, such as plush or velvet, perhaps beaded, or they could be worked in various techniques such as crazy patchwork or canvas-work. At Wightwick Manor there is still a valance, not depending from the mantelpiece itself but from the top of the chimney opening, which must have been a summer decoration, slighter, but akin to that made by Elizabeth Ames.

Bell-pulls were another item which lent themselves to needlework. With a large decorative tassel and beautiful fabric or work they were yet another element in crowded Victorian reception rooms.

During the nineteenth century it was considered important that every piece of furniture should have as much of its wooden structure covered as possible and, to this end, tables had covers reaching the floor, sometimes with a Berlin wool-work surround, sometimes in gay striped plush, while sofas and *chaises longues*, footstools and stools, were covered with beadwork, Berlin wool-work or had brightly coloured afghans and throws over them.

Towards the end of the century the techniques changed, largely due to the ascendancy of William Morris and his colleagues, and in houses like Standen the decorative needlework took on a totally new look, far removed from the canvas-work of earlier decades.

A description of a Manchester drawing room in the late 1840s puts all the objects described in this chapter in focus:

Antonia's drawing room was furnished in the modern manner with rose-trellised carpet, rosewood furniture of shocking design, rep curtains, an upright piano with a silk front, ... a gentleman's chair, and a lady's chair, each with an antimacassar ... an ottoman with a top of cross stitch, a rosewood work table, from which hung a bag of pleated magenta silk, adorned with tassels, and bell pulls of cross stitch enriched with glass beads.[170]

At no other period were textiles so important in a house.

Thirteen

CARPETS AND FLOOR COVERINGS

TABLE CARPETS

There may not appear to be any obvious connection between carpets which lie on tables and cupboards, and carpets which lie on floors, but in fact one developed into the other. Until the eighteenth century, the word carpet was applied to coverings for furniture and only later to coverings for floors. As late as 1727 *Chambers' Encyclopaedia* defines the word as 'a sort of covering to be spread on a table, trunk, an astrade [dais] or even a passage or floor', implying that its use on floors was minimal. In general, however, the word changed its meaning in the seventeenth century. On the rare occasions in the fifteenth and sixteenth centuries where carpets are found on the floor, they are generally referred to as 'foot carpets'.

One of the most decorative elements in any room in the fifteenth century must have been these coverings for tables and cupboards. The reason for their being there at all is unclear, but what is crystal clear is that as far down the social scale as yeomen's homes, at least, and often in the homes of shopkeepers and quite humble people, the provision of some kind of covering for tables and cupboards was considered a necessity. The fabrics used varied widely, according to the purse of the house-owner. The very rich had superb carpets from the east, especially Turkey and Persia, and often the English equivalent, turkey work (see illus. 3). Others used tapestry, possibly cut down from larger, worn-out pieces and poorer homes used darnix, say, drafte-work (probably cross-stitch), Danske- or Danish-work, frizado or kersey. One of the favourite colours was green.

Robert Morton in 1488 had three coverings of green say for chests, and in the chapel chamber six little carpets of various kinds.[125] In 1523 Dame Agnes Hungerford[116] had six fine carpets for cupboards, three great carpets for tables (of which two were of fine arras and one of verdure – all tapestry), as well as seven 'bastard carpetts' for cupboards and tables of poorer quality, possibly cut down from worn-out hangings.

While most carpets were designed to be used on furniture in the sixteenth century, there were a few made for floors. An inventory of 1543, taken after the death of Thomas, Earl of Rutland, includes five long table carpets of 'Turky makyng'; one foot carpet also made in Turkey, along with thirteen cupboard carpets of 'Turky makyng' and two of needlework, made for cupboards.[11] Robert Dudley, Earl of Leicester, one of the richest and most influential men in England, had many Turkey carpets at Kenilworth in 1583.[119] By this date the Levant Company brought goods from the Near East, though they were very expensive. It appears from the Kenilworth inventory that designs must have gone out from England to be worked into carpets in Turkey which were then brought to England, just as designs were later to be sent to China and India: one of the Leicester carpets was worked with roses in the middle and the Stafford knot at each end – clearly a case where the design would have had to have been sent to Turkey. Another of his carpets must surely have been for the floor, even though it is not called a foot carpet, as it is described as a 'greate Turkey carpett, the grounde blewe withe a lyst of yellowe at each ende, being in length tenne yardes scant and in breadth iiij yardes dis. quarter'. It does not seem possible that a carpet thirty feet in length and fourteen feet wide could be for a table, however large.

He also had a small 'Turkey carpett of Norwiche make', referring to the English equivalent of the oriental knotting. In all, his lordship had twenty-one Turkey carpets big and important enough to be described individually in the inventory, besides twenty-six small, ordinary ones. A very large number to have at this date. But the range of carpets was not restricted to the higher end of the scale. While Robert Dudley's table carpets ran into thousands of pounds, in 1591 Nathaniel Bacon paid just 2s. 6d. for a 'darnicke carpet'.[1]

In the seventeenth century there were still carpet coverings for furniture, but gradually more came to be used on the floor, and there is reason to assume that as fashions changed so pile carpets, whether English turkey work or imported from abroad, moved from the furniture to the floor. It is quite possible that where an inventory of, say, 1600 refers to a Turkey carpet on a cupboard, this is the same carpet referred to, in a 1640 inventory, as a Turkey foot carpet. At this period Hengrave contained mostly turkey-work carpets, described variously as carpet-work, set-work and English-

89. Detail of an early Persian carpet made in Goa.
Early seventeenth century. Knole

work.[113] If there was a difference between these four terms, it is now no longer understood. Sir Thomas Kitson of Hengrave had, in his Great Chamber, a long carpet of English-work with his arms, one for the 'bord' table, (a table on trestles), and another of the same kind for his cupboard, together with twenty-four high joined stools covered with similar carpet-work. Again, we presume that the first-mentioned carpet is for the floor, as the inventory does not say specifically what it was covering. In the Summer and Winter Parlours the same thing applies: a carpet for the floor as well as others for cupboards and tables. One, in the Chapel Chamber, was rather charmingly 'wrought with butterflies'.

By the time the Ham House inventory was taken in 1654, [111] table carpets were starting to be seen as part of the general decor, rather than isolated textiles. In one of the parlours four tables of various shapes had matching carpets of red cloth bordered with gilt leather, which also matched the wall panels, curtains, a couch bed and eighteen chairs. The room must have been a welter of scarlet and gold.

Though table carpets continued to be used, and in one sense continue to exist today in the form of cloths and runners, they gradually ceased to be of the type which can be compared with floor carpets.

FLOOR COVERINGS

In early houses there were no textile floor coverings. Rushes or straw were strewn on the floor, as well as herbs and sweet-smelling flowers in summer, all of which could be swept up when required. They were put down as elementary hygiene, to make the task of sweeping and keeping the floor clean easier, in much the same way as, later on, tea leaves were thrown on the floor before sweeping to collect the dust. The provision of rushes might appear a simple matter, but it could be quite involved, and various people needed to be employed, as a series of items in the Rutland accounts for 1536 makes clear.[11] There had been a wedding at Hollywell, and 8d. was paid for 'makyng clean the house'. This implies the sweeping up and burning of the old rushes which would have been filthy after the 'maryage'. Then 12d. was paid for 'repyng a lode of rushes at Endfild Park'; apart from the actual reaping it cost 7s. 9d. for five dozen bundles of rushes, three dozen bundles at 18d. and two dozen at 20d. Presumably the rushes were of two qualities. Next, 7d. was paid to watermen for carrying the same rushes from the waterside to 'Schordyche'. And, lastly, 3s. 5d. was paid to a carter or waggoner for taking the 'same rushes' from London to the house.

Four years later, in 1540, nine bundles of rushes were needed for the Great Chamber; two for the chapel; two for the wardrobe and an unknown quantity for the nursery, Lady Nevill's chamber and 'Maister Tresorar chamber'.

The next stage in the development of floor coverings was to plait straw or rushes into mats, which could be put down when and where required. These were for the important rooms of the house – not the bedrooms where, except for a mat beside the bed, no floor coverings are found until the eighteenth century, and not always then. Plaited rush and straw mats were in general use; in 1577 Lord North bought '12 score Yards of Matts

90. Plaited rush matting. Hardwick Hall

for the Great Chamber' at Kirtling, for which he paid £3 10s.[15] These mats would be from eighteen inches to two feet broad, sewn together to make one large floor covering, so 240 yards is not as much as it sounds. Bedfordshire mats were noted for their quality and Lord North bought his from there, giving the men who brought them and put them down 6s. 8d. for their 'paines'.

The Rutland account for 1611[11] gives a very good indication of the provision of mats. It states clearly that at Ferningham, mats for chambers cost 13s. 4d. the roll and that a roll consisted of eighty yards: 'it is but halfe yeard broad, so that ij yeards in length's one yeard square; which yeard square costs 4d. the yeard'. The earl used eight rolls a year.

Bedside mats were universal. At Stiffkey in 1587, with no other floor coverings mentioned, the steward bought 'A matt to laye at my masters bedsyde' for 3d.; four years later, either as a result of inflation or for a larger mat, he bought another for 6d.[1]

In the seventeenth century floor carpets made of different materials were available. The 1641 inventory of Tart Hall[115] gives a varied selection, and one of the most surprising materials used is leather. The Drawing Chamber had a 'foote carpett of read leather', and in Mr Thomas Howard's room the bedstead stood on yellow leather. In another room the floor was covered

91. A Savonnerie carpet, c. 1683. Waddesdon manor

with a 'Carpett of yellow leather', and in yet another with white leather, as was a table. White leather seems very impractical, even for a closet. 'The carpet to goe around about my lord's Bed' was of red baize, and the bed in what 'was my Ladyes Bed-Chamber' stood on an Indian mat. In store at Tart Hall were three large Persian carpets and seven small ones, as well as eleven large and seven small Turkey carpets, but whether these were for floor or furniture is unclear.

In the eighteenth century the use of carpets became normal in most houses, and it is from the middle of the century that the English tradition of knotted carpets – Brussels, Wilton and Axminster – started. Carpets had been woven earlier, using a cloth-loom with heavy, cheap wool making what was known as Ingrain carpets. These, also called Kidderminster or

Scotch carpets, had no pile. They were generally woven in stripes or a plaid design on a cloth-loom, using a worsted warp and woollen weft, and were reversible. Kidderminster and Ingrain were two-ply, as were Scotch carpets originally, but in 1824 a method of weaving three-ply carpets was evolved at Kilmarnock, which made for more strength, was brighter in colour and was both thick and cheap. This must have added considerably to the warmth of the rooms.

92. Detail of a Wilton carpet, c. 1760. Uppark

About 1740 Brussels and Wilton pile carpets were produced in England. Brussels carpeting had a looped pile and Wilton a cut, but they were both made in strips sewn together, on adapted cloth-looms. It was not until 1754 that Thomas Whitty, a cloth-weaver of Axminster in Devon, decided to try and copy the eastern seamless carpets. He managed to copy the knot used in Turkey, but on his cloth-loom could only weave a narrow width. It was not until he had made contact with some French weavers who had worked at the Savonnerie factory in France that he realized that the answer was to work on an upright loom, like a tapestry loom. At the same time Thomas Moore of Moorfields in London had come to the same conclusion, and for several years the two men vied for the premiums offered by the Royal Society of Arts. Whitty, however, was the better businessman, and eventually the Axminster became the best-known carpet in England.

Another manufacturer, a Frenchman named Claude Passavant, set up a similar factory in Exeter and, though it only worked for nine years between 1750 and 1759, the carpets were very fashionable, and most diaries and letters of the mid-1700s, where they refer to carpets at all, refer to those made in Exeter. One of the finest Exeter carpets to be seen today is at Petworth, an imitation of a Savonnerie, made in 1758.

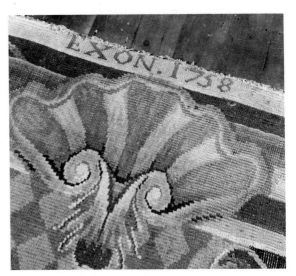

93. Detail of an Exeter carpet, signed and dated 1758.
Petworth

Pile carpets were not for everyone, and in the same way as painted cloths had imitated tapestries in the sixteenth century, so painted floor-cloths were used by the less well-off in the eighteenth century. In fact, the variety of floor coverings then available was considerable. The trade cards of upholsterers in the second half of the eighteenth century refer to painted floor-cloths, hair cloths, English and Dutch mats, and list carpets besides Turkey, Wilton and Axminster.[87] Frances Thompson advertised that he sold 'painted floor-cloths of all Sorts and Sizes, of the newest Pattern, warranted to be done well in Oil and wear well'; these cloths were also exported to the colonies. In 1769 and 1770 among the goods which John Norton the tobacco merchant sent from London to his customers in Virginia were Kilmarnock carpets, Scotch carpets and painted duck floor-cloths.[56]

Floor-cloths — in use in many houses from the early eighteenth to the late nineteenth century — were made by painting duck or strong canvas with oil paints. These took a very long while to dry – several months – and an even longer time to harden, so that they could be walked on and cleaned without damaging the paint. Unless a customer was prepared to wait for a year to two for their cloths they would have to buy from stock rather than have a design of their own choice. There were books of designs available from 1739, but evidently in the nineteenth century the designs deteriorated, and Eastlake in 1878 was, as usual, forthright. He says that the designs began with imitations of marble pavements and parquetry floors but 'A floor cloth ... should seem to be what it really is ... There are endless varieties of geometrical shapes which could be used for floor cloths without resorting to the foolish expedient of copying the knots and veins of wood and marble.'[69]

Large rugs and small carpets were also worked domestically, mostly in cross-stitch, and there are superb examples of these at Clandon in Surrey. It is not usually known who made them, but Mrs Boscawen, writing to Mrs Delany in 1774 from Holkham, says, 'I think it curious to see my Ly Leicester work at a tent stitch frame every night by one candle that she sets upon it, and no spectacles. It is a carpet that she works in shades – tent stitch.'[46]

By the end of the century most houses had carpets in the middle of the room at least, though they were often put down only in winter. Mrs Boscawen again, in 1787 gives instructions about the carpeting in her villa, which tells us a good deal about the standard of housewifery at that date.[23] She says:

Let Dan Martin, therefore, take up the carpet; let it be turned out upon the lawn so soon as this rainy weather has given place to sunshine and dryness. Then let it be shook and beaten without mercy by the strong hands of both gardeners. During its absence let the floor, whose dirt it has so long concealed, be finally and totally rid of said dirt by means of a good scouring ... once and again until it becomes perfectly clean; after which it may be dry-rubbed by the gardeners wife ... Then ... put the carpet anywhere, for when I come down I shall bring mats, for I hate a carpet in summer ... Besides that, covering the whole room is not only now entirely disused, but it is really odious, not neat nor agreeable in any respect.

This habit of taking carpets up in summer in favour of mats or simply plain floors continued for most of the nineteenth century. The interior sketches by John Harden in 1827[76] show no carpets in summer, and in 1842 in *Letters to Mary* her daughter says, 'Ma is now putting down our winter carpet, do. curtains.'[40]

The 1793 inventory of Blickling Hall[96] shows a great variety of floor

*94. Motif from an Axminster carpet, c. 1790,
in the Peter the Great Room, Blickling Hall*

coverings. The bedrooms, even then, only had bedside mats, but the main rooms had Turkey carpets, floor-cloths, a 'very large Axminster Carpet' in what is now called the Peter the Great Room and, in the State Bedroom, a 'flowered Bed Carpet and 1 square Do'. These are still there, the flowered bed carpet being a strip which goes round three sides of the bed and which matches the border of the very large carpet in the room.

Axminster carpets were often designed for a specific room; and in many cases the design was a copy of, or related to, the ceiling. When Chippendale and Haig were refurnishing a house for Sir Edward Knatchbull, a letter of 1778 says:

You have likewise a design for an Axminster Carpet to correspond with your Ceiling to go into Bow and at equal distance from the plinth all round the Room, the Expense of it will be according to their best price about £100. They will have a Painting to make of it at large and the Colours to dye on purpose, but if you chuse to have it made square, like your other carpet it will be proportionably less in price, and if you or Lady Knatchbull chuses any alteration in any of the Colours, by describing it properly, it may be done.[38]

95. *Axminster carpet. State Bedroom, Blickling Hall*

96. *Detail of a bed carpet matching the border of the large carpet.
State Bedroom, Blickling Hall*

Fashions in the size and shape of floor coverings varied considerably between covering the floor completely and leaving a wide border of wood, which might be board, parquet or even stencilling, around the edge. Loudon, writing in 1833 of his beau ideal of an English villa, insisted on a bordered carpet in the saloon, with a yard of polished oak boards around it. He suggested Axminster for the drawing room, Turkey or Axminster with a matching hearth-rug for the library, Turkey for the dining room and, as late as 1833, 'Floors that should be washed; i e not polished oak, and should not have the whole covered with carpet',[157] in the bedrooms.

Maria Edgeworth is as lively as ever in her letters and in 1818 she describes one house where Francis had bought a very pretty carpet patterned in brown leaves on a blue ground. She goes on to say how pleased Mrs Wilson was with it and that Francis had had the footstools covered in the same fabric: 'The only inconvenience that being the same as the carpet none but lynx eyes can see them and they will break all shins. I hope Alicia will not stumble over them. The red morocco strip round them and brass nails thereon her only chance of escape.'[47]

In 1821 Maria was visiting Wycombe Abbey and comments: 'When I say we shall leave Wycombe Abbey on Wenesday sennight I ought to add provided we do not some of us or all of us break our limbs or our necks on these horribly slippery beautiful floors and stairs ... The carpets on our bedchambers and dressing rooms skate about and we upon them just as the mat on the ice at Kilbuxey ...' This was something of which Loudon did not approve.

In *Hints on Household Taste* Charles Eastlake discourses on floor coverings as well as on other household matters.[69] He would rather have had cheap hand-knotted Turkey or Scinde carpets than the machine-made ones which came into use about the middle of the century. He approved of parquet or plain wood borders and thought that a bedside rug and a bare floor was better in a bedroom than the current fashion for large carpets. Ward Lock's *Home Book*[89] (c. 1880) agrees and says that the old style (of c. 1850) of covering the floor of a room entirely was now giving way to the 'more cleanly and healthy' mode of laying down a square of carpet in the centre of the room and having the surrounds 'stained and varnished or polished with beeswax in the French style'.

As furniture and chairs were protected by case covers, so carpets were protected by painted cloths, druggets, baize and other fabrics. Sometimes the cloth was painted with the same design as the carpet, sometimes there was a quiet, non-committal pattern, and right down to the middle of the

97. *Carpet designed by Adam with motifs related to the ceiling ornament, made by John Whitty at Axminster in 1770, costing £126. Saltram*

98. An Aubusson carpet, c. 1783. Waddesdon Manor

present century a square of drugget called a crumb cloth was often placed under the dining-room table and chairs to protect the carpet.

There remained the problem of floor coverings for those parts of the house where a carpet was either unsuitable or too expensive: nurseries, servants' rooms, passages. What was needed was something both hard-

99. Drugget used to protect the carpet in the hall at Felbrigg

wearing and attractive, which was easy to clean and warmer and safer than bare boards, bricks or flags. Even with servants there was a limit to the amount of daily or weekly scrubbing that could be done. Floor-cloths, which were made of thick coarse fabric painted or stencilled, were one answer, oilcloth was another. This was made of coarse canvas treated with oil and painted. When the oil, with resin or gum lac added, had dried, the fabric was impervious to water and could be easily swept and washed.

The next invention was named Kamptulicon, and was made from india rubber softened and impregnated with cork. It was used by Charles Barry for the new Houses of Parliament. After Kamptulicon came linoleum, which was used for a very long time indeed, and was not superseded until after the Second World War. It was invented in 1863 by Frederick Walton, and was made from linseed oil which was oxidized, mixed with ground cork and rolled onto a canvas backing. This was found to be the most useful, cheapest and longest lasting of all floor coverings with the exception of carpet, but it did have one big disadvantage: while it was impervious to spillage from above, it was also impervious to damp from below, and because it could not breathe, it could not dry out. So before very long, where it was used on bricks and flagstones, especially in basements, it began to rot and then there would be an unpleasant smell of damp, mildew and decay.

Fourteen

TECHNIQUES

NEEDLEWORK

During the centuries under review a great many of both the larger and the smaller items in a house were embroidered. The work ranged from curtains and bed hangings to cushions and footstools; in fact, everything which

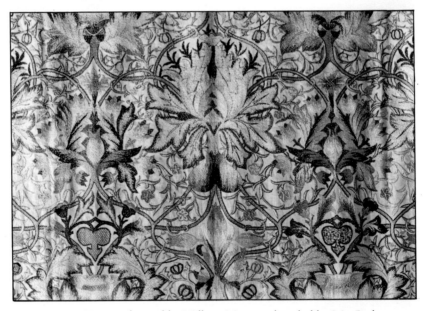

100. Hanging designed by William Morris and worked by Mrs Beale.
Late nineteenth century. Standen

could be covered by a fabric has at some time been embroidered in a variety of techniques. One of the problems in assessing the work of embroiderers has been to decide whether they were amateurs or professionals. On looking carefully at some pieces it is clear; there may be a professional gloss or lack of spontaneity which suggest a workshop practice. Equally at the other end of the scale there may well be mistakes in technique or a crudity of design which betrays the amateur. It is in the great gap between these two extremes where doubts creep in.

There were many superb needlewomen (the amateurs were generally women), whose work rivalled that of the best professionals who, until the nineteenth century, were generally men, and there were often extremely dull and uninspired professionals who produced very pedestrian work. Often it is impossible to distinguish between them. Some techniques never seem to have been attempted by workshops: patchwork quilts for example, and canvas-work coverings for furniture were generally, although not always, done in the home. But there are many areas where it will probably never be known who did the work.

Often it was a collaboration. Kits are nothing new and it was always possible to buy fabric with the design drawn on it, ready for working. In fact, many eighteenth-century upholsterers advertised that they 'drew for all sorts of needlework', and sold 'painted patterns and shades of Silk and Worsted for such works'. In France the same thing applied, as Saint-Aubin explains in his book, L'Art du Brodeur (1770).[179] In his discussion of canvas-work and its technique he says that 'some merchants in stores selling chairs and sofas have canvas on hand on which shaded designs are already embroidered. Only the background remains to be filled in to amuse those who do not wish to expend too much effort.' This work would probably be passed off as having been completely worked by the lady who did the simple ground.

In the first half of the eighteenth century some of the canvas-work for chairs and sofas consisted of vignettes of mythological or pastoral subjects, worked in fine tent-stitch over one thread of canvas, with a surround of foliage in large stitches worked over two threads. A set of chairs and a sofa at Montacute are examples of this, and there are others at Clandon Park and Canons Ashby. These appear to be professional work, while the large canvas wall hanging at Anglesey Abbey is almost certainly amateur.

In the nineteenth century pattern-drawers travelled round the villages where quilts were made, drawing the designs for the quilters to work, and earlier Walter Gale, a Sussex schoolmaster, added to his meagre income by drawing designs for ladies. He writes in his diary in 1751 that he 'finished drawing Miss Ann's handkerchief and carried it home to her receiving 1s for my labour'. In the early nineteenth century J.H. Priest of Norwich

101. Detail of canvas-work on a George I walnut and parcel gilt chair.
Montacute House

102. Early eighteenth-century settee with canvas-work upholstery.
Canons Ashby

manufactured and sold 'Worsteds, Patterns and Canvas worked and drawn for Urn and Tea-Pot Rugs, Bell Pulls etc.', and this list could be extended indefinitely.

The owners of great houses often had an embroiderer on the payroll, and Bess of Hardwick, no mean embroideress herself, had Webb the 'embroiderer' living in the Hall, who was paid 18s. 4d. a quarter. Mark Girouard says[81] that, according to Bess's own evidence, the famous hangings of classical matrons and accompanying Virtues now in Hardwick Hall were made at Chatsworth by her grooms, women and some 'boys she kept' with the assistance of a professional embroiderer.

In 1536 a gentlewoman was recommended to Lady Lisle largely because of her ability as a needlewoman: 'Also there is a gentlewoman which is a maiden and unmarried but lately dwelled with Lady Waldon, and is of XXX years, a good needlewoman and also she can embroider very well and will be content to work and brush and do anything else that your Ladyship would put her to. She demandeth xls and a livery.'[54] She would probably

103. Detail showing the front and back of an eighteenth-century canvas-work hanging. Anglesey Abbey

have embroidered caps, coifs and smocks for all the family, as well as working cushions and possibly bed hangings.

Often several people in a house worked on the needlework. In the seventeenth century it would be gentlewomen, later daughters and indigent relations who lived there as part of an extended family. Roger North, discussing a visit to Beaufort in Gloucestershire in the seventeenth century, said that 'the ordinary past time of the ladies was in a gallery on the other side where she [the Duchess] had divers gentlewomen commonly at work upon embroidery and fringe-making for all the beds of state were made and finished in the house.'[166] But this was exceptional; such spectacular furniture as State Beds were nearly always professional.

104. Further detail of a canvas-work hanging.
Anglesey Abbey

Needlework carpets were items which were often homemade. In the Rutland accounts for 1600 various floss silks and Spanish silks were bought and sent to 'Mrs Fayrebarn to make up the carpet which was begun by my late lady'.[11] The silks cost the not inconsiderable sum of £7 18s. 8d. and were for what must have been a richly worked table carpet. Floor carpets and rugs were also tackled by the amateur. Mrs Delany both worked them herself and helped her friends: 'My candlelight work is finishing a carpet in double cross-stitch on very coarse canvas to go round my bed.'[46] This perhaps was charming, but when writing from Ireland in 1751 she says that she 'went to Dublin, was two hours and a half choosing worsteds for a friend in the North who is working *a fright* of a carpet'!

*105. Penelope, one of the set of heroines and Virtues,
embroidered and applied. Late sixteenth century. Hardwick Hall*

Mrs Delany was a great friend of another eminent needlewoman, the
Duchess of Portland, who seems to have been a true craftswoman, able to
work successfully at any technique. She writes that 'the Duchess of Portland

has in hand twelve toilettes, a carpet to go round her bed, knotting of various kinds, besides turning which goes on successfully.'[46]

It would be very interesting to know how much of the many beds worked by ladies was done by them personally. Again, Mrs Delany, obviously a very quick and dedicated worker, embroidered her blue linen bed with a design of white oak leaves herself, but it seems almost impossible that the bed which Celia Fiennes saw at Burghley was one person's work: 'A green velvet bed, the hangings are all embroidery of her mother's work, very fine, the silk looks very fresh and the figures look natural.'[48] Figure-work is one of the most difficult techniques.

In 1621 Lady Anne Drury bequeathed 'my clothe bed of my own workinge with all the furniture to it ...'[138] and much later, in 1763, Horace Walpole, when speaking of a visit to Drayton, says that in the apartment 'called the Duchess of Norfolk's is a rich bed of her work ...' It is generally impossible to identify these embroideries now, as in most cases they have either deteriorated and been thrown away or cut up, or their provenance has been lost, but occasionally the embroideress signed her work, or it has remained in the same place since it was worked. Mary Holte's beautiful hangings at Aston Hall near Birmingham are an example of signed work, and the wall panels worked by Lady Julia Calverly at Wallington of work which has not been moved.

The techniques most suited to amateur work were canvas-work, patch-work, and all kinds of linen embroidery. As a general rule, gold-work, in its various forms, and often silk embroidery were better left to the pro-fessional. It is clear that not all amateur embroideresses were successful in what they undertook. Pepys in 1663 had one of his usual wrangles with his wife and said, 'She and I did jangle mightily about her cushions which she wrought with worsteds the last year, which are too little for any use ...'[58]

There were workshops where some of the finest embroideries were made and occasionally there are groups of embroideries which clearly come from the same workshop. One such group dates from the 1730s or so, and consists of sets of counterpanes, pillow beres and cushions, all worked on white satin with baskets and sprays of naturalistic flowers, with the baskets in intricate gold-work. There is one of these sets in the Bowes Museum, one at Longleat and one at Blickling and there are probably several more. They are perfect professional work with their gold-work, long- and short-stitch and straight-stitch in silk for the flowers. Exquisite, but soulless.

As well as the workshops there were men working on their own or with a son or apprentice who went around to different houses and stayed there doing the work required. One such, Rofe the embroiderer, went to Stiffkey to do work for the Bacon family in 1593. At one point he was working on the hangings for a bed and at another working on gowns and stomachers. He received as wages 16d. a day and his son and apprentice 12d. a day.

106. Embroidered pillow beres matching the quilt (illus. 48). Blickling Hall

This was considerably higher wages than those of a tailor, who also worked for the Bacons, who only received 6d. a day. Sometimes Rofe seems to have been paid by the day and sometimes by the articles; for example, for working three gowns and stomachers – probably elaborate ones, as they were wedding garments – he received £4 7s., and for another single gown 16s. Rofe was also one of those willing and able to help the amateur: in 1591 he bought silk for the household to embroider a cushion cloth and was paid 12d. 'for the drawinge of it', and in 1593 he was paid 3s. 4d. for 'drawinge your things'. In 1597, when Winifred Bacon was to be married, an unnamed embroiderer worked on two of her gowns, one presumably her wedding dress, and was paid the very large sum of £13 10s. for his work.

By 1747 Campbell in *The London Tradesman*[30] had little good to say of the embroiderers who, he said, were by then nearly all women. He did not consider that they came anywhere near the French and Italians in ability, because they were short of the 'Bold Fancy; they may go on a dull beaten Tract, or servily imitate a Foreign Pattern, but know not how to advance the Beauty of the old or strike out a new Invention worth notice'. He said they might be reckoned among the dependants of the lace man, and altogether thought little of them. At present the whole question of embroidery workshops has had little attention and there must still be a lot to discover about them.

Embroideries, especially those worked with expensive metal thread, could be used again. In 1614, in the accounts of Henry Howard, the flower slips and borders of a cloak worked in silver were 'cutte forth into pieces to imbroder some furniture for the house withal', at a cost of £3.[114] Perhaps they were put onto cushions, as there would scarcely have been enough for beds.

The question of professional versus amateur will never be resolved, but there is another problem which will be even more acute in the future than now. Owing to the prevalence of reproducing old designs today, particularly for seat furniture, how are future generations to recognize contemporary work? To some extent this question has to be considered now, as the Victorians and certainly embroiderers in the 1930s reproduced many earlier patterns. In the case of nineteenth-century work there always seems to be an atmosphere about it which proclaims the fact that it is not seventeenth- or eighteenth-century, and where the reproduction of eighteenth-century crewel-work is concerned, though fabric and thread may be similar, the technique is often too accurate and the scale of design wrong. It is in the realm of canvas-work seat coverings that doubt creeps in. Modern crewel wool is similar to the old and in spite of all that is said about modern dyes it takes a very acute eye to detect the difference. If the work is in good condition the canvas cannot be examined, and where a certain amount of time has elapsed and dirt, fading and wear have dulled the surface, it is easy to be deceived. The chair worked by Tess Hope in the 1930s, for example, would pass any but the keenest eye as being eighteenth-century. Some work, however, is more obvious, such as a chair at Lanhydrock which was re-upholstered in nineteenth-century cross-stitch in a design that would not have been seen when the chair was made. Perhaps one should say 'Does it really matter?' What is important is that all reproductions should be documented, preferably inside the work itself, rather than have the fact left

107. Eighteenth-century chair with embroidered covers by Tess Hope, 1930s. Private collection

to word of mouth. What starts in good faith as a stated reproduction can so easily have its origins forgotten.

Peter Thornton has drawn attention to the fact that there are few crewel-work hangings listed in seventeenth-century inventories. This is certainly puzzling, as these hangings have in many cases come down to the present day and can be seen in museums, houses open to the public and private houses, even if they have been cut up .and re-used. These hangings were

108. Seventeenth-century chair with cross-stitch covers
from the nineteenth century. Lanhydrock

always worked on a union twill of cotton and linen, probably imported from Bruges. Richly dyed crewel wool was used and the designs were generally of branched trees with large, exotic leaves and flowers growing from a series of mounds, with rabbits, stags and other animals. The designs derive from the verdure tapestries of earlier centuries. As there was no fast green dye in the seventeenth century and green was made from yellow overlaying blue, the yellow has often disappeared, leaving the embroidery apparently worked in shades of indigo rather than green. This type of work (erroneously called Jacobean) was popular for about a hundred years,

109. *Crewel-work bed hanging, made, in the 1930s,
from a large, early eighteenth-century bed curtain. Blickling Hall*

starting from the first half of the seventeenth century when the designs originally covered almost all the linen, gradually becoming lighter in both weight and colour in the eighteenth century. One item in the inventory of Gosfield Hall, taken in 1638, is '1 large counterpointe for a bed of Holland wrought in collours of needleworke of waving worke of wostead',[101] and this may well be a crewel-work embroidery. This whole subject of crewel-work is one of those rare cases where there are more actual objects to be seen today than there are literary references, though James Ayres quotes from John Wood of Bath, who said that about 1727 'the Matrons of the

110. *Detail of preceding bed curtain, showing why so many embroideries have been re-used. Blickling Hall*

City, their Daughters and their Maids [were] flowering the latter [coarse Fustian] with Worsted, during the intervals between the Seasons to give the Beds a gaudy Look.'[24]

The practical question that arises is how embroideries for the house were actually ordered. Did the upholsterer produce designs, either on paper or worked, or was the design outlined in discussion and then left to the workshop? Did the customer always get what he wanted or hoped for, bearing in mind that with country customers in particular the whole transaction might be laboriously undertaken by letter or via an intermediary? The method by which Mrs Purefoy acquired the quilted hangings for her bed has already been described but while it might seem comparatively simple to send patterns of quilting to a customer, it must have been much more difficult with such things as chair and sofa coverings in canvas-work, for example. In those cases it must have been drawn and coloured-paper designs were sent or shown to the customer.

Bed-linen was sometimes embroidered, different techniques being used at different dates. In the sixteenth and seventeenth centuries the ends of top sheets and pillowcases were worked in Holbein- or double running-stitch in the type of pattern so often seen on collars, cuffs and shirts in the paintings of Holbein and his contemporaries. As well as her crewel-work counterpane, Anne, Viscountess Dorchester, had at Gosfield 'a linen sheet worked in black worsted of a running worke'. Silk was more usual than worsted in this technique, but she also had another sheet worked in silk with two matching pillow beres, and one little table cloth 'wrought in worsted'.

In the eighteenth and nineteenth centuries these sheets would be delicately embroidered in whitework using a variety of flat stitches which would stand hard wear and washing, but the enthusiasm for drawn thread-work at the end of the nineteenth and early twentieth centuries made for a much weaker edge which has not always stood the test of time.

KNOTTING

Knotting is a craft allied to both macramé and tatting. It is like macramé in that a series of knots are made in a length of thread, though the tool used is not the fingers but a shuttle very like a tatting shuttle but larger, with rounded rather than pointed ends. The shuttle had to be large in order to accommodate the thick thread often used. One of the finest collections of French knotting shuttles can be seen at the Wallace Collection in London.

Having made the knots, either closely or widely spaced, the resulting thread could be used in several ways. The most general use was for fringes, either looped or cut. These were sewn on light articles such as *toilettes*, or heavier ones, such as curtains for beds or windows. The knotted thread could also be used to outline a design: Mrs Delany made the complete furniture for a bed of dark blue linen which had a pattern of white oak leaves applied, with veins, stems and edges in knotting, which must have looked extremely attractive.[46]

There was yet another use as was explained by M. de Saint-Aubin in *L'Art du Brodeur*. He says, referring to the craft in a kindly, dismissive way, 'Dresses and furniture are embroidered by sewing, with little stitches, the knots which ladies make with their shuttles to amuse themselves ... There are few works as sturdy. When the objects are rather large, one can space the knots as with silk thread...There are knots of different thicknesses; they are made in wool, in thread, or in silk.'[179] Saint-Aubin seems to be implying that the knots, having been made by the ladies, were then used by the professional embroiderer, and probably this did happen unless the knotter was also a good needlewoman.

111. One of a set of chairs with knotted covers.
Early eighteenth century. Cotehele House

This use is exemplified in a set of chairs at Cotehele House in Cornwall. The chairs, straight-backed Queen Anne, are completely covered with a design of rioting flowers in knotting, the knots so close that they resemble a fabric themselves.

The technique, however, goes back a great deal further than this. One

112. *Detail of close knotting. Cotehele*

113. *Cushion with knotted fringe and decoration, said to have been given to Gonville and Caius College by Dr Caius, in 1558*

of the earliest known pieces is the decoration on a cushion said to have been given to Gonville and Caius College, Cambridge, by Dr Caius himself in 1558. The cushion is of yellow satin and the fringe is of knotted, thick brown silk, each strand of knotting being crossed between the knots by other short knotted lengths. This open-work fringe is also formed into four rosettes, one sewn to each corner of the cushion, with excellent decorative effect.

By the early eighteenth century at least, knotting was becoming a pastime for the woman who did not like having her fingers unoccupied. One may smile at the uselessness of the result; indeed, Dr Johnson said, 'Next to mere idleness, I think knotting is to be reckoned in the scale of insignificance ...' but it should not be forgotten that many women have a compulsion to use their hands all the time, and there were not many ways of doing this when moving about or sitting in a strange house, except by knitting, later on by crocheting and tatting, or by knotting. It was also a very elegant pastime, the turn of the wrist as the knot was made was particularly becoming, so much so that portraits can be seen of grand ladies knotting, for example the Countess of Albemarle in the National Gallery or Lepel, Lady Mulgrave, by Zoffany, at Ickworth.

These ladies were following royal fashion. Queen Mary, wife and co-monarch of William III, was such a devotee of the craft that Sir Charles Sedley wrote a poem about the two of them which said that:

> While he (by valour) conquers France,
> She manufactures does advance
> And makes thread fringes for ye. [...]
>
> For here's a Queen now, thanks to God!
> Who when she rides in coach abroad,
> Is always knotting threads.

It would be nice to know whether Queen Mary was a compulsive finger-user or whether she felt she was setting a good example by her industry. It seems possible that with slow, lumbering coach travel knotting was a way of lessening the boredom of a long journey. Apart from Queen Mary, Cassandra, Duchess of Chandos, in a letter written in 1737, says that she has not done much knotting of late as she has been on very few coach journeys.[26]

Mrs Delany, like so many other ladies of the eighteenth century, was a great knotter. She found it very restful to her eyes when she had been doing more intricate work, and she was also able to continue with this

LEPEL LADY MULGRAVE

114. Portrait of Lepel, Lady Mulgrave, knotting, by Zoffany.
Ickworth

when her eyes began to fail as she got older. From her remarks in her letters it is obvious that there was a lot more to knotting than we today realize: it is certainly a forgotten craft. In one letter she says, 'I am sorry I have no knotting of the sort you want done. I cannot promise too much for you till I have finished a plain fringe I am knotting to trim a new blue and white linen bed I have just put up; as soon as that is finished I will do some sugar-plums for you; ... send me the sized knotting you want.' The sugar-plums apparently were the knots that were sewn over and over, making a raised mound, and the linen bed she refers to is the one already described, which obviously had a knotted fringe as well as the applied work.

Queen Charlotte, in the late eighteenth century, not only knotted but also encouraged poor girls to make a living by it. Sophie von la Roche, who went to Windsor Castle in 1789, says, 'another Chamber is entirely hung with knotted tapestry. The knotted threads are made by the women at Court here and a woman in Germany, very respectable, whose circumstances are not too happy, makes hangings out of them for which the Queen pays and supports her; thus the Court ladies are kept diligently employed.'[177] These hangings probably resembled the Cotehele chairs in technique and it would be nice to know how many other hangings were made in this particular style.

In 1782 Mrs Delany went to see Queen Charlotte, and said that she 'was quite alone in her dressing room. She was making a fringe in a frame, and did me the honour to show me how to do it, and to say she would send me such a frame as her own, as she thought it was a work which would not try my eyes.' One day, referring to a special occasion, Mrs Delany says that she has 'put on all my birthday gear, new white satin best covers on my chair, and the knotting furniture of my bed chamber, with window curtains of the same'.[46] As well as making all the bed curtains in the blue linen with the white oak leaves, she had worked window curtains in the same technique, with the knotted fringes and outlines. A most industrious lady!

NETTING

Nets have been made from the early days of mankind for fishing, snaring birds and animals and carrying goods of all kinds. Later they were used for protecting fruit from the ravages of birds and, later still, they began to be used in a purely decorative way. It did not take the upholsterer long to discover that fabric seen through an open-work net was very attractive.

One of the advantages of netting is that it can be coarse or fine and so is suitable for a very wide range of articles from cauls for the hair to linings for bed curtains. The craft is simple and the only tools needed are a netting needle and a gauge or mesh the size of the hole required; probably because of its simplicity there never appears to have been a netter's guild or tradesman's confederacy. The netting which formed the basis of the six-teenth- and seventeenth-century filet lace may well have been made by amateurs as well as lace-makers and in the eighteenth century the craft became one which the lady took out visiting; in the nineteenth century the innumerable netted purses, doilies and other knick-knacks were worked by those with time to spare.

From the point of view of the upholsterer netting was at first used chiefly to lengthen a fringe. The end warp threads of a cloth could be netted with the fingers to produce a tasselled fringe, or the same thing could be made with a heading and then sewn on to the netting. This, made with either thick or thin thread as the fabric demanded, was a good-looking, plain decoration and was certainly used early in the sixteenth century if not before.

Mary, Queen of Scots, netted, and in 1567, while imprisoned, she was sent needles and gauges to make 'le reseau' – probably the groundwork of filet lace (lacis). Often these small individual squares of filet were used as insertions to put into cushions or make into a decorative border for a cloth, but Mary left, after her death, the 'furniture for a bed, of network and holland, not half finished'. This 'network' was, in fact, squares of filet joined to rectangles of linen.[185]

Netting could be plain or it could be very decorative. The description of a bed at Tart Hall in 1641 sounds charming, though the bed curtains were only of frieze, not an exotic material: 'the Curtaynes are lyned with Networke and edged about with a Silke and Golde Fringe, Bottones and loopes ...' It would be nice to know of what the 'Networke' was made; was it plain cotton yarn or perhaps gold to match the fringe? This bed with its net-work lining foreshadows the bed in the Lord Chancellor's Room at Wimpole. The bed, of about 1780, has a central canopy with Prince of Wales' feathers at the four corners and on top of the dome and, according to writing found on the inside of the dome when the bed was conserved in 1979, had been re-upholstered in 1852. The hangings, which fall from the dome and are looped up around the top of the bedposts in the style known as *lit à la polonaise*, are of crimson satin entirely covered in coarse white netting. This netting also covers the head and foot of the bed as well as the counterpane, and is everywhere edged with a braid made from knotting in the same white 'dishcloth' cotton. The very deep heading to the fringe is also knotted and netted and the fringe itself is knotted. Netting for the tops of fringes was very prevalent in the early nineteenth century and many of the furniture designs of Thomas Hope have plain netted

115. Lit à la polonaise at Wimpole Hall.
The crimson satin is covered with coarse netting with knotted braids
and tassels. Late eighteenth century

fringes,[90] so it is not easy to tell whether the decoration of the Wimpole bed was rather before its time, or if all the netting was put on at the restoration of 1852, when it might be considered old-fashioned.

Hand-netted curtains were used in the early nineteenth century, both as inside curtains or alone, but the necessity to produce net for upholstery went when machine-made nets, especially those known as Nottingham lace, became fashionable. These were cheap, decorative and fulfilled their purpose admirably.

PASSEMENTERIE OR
TRIMMINGS

Passementerie is a word for which there is no exact equivalent in English; the nearest is really trimmings. The term embraces braids, tassels, fringes, laces and gimps. The word lace must here be used with care. Santina Levey has pointed out that lace as we understand it today has not really got a name of its own. The original laces were braids which were sometimes made with the fingers and sometimes on a loom, and were often light in character; it was these laces which, in the sixteenth century, developed into the bobbin and needle laces which were to become so famous. Even in France, where all the early braids were known as *passements*, early bobbin lace was known as *passement dentelé*, in other words 'toothed' or 'indented', and it was only later that the word *'passement'* for bobbin and needlepoint laces was dropped and they became *'dentelle'*. All this must be borne in mind when reading old records and inventories, as 'laced' can imply the use of braids, or the use of cords to 'lace up' something or, a little later, decoration with bobbin or needlepoint lace.

All these trimmings made a tremendous difference to the look of the upholstered article, giving richness and colour. Sometimes they are understated, but in the seventeenth and eighteenth centuries particularly, they were decidedly overstated, and gave a look whose richness can today scarcely be believed. Unfortunately, because of the weight of these trimmings, the tassels and bobbles on so many of the articles have disappeared, as have the fringes themselves. In fact, in England these very ornate trimmings are no longer made — one can buy ordinary braids, but nothing approaching the seventeenth- and eighteenth-centuries makes — and even in France, where they do still have the most beautiful braids and trimmings, the price puts them out of most people's reach.

The original *passementeries* were fringes made by tying off the warp threads at the ends of pieces of weaving, whether they were linen for a cloth or even a heavier rug or coverlet. Loose warp threads when cut off could very easily unravel and weaken the end of the work, and so it became the practice to knot these ends, making some form of fringe, which was more or less ornamental. In some cases it became just like the technique of macramé, which is also known as finger-knotting. From this it was not a very big step to the making of fringes with their own headings, which could be sewn or nailed onto a piece of upholstered furniture, be it cushion, chair or bed hanging.

This is where the braid-makers and *passementiers* came into their own. Braids, laces and orris (which was lace woven from gold and silver thread) were used in many ways; they could cover seams, be used as insertions, edge articles and also make patterns over plain material. Here again, care in terminology is needed. The expression that seams are 'laced' does not mean that they are joined with faggotting, or that the lace is an insertion, but that lace is laid over the join to hide it and provide decoration.

Besides metal threads, silk and sometimes wool were used, often in combination, and any amount of fantasy was employed with different-length fringes, silk and wool threads, tassels of various shapes being used often all at once. The making was slow and painstaking and this was reflected in the price. The trimmings of a bed or a chair generally cost far more than the fabric and the making put together.

These trimmings were sold by the lace men who, according to *The London Tradesman* of 1747, sold 'all Sorts of Gold and Silver Lace, Gold and Silver Buttons, Shapes for Waistcoats, Lace and Networkes for Robeings and Women's Petticoats, Fringes, Bugles, Spangles, Plates for Embroidery and Orrice, and Bone-Lace Weavers, Gold and Silver Wire, Purle, Slesy, Twist etc.' Campbell tells us that orrice is made on a loom on the same principles as damask but needs much greater strength as the loom is heavier, and he added that 'a dry cold hand, free from Sweat, is likewise absolutely necessary; because if they tarnish their Work, so as to put it past Sale, they are obliged to pay for the stuff and lose their Labour.'[30]

Campbell also says that 'The Fringe, Frog, and Tassel Maker is likewise employed by the Lace Man. Some of the Button Makers perform the Work; but it is chiefly done by Women, upon the Hand, who make a very handsome livelihood of it, if they are not initiated into the Mystery of Gin-Drinking.'

Added to the hazards of weight, housemaids, dogs and cats and time,

116 (opposite). *Corner decoration of bed, and stylized loops in braid, wire and silks. Seventeenth century. Cotehele House*

117. *Fringe and tassels on the seat and arm of a chair. Seventeenth century. Knole*

118. *Embroidery, fringe and tassels on State Bed, Osterley Park*

re-upholstery has taken its toll of trimmings. Where the trimmings were nailed to the bottom of a chair, for example, and have had to be taken off to release the fabric, it has often not seemed worthwhile to replace them, especially as they might then be the wrong colour. Thus they have been lost, and we have few examples left to show us their richness.

But there are some left which, even if tattered, give an idea of the invention and care which went into the making. The valance trimmings of the bed in the Red Room at Cotehele are breathtaking, and the corner urns seem to owe something to the technique of stump-work. The State Bed at Dyrham has sumptuous fringes, as do many of the pieces of seat furniture at Knole. More restrained but no less beautiful is the decoration on the State Bed at Osterley.

PATCHWORK

How much patchwork was used for hangings in the sixteenth and seventeenth centuries is uncertain. It is unlikely that it became a generally accepted craft until the appearance of Indian cottons in the second half of the seventeenth century, as it is work far more suited to close-woven cotton than to wool or linen. In the sense that, as an economy measure, old fabrics must always have been cut up and rejoined to be made into fresh bed hangings or curtains, patchwork was always in existence. In those cases, fabrics which had worn out would be taken down, the bad pieces cut out and the good saved, and eventually various parts were joined together to be made into hangings or bed covers for children's or servants' rooms. Equally, in smaller houses the fashionable paned hangings may well have been achieved by covering the worn out parts of a fabric with strips of another fabric.

In this connection an item in the 1741 inventory of Sir John Smyth of Long Ashton in Somerset may be relevant.[132] He had, in the Hall Chamber, 'two old bedsteds with ragot furniture', eighteen large damask napkins and '17 old ragot ditto', as well as five pieces of 'ragot linens'. Ragot was another word for patchwork, but it does sound as though Sir John's articles were of the economy rather than the craft variety – patched instead of patchwork.

Patchwork as we know it today probably started in the late seventeenth century, flourished in the late eighteenth and early nineteenth centuries, then fell into disrepute as a cottage craft only fit for the poor until it

119. Patchwork quilt. Second half of the nineteenth century.
Cragside

emerged in the second half of this century as an art form. It was generally tied to economy and the satisfaction of producing something both useful and attractive with the minimum of outlay, with the buying of new fabric considered unethical, but now the designs are considered the most important thing, and much new fabric has been bought.

The earliest known set of patchwork hangings in England are those of Levens Hall in Westmorland, which have been dated 1708. There were also, at Stow Hall in 1709, two 'Elbow Chairs of patchwork'.

Considering the many patchwork quilts which have survived from the late eighteenth and nineteenth centuries and the many hundreds more which must have perished from hard wear and old age, it is surprising that so few are mentioned in letters, diaries and inventories. However, again at Stow Hall, the sale catalogue of 1831 lists three. The lack of documentation is on a par with that of seventeenth-century crewel-work, in that the only objects of which we have a considerable number are those which are seldom

120. Crazy patchwork tablecloth. Second half of the nineteenth century.
Cragside

mentioned. However, there are enough patchwork quilts both here and in America for us to know exactly what they were like. At the end of the eighteenth century they were mostly of the applied variety, while those of the nineteenth were usually pieced. Applied patchwork consists of a design made up of pieces of all shapes and sizes being sewn (applied) onto a ground fabric, while pieced patchwork consists of regularly shaped pieces of fabric sewn together so closely that they form another fabric. Occasionally the two methods were combined.

In the last half of the nineteenth century yet another method became fashionable, when scraps of unrelated fabrics, silks, ribbons, satins or velvet were sewn onto a backing, each shape being outlined with feather stitching in thick silk, often of a gold colour. This was known as 'crazy' patchwork, and was an essential part of the late-Victorian home, being used for quilts, table coverings, cushions, handkerchief and nightdress cases and anything else which ingenuity might suggest.

PULHAM-WORK

Pulham-work was a type of needlework about which nothing is known except that it was very popular in the sixteenth century. Pulham Market and Pulham St Mary were two adjacent villages in south Norfolk which had flourishing industries in the rather different crafts of the making of felt hats, darnix weaving, and the making of coverlets which were known as Pulham-work. In 1552 an Act was passed for the benefit of the citizens of Norwich which forbade anyone outside the city – except certain corporate or market towns – to make these things, Pulham excepted.

The hats and darnix fabrics have never been identified, but Pulham-work appears in many inventories, not only in Norfolk, but also further afield. In 1522 the L'Estranges of Hunstanton paid 6s. for a 'coverlet of Pulham work',[13] and the hangings in the Queen's Chamber in Sir Roger Wodehouse's house at Kimberley in Norfolk also had 'hangings of Pulham work'.[141] In some ways this work (was it weaving or embroidery?) seems to have been connected with bird-work, which also often appears in sixteenth-century inventories, sometimes in the same room as Pulham-work. One can only imagine that it was a particular type of design featuring birds, but so far fairly exhaustive research has not come up with any answers.

TURKEY WORK

Turkey work was the English weavers' attempt to rival the very expensive carpets which came from Turkey, Asia Minor and Persia. Carpets in the east were used more as hangings and coverings than on the floor and, as we have seen, this was how a carpet was originally used in England. Practically all inventories differentiate quite clearly between the imported carpet and turkey work, so it soon becomes clear that the late sixteenth, seventeenth and early eighteenth centuries saw an enormous amount of this type of carpeting being made in England.

Strangely enough, it is not known where these carpets were made, although it has long been thought that there was a considerable industry in East Anglia, somewhere in or near Norwich. Inventories like the one of

Kenilworth of 1588 refer to 'A Turquoy carpette of Norwiche work';[119] at Hatfield House there was in the 'Greate Parlour' 'A large Norwiche Carpitt lyned with buckrome'; at Salisbury House in the Strand there were both a long carpet of Norwich-work and a cupboard carpet of the same work in the Great Chamber. A rather puzzling reference from Hatfield House refers to 'Two fyne Norwich silke Carpitts of diverse colors lyned with black buckrome'. All known turkey work is made from wool and no other one of silk has been noted. Whether this was actual turkey work or a different type of work is not known.

The earliest reference to turkey work so far found is from Leeds Castle in Kent,[121] where in 1532 there were two small carpets of the work on two cupboards. However, there are considerably earlier references to carpet work and, bearing in mind that chairs upholstered in turkey work were also known as carpet chairs in the seventeenth and eighteenth century, it seems certain that carpet and turkey work are the same. In the sequestration inventory of Edmund Dudley in 1509[104] are '23 Cussins of carpett work' and '3 couerynges for cussins of carpett worke', and in the slightly later (1513) inventory of John de Veer, Earl of Oxford,[146] there are 'viii Cussheons of carpett worke' as well as 'Carpett Cussheons'.

Another entry in the same inventory refers to two little carpets with knots 'of beyonde see makyng'. This gives a clue to the existence of carpets made in Turkey or Persia which found their way to England to serve as early models for the technique copied so assiduously during the sixteenth and seventeenth centuries. The great influx of eastern carpets came in the 1520s, when Cardinal Wolsey was so overwhelmed by their beauty that he acquired, by somewhat dubious means, a number for Hampton Court Palace.

A number of big houses had these carpets in the sixteenth century but in the seventeenth it appears that virtually every house down to the level of the yeomanry had their complement of turkey work, especially as chair coverings. The greatest number of chairs in the first half of the sixteenth century were of the so-called Farthingale type, often used as dining chairs. They had square seats, and were like a stool with a short back with a padded strip across it which would just about reach the small of the back. Margaret Swain in her lecture, 'Textile covers and the Farthingale Chair', showed that the backs and seats were woven and then the frames of the chairs were made to fit the covers. A set of chairs at Holyrood House in Edinburgh are all of slightly different measurements but all fit their covers exactly. This method would also make export very much simpler: the fabric

121. Turkey work foot carpet. Seventeenth century. Knole

was simply rolled up and sent, rather than sending the chairs themselves to America (where they were very popular) or the continent. In this connection, the Fairfax inventory of 1624 has a tantalizing reference to turkey or set-work. In the cypress chest were 'Two dozen of cushions, one long cushion, and 2 armes for a couch chare all of set work to make up, cushions and a long cushion of Irish stitch to make upp'; also, 'one Nedle work Cushion, not all sewed'. This would seem to imply that all the cushions, whether of turkey work, Irish-stitch, or the unspecified needlework had been made in the house and were waiting for the attention of the upholsterer to be made up and stuffed.

Turkey work was done on a loom, using a strong linen warp. Between each row of weft, or sometimes between two rows, wool was knotted, using the same knots as were used in real Turkey carpets. This gave rise to very angular designs, as the work was too coarse to take good curves, and though generally flowers, leaves and foliage were used in the designs (the English keeping to their well-loved flowers, rather than copying the geometrical designs of the east), they were always stylized and angular.

Turkey work made a very strong covering – there is ample proof in the fact that there is still a considerable amount to be seen today. It was also

122. Detail of very worn turkey work on church hassocks.
Seventeenth century. Felbrigg Hall

soft which, for people who had not been used to upholstered furniture, must have been a very great blessing.

Towards the end of the seventeenth century cane-seated chairs with high backs which did not need wool seats became fashionable, and the distress to the wool merchants made them petition Parliament asking it to prohibit 'the making and Vending of cane Chairs, Stools and Couches'. This petition further stated that 'there were yearly made and vended in the Kingdom about five thousand dozen of sett worke (commonly called Turkey worke) Chairs though made in England'. This is an enormous number, even allowing for the exaggeration found in most petitions, and if anything like that amount was made each year it is not surprising that the wool merchants should very much dislike the idea of any other covering or indeed any other type of chair being made. However, these low-backed chairs were eventually superseded, though not until towards the middle of the eighteenth century.

Apart from its use on the chairs bought by so many people, including Pepys ('having bought Turkey work chairs etc.'), this form of weaving was used for other things. Mary Chapman of Bury St Edmunds, the wife of a grocer, made a will in 1649, in which she refers to my 'posted settworke bedsteade'. Separate cushions were also made. A set, now broken up and in Norwich Cathedral, the Victoria and Albert Museum and Stranger's Hall Museum, Norwich, was made in 1651 and given by Mayor Barrett to the City Council, which was then meeting in Blackfriars Hall. These have the Norwich Arms – the castle and lion – as the design, and though the gift is minuted in the records of the city, there is no mention of where they were made.

In 1588 Sir Roger Wodehouse had quite a considerable variety of turkey work at Kimberley, including a large carpet and cupboard cloth, a window cloth, which might have been used on a window-seat or, more likely, was hung before the window to keep out the cold, another cloth for a square table, five cushions and six cushioned stools. Yet another use was for church hassocks and, originally in Felbrigg Church but now in Felbrigg Hall, there are turkey-work hassocks with a design of tulips and other flowers.

A GLOSSARY OF
UPHOLSTERY FABRICS AND TERMS

It is easy to assess, from inventories and early writings, the importance of various fabrics. What is less easy is to guess what they actually looked like. There are few early textiles in existence, and those which can still be seen are those originally considered the most valuable and were therefore the most carefully looked after and preserved. Ordinary domestic furnishings have worn out.

In many houses, some belonging to individuals, others in the care of organizations such as the National Trust, there is now a policy of sympathetic reproduction where appropriate and possible, but how, for example, could one reproduce the furnishings for King Charles' Room at Dunster Castle, as cited in the 1690 inventory: 'Gold coloured Mohair bed lined with blew sarcenett, one quilt of the same ... 4 white window curtains'. What shade of gold, was the mohair silk or wool, what shade of blue, and what were the window curtains made of? The Rev. William Cole, of Bletchley Parsonage in Buckinghamshire, in 1765 gave a most clear description of the bed in the 'Next Best Bedchamber': 'the Bed is a most beautiful stained cotton of Crimson and White by a Copper Plate, having Parrots, Baskets of Flowers etc.' A wonderfully accurate description of the fabric, which must have been one of the fairly new, single-colour plate-printed cotton/linens, but what about trimmings and what style of bed were they for?

Sometimes it is possible to find, under layers of fabric on chairs or sofas, tiny fragments of the original fabric, which were not completely removed when the piece of furniture was re-upholstered; these can often be reproduced to a greater or lesser extent. Lesser, because it is difficult for modern machines and technicians to weave in the same way, using the same yarns as was done one or two hundred years ago. Luckily, there are a few firms now willing or able to try.

The most difficult problem of all is knowing what is meant by the name of a fabric. For example, one of the commonest words found in sixteenth- and seventeenth-century inventories is 'fustian'. This is generally taken to mean a fabric woven as a twill with a linen warp and a cotton weft, but it could also have a wool weft. Apparently it could be smooth or napped; the word could also include other fabrics, or be a generic name for a whole range; and it could be applied to such varied articles as blankets, bed curtains, petticoats and waistcoats. Like many other textiles, it changed components but kept the same name. Equally, the reverse could happen: when manufacturers were left with a fabric which was selling badly, they tended to leave it alone, but give it a different name – an advertising puff – and hope for better sales.

The most that can be done is to put all the available information together and hope that a coherent picture emerges. Luckily, many people are now doing just that. Museum curators here and in America, textile specialists at the Victoria and Albert Museum, members of the Furniture History Society and the National Trust, are all working towards a more complete understanding of the textiles of the past.

Attempting to assess fabrics by the prices charged is another pitfall for the unwary, due to the different methods of measurement. In England up to the nineteenth century fabrics could be measured by the yard (36 inches) or the ell (45 inches). Harrison, in his *Description of England*, written in 1587, says that '[We measure] by the yard our woolen cloth, tapestry, arras, silks and laces, but our linen by the elne [ell].' How long this rule, if it was a rule, went on is difficult to say: certainly as much or more tapestry was measured by the ell than by the yard. The inventory of a shopkeeping chapman of 1588 shows holland by the ell, but brown holland by the yard, with dowlas, cloth, osnaburg and Lancashire cloth by the ell, and canvas by both ell and yard. There appears to be no rhyme or reason. In a chapman's inventory for 1691, a case can be made out for imported fabrics being measured by the ell (but a French, Flemish or English ell?) and English by the yard, but that theory falls down on '26 ells of Osenbrids (osnaburg) at 9 the ell', and, next to it, '2 yards of blew ditto at 1s. 6d. yard'. For the time being, it must remain a mystery.

There were also very subtle variations in the quality of cloth – so slight and so subtle that they are difficult to visualize today. William Mackerall, a shopkeeping chapman of Newcastle-upon-Tyne, had a very extensive stock of goods and carried linen cloth priced variously (by the yard) at 10d., 12d., 14d., 16d., 18d., 1s 8d., 1s.10d., 2s., 2s 2d., 2s. 4d. and 2s. 6d.: a range of prices in one fabric which is inconceivable today. His bone or bobbin lace was valued at 3d., 4d., 5d., 6d., 7d., 8d., 10d., 11d., 1s. 2d., 1s 6d., 1s 11d., 2s. 4d., 3s., 3s. 3d., 3s. 4d. and 3s. 8d. a yard. This last can be more easily accounted for by variations in width, but it is still a very wide range.

Stocks of fabrics were not always measured by the yard or ell, but, where there was a large quantity, by the piece. Different cloths, however, were sold in different piece lengths. In 1578 baize was sold in thirty-four-yard lengths, grosgrains in fourteen yard; mackadoes in fourteen yard; Naples fustian, fourteen yard; and linen in twelve-yard lengths. Devonshire kersies and some in Yorkshire were known as 'dozens', being twelve yards long in the piece. Even today bolts and rolls of fabrics come in different lengths.

A further complication to the understanding of the use and type of fabric is the habit of naming it according to the town where it was first made – for example, Lucca velvet, Naples fustian, Bruges satin, etc. Before the New Draperies at the end of the sixteenth century it could be assumed that the fabric was imported from the place named; but after the coming of the 'Strangers', who brought their skills from their various home towns, the fabric was more likely to have been made in England in the style of the foreign town – but it is impossible to be certain.

Despite these varied problems, certain premises can be allowed, and certain distinctions made. What follows is a very brief outline to some of the fabrics and terms mentioned in the book.

ATLAS. A satin or silk fabric. Beck says that the German, Dutch, Russian, Polish and Danish for satin is *atlas*; but it was also imported from India. Celia Fiennes saw it at Fetcham Park in Surrey in 1703; '... only one ground bed chamber which was an Indian atlas, white very fine', and at the same date there were twelve atlas cushions in a room at Dyrham Park.

BAIZE (Bayes). A lightweight, open woollen with a nap, not unlike flannel. It was said to have come into England with the Flemings in the late sixteenth century, but had certainly been made in England earlier than that, though perhaps not in quite the same way. It was made throughout Essex with Colchester as the centre of the industry, though it was also made in the West Country. Celia Fiennes was interested in the weaving of baize and noticed that at Dunmow they were 'altogether taken up about the spinning and preparing for the Bayes'. When she reached Colchester she described the Market Cross and Town Hall with its stalls on which the merchants laid their 'Bayes when exposed to sale', before going to London 'in Bales'. She watched them carding the wool and, after weaving, bringing up the nap with teasles grown locally for that purpose. Lastly she noted that the 'low grounds all about the town are used for whitening their Bayes' – the bleaching fields. Baize in its various qualities never went out of fashion. It was listed in most upholsterers' trade cards of the eighteenth century, and in the nineteenth century in its superfine quality it was, and still is, used for covering billiard tables.

BLANKET. Both an article of bedding and a fabric, the article made from the fabric. It is an undyed woollen cloth, loosely woven and soft. In 1520 the L'Estrange family bought twenty-five and a half yards of blanket at 7d. the yard and also an ell of blanket for 11d. to make 'ye boye of ye kechyn [kitchen] a payer of hose'. Blankets for beds in the sixteenth century were either of fustian or, more rarely, Spanish blankets, woven from the wool of Spanish merino sheep.

BROADCLOTH. Probably the best-known of all English fabrics, famous all over Europe and America and woven in the West Country. Woven on a broad loom and fulled before finishing, the fibres closed together and made it virtually impervious to the weather. There were many different qualities and it was used for covering furniture as well as for outdoor clothes, and in a finer quality for men's suitings. In 1523 livery broadcloth cost 3s. 4d., 3s. and 2s. 10d. a yard. In 1573 the Bacon family bought a piece of broadcloth from which was made three pairs of livery blankets, one larger pair, with eight yards left over. The piece cost £3 18s. 8d., but it was two yards wide. Joseph Clarke of Roxwell in Essex was a grocer and draper and in the list of goods in his shop, made at his death in 1692, he had a broadcloth at 5s. a yard in the piece or 4s. a yard in remnants.

BROCADE. A flat fabric with a slightly raised pattern of flowers, etc. The pattern can be woven in metal threads or thick or fine silk in a variety of colours. Though most brocades were silk, the term 'brocaded' could be used to refer to the technique rather than the thread.

BUCKRUM. A cheap, coarse, loosely woven cloth made from hemp, often used for linings. In a draper's inventory of 1692 it was classed with linens at 8½d. a yard, but in 1533 it only cost 6d. a yard and in 1592 black buckram was 11d. a yard. Peter Thornton says that in the seventeenth century, because it was so loosely woven, it was frequently used for sun curtains, but if used this way, it was probably not stiffened and gummed, as was usual.

BUSTIAN. Fabric originally imported, later one of the New Draperies. The early cloth seems to have been a cotton or cotton/linen mix allied to fustian, while the later fabric was a woollen.

CAFFOY (Caffa). Usually a wool fabric imitating silk furnishing damasks, but in the sixteenth century it may have been made of silk. In a pageant commemorating Queen Elizabeth's visit to Norwich in 1579, the weaving of caffoy was shown along with other fabrics. It was popular during the seventeenth and early eighteenth centuries and was used at Ingatestone in 1600, where a bed had a blue caffa canopy and valance with birds and beasts in white silk and gold upon it. This implies a plain fabric; certainly not one with a raised pile. Later, in 1731, John Loveday saw the fabric at Houghton where 'the Salon is hung with Scarlet Caffoy'; Sir John Smyth's house in 1741 had a 'Bedstead and blue Cawfoy furniture, lin'd with strip'd Stuff'. Some of the early wallpapers imitated caffoy. Mrs Delany wrote that 'my "dining room" vulgarly so called is hung with mohair cafoy paper, (a *good* blue) ...' Caffoy has been positively identified as the fabric on a set of chairs, listed in an inventory at Erddig, near Wrexham.

CALAMANCO. A worsted material, hot-pressed. There were many types of calamanco and they could be striped, brocaded or plain. They were sometimes used for dresses and petticoats, but more particularly for upholstery and hangings. In 1765 the parson at Bletchley 'hung the Room entirely with a very good deep blew Callimanco Stuff'. In the 1771 inventory at Felbrigg Hall there is green calamanco in a trunk, for the window curtains. Many styles of the fabric were made in Norwich and pattern books in the Bridewell Museum there show that the stuff was exported in large quantities to Italy and Spain as well as being used in Britain.

CALICO. A cotton cloth, originally imported from India. It could be plain – chiefly used for undergarments – or printed – used for dresses and hangings. It was not until the last quarter of the eighteenth century that calico equal in quality to the Indian could be made in England, but from then on it rivalled and surpassed it. In 1628 calico cost 11d. and 15d. a yard; in 1690, 12d.; in 1712, 16d.; and in 1714, blue calico was 1s. 7d.

CAMLET. A tabby-weave fabric made from a variety of threads, either singly or mixed, including goat hair, but the most commonly used thread was worsted mixed with hair. Camlet could be comparatively cheap (2s. 4d. per yard in 1538), though when coloured and figured was more expensive. Katharine of Aragon had silk 'chamlette' bed covers at Baynards Castle at this date – silk camlet in 1522 costing 4s. a yard. In England it was largely made in Norwich and in the seventeenth and eighteenth centuries was sold to the East India Company for export to India and north China as well as to various places in Europe, but towards the end of the eighteenth and beginning of the nineteenth centuries the demand dropped, giving much unemployment in the district.

The plain fabric could be finished in many ways, chiefly by hot-pressing, and the different finishes gave rise to different names such as harrateen, moreen, grograms, etc. These, however, are all basically camlets and all used in upholstery, being very hard wearing.

In 1698 Celia Fiennes saw camlet and mohair beds at Cupola House in Bury St Edmunds, and in 1715 Lady Grisell Baillie in Scotland had a sea-green camlet bed, while later, in 1771, in a chest at Felbrigg Hall, was 'enough brown camolet for a bed'.

CANVAS. A fabric which could be woven from cotton, hemp or linen, varying from very fine to very thick. It could be closely woven or open-weave. A rather surprising entry in the 1641 inventory of Tart Hall is, 'Canvas for 2 Beds to keep Gnats away'. This must have been an early form of mosquito net using an open-weave canvas.

CHENY. *See* **Philip and china.**

CHINTZ. Today the word chintz is taken to mean a highly-glazed cotton printed with large flowers and leaves, but this was not the original meaning. The word 'chint' in Hindi means 'spotted cloth' and the English factors in India made the plural, 'chintes', which in England became 'chintz'. This applied to any painted or printed cloth from India, with no glazing. So both pintadoes (q.v.) and palampores (q.v.) are technically chintz. The Indian fabric in its various forms became very popular for wall hangings, bed hangings, furniture upholstery and window curtains, as well as dresses from the mid-seventeenth century to the end of the eighteenth century. Mrs Lybbe Powys described the library at Heythrop as having 'the sofas, chairs and curtains fine chintz, a present from the late Lord Clive, a bed and furniture the same above stairs.' Referring to Mawley, she said: 'I think Lady Blount has more chintz counterpanes than in one house I ever saw; not one bed without very fine ones.' The British calico-printers copied the Indian chintz from the end of the eighteenth century onwards, but in the nineteenth century the designs became more English in style and the fabric was highly glazed.

CLOTH OF GOLD/SILVER. A sumptuous fabric woven from silk with gold or silver threads and imported from the east. A draper's bill for 1538 itemizes cloth of silver 'with workes' at the very high price of 36s. 8d. a yard. 'With workes' generally means embroidered, but this appears to have been brocaded.

CLOTHIER. Generally, a man who employs others to weave cloth and then sells it. In the fifteenth and sixteenth centuries clothiers were very influential in cloth-making districts, as they had the capital to buy wool, and employ spinners and weavers, fullers and dyers to produce the cloth. This meant that whole areas of the country were dependent on the business sense and solvency of the clothiers.

CLOUDED. When applied to a fabric, 'clouded' implies that the edge of the design is soft and slightly indefinite. This was achieved by printing the threads before weaving. Many fabrics were clouded or chiné, both woollen and silk, and in the seventeenth and eighteenth centuries clouded silk was a popular fabric for bed hangings and curtains. In the eighteenth century calamancoes (q.v.) were frequently clouded, as is cretonne (q.v.) a favourite nineteenth- and twentieth-century fabric.

COSTRYNGES. A word, found in early inventories, meaning hangings, especially those for a hall.

CRANKY. A North Country word applied to a stout linen fabric striped both ways, i.e., checked, blue on white. It was used for working aprons and also as mattress coverings. In a letter to Thomas Leigh of Stow Hall in 1790, the firm of Gillows, based in Lancaster, refers to a 'cranky mattress'. The 1831 sale catalogue for the same house has several lots which include the word cranky, such as 'a wool mattress in a cranky case', so the word must also have been used in East Anglia.

CRETONNE. Fabric originally made from hemp and linen, but later from cotton. It is supposed to have been introduced in 1825 by a French linen manufacturer M. Cretonne, but it also appears to have been known earlier – probably in a different form. In the nineteenth century it gradually superseded chintz as an upholstery fabric, and Eastlake, writing in 1878, said it 'made a good substitute for chintz and will wash'. It had a warp thicker than the weft and so had a slightly ribbed appearance.

CREWEL. A two-ply yarn spun from long-staple worsted. This thread has been used for embroidery from at least the seventeenth century (probably earlier) until today. It was used exclusively for the embroidery worked on bed curtains, etc., in the seventeenth and eighteenth centuries. This is generally known as crewel-work, though there has been a regrettable tendency in the last fifty years to refer to it as 'Jacobean-work.'

DAMASK. A reversible fabric, woven from either silk, flax or wool in the past, and today from virtually any thread or combination of threads. Silk damask was the most expensive, and was woven with large trailing flowers and used for dresses and petticoats in the eighteenth century. Wool damask was used for upholstery and linen damask for table-linen. Scotland produced most of the damask woven in the seventeenth and eighteenth centuries, but the name comes from Damascus, where the most beautiful damask was woven from the twelfth century on. In a bill of 1538, white damask was priced at 6s. a yard, and black at 8s. In 1587 it was 12s. a yard, and in 1591, 13s. 4d. Horace Walpole lined the walls of the gallery at Strawberry Hill with crimson Norwich wool damask, and also covered the black and gold furniture supplied by William Vile in the same material.

DARNIX (Darnick, Dornock). A fabric of linen and wool, used in particular for household linen – both bed and table – though it also had many other uses. It was originally made in Flanders at Tournai (in Dutch, Dorneck), and by the middle of the sixteenth century was also made in Norwich. In 1591 two 'darnicke' coverlets cost 12s., and a darnicke table carpet 2s. 6d.; in 1596 four darnick coverlets bought at Binham Fair in Norfolk cost 27s. In an inventory of 1626 a fairly small home lists darnix carpets, coverlets and curtains. Next to fustian it was probably the most common word relating to textiles in sixteenth-century inventories.

DIAPER. This refers to both a pattern and a fabric, generally combined. The pattern consists of tiny lozenges woven into a fabric in diagonal lines. Any fabric can be 'diapered', but diaper generally referred to household linen, be it cotton or linen, used for towels and tablecloths. Virtually every inventory of any date which includes household linen includes such items as, 'Three large diaper tablecloths; six dozen of diaper napkins; five diaper towelles'. These from the Standen inventory of 1623 are listed in contrast to two dozen damask napkins and three dozen plain napkins.

DIMITY. Today a white cotton fabric, tabby weave, often with a slight corded self-stripe. At various times it has been thick or thin, plain cotton, lined or mixed, and it has been described as a sort of fustian (q.v.). It could also be patterned with coloured satin stripes, or even flowered. It was originally imported from India, but from the eighteenth century was also made in Lancashire. In 1778 Mrs Delany writes: 'I have been at as great a loss to get you a few yards of true Indian dimity. Your neighbour, Manchester, has brought the manufacture to so great a perfection that it is difficult to know which is the right.'

DOILY. Mr Doily was a linen-mercer in the Strand in London in the late seventeenth century who made a fortune by 'finding out Materials for such Stuffs as might at once be cheap and genteel'; these included a thin woollen stuff for summer wear which was named after him. In the eighteenth century a doily was a fringed napkin, presumably made from the same fabric, used for wiping the fingers at dessert, and it was not until the nineteenth century that it became a general term for any round linen or cotton mat placed on plates under cakes, bread and butter, or sandwiches. An entry in the 1790 inventory of Stow Hall is for, '10 hand towels, 2 round ditto, 2 toilet covers and 28 doyleys'.

DRUGGET. Like many other cloths, drugget has changed over the years from being a narrow, cheap cloth of wool, or wool and silk, used for coats and other outer garments, to a cloth used to lay over carpets for their protection, especially in houses open to the public. It was also used in upholstery; a bed at Dyrham (1703) had drugget hangings.

DURANT (Durance). A glazed woollen stuff, allied to tammy, and very hard-wearing. In 1771 a fine durant was used for backing the Moor Park tapestry suit at Temple Newsom.

ELL. The measurements of length given in the *Finchley Manual of Industry* (1860) are: '$2\frac{1}{4}$ Inches make 1 Nail. 4 Nails make 1 Quarter. 3 Quarters make 1 Flemish Ell. 4 Quarters make 1 Yard. 5 Quarters make 1 English Ell. 6 Quarters make 1 French Ell.' To add to the difficulty, a Scottish ell is 37.2 inches, which is unrelated to the quarter altogether. When comparing prices of different fabrics it is necessary, but generally impossible, to know in which country they were measured, and also to know whether or not the measurements were ever translated into the English ell.

FILET. Also known as lacis or darned netting. The earliest kind of net lace, which is really a compound of netting and embroidery. First a net with a small mesh is made, and then a pattern or design is darned into it. Filet was popular in the sixteenth and early seventeenth centuries and then again in the late nineteenth and early twentieth centuries.

FLANNEL. A loosely woven woollen fabric, often napped, not generally associated with upholstery, but in 1603 at Hengrave, in the Tower Gallery, there were 'hangings of green flannel complete, with a vallence indented, with lace and bells'.

FRIEZE. A woollen cloth napped and sometimes curled as well. Any woollen cloth could be *frisé* or friezed, and a Yorkshire pattern book of about 1770 shows swatches of broadcloth (q.v.) 'Frized', at 2s. 9d. the yard. It was a fabric used for warmth both in clothing, where it was usually used for greatcoats, and upholstery. The Arundel inventory of Tart Hall in 1641 has many curtains, bed and wall hangings of frieze, and obviously the fabric, even if plain and dull, could be treated as though rich, as in the four back armed chairs, covered with frieze and edged about with a 'broad Embroydered lace of Gold'. In 1591 frieze of the 'best sorte' cost 17d. the yard, and of the 'worst sorte', 13d.

FULL. To thicken cloth by kneading it in water. Cloth, which is woven from short-staple wool, is made weather-proof and thicker by fulling. Originally this was done by treading cloth in water with the feet, but later fulling mills were built on rivers which turned wheels with paddles that came down onto the cloth, squeezing and kneading it.

FURNITURE. A word with many meanings. It can refer to all the movable articles of a house as well as to some immovable accessories, such as finger-plates or latches on doors. It also refers to the draperies and linen for beds, but not specifically to the mattresses. It includes any embellishments of a room, such as curtains or carpets. The modern word 'furnishings' is generally used for all fabrics in a room and furniture today implies solid but movable articles.

FUSTIAN. A word which crops up frequently in inventories and accounts from medieval times. It was a mixed fabric with a linen warp and cotton weft, generally napped, but it could have wool in it as well. It is difficult to identify as there were a large number of fabrics which came under the general term, and jean fustian (from Genoa), myllion fustian (from Milan) and holmes fustian (from Ulm) are among those used for upholstery as well as clothing. Most blankets in the sixteenth and seventeenth centuries were made from fustian, but the yarns are generally unspecified. In 1520 black fustian for a doublet cost 8d. the yard, and in 1591 it was 3s. 6d. the yard. In 1692 coloured fustian was 9d. and white narrow, $6\frac{1}{2}$d. In 1703 there was at Dyrham a 'white fustian wrought bed'.

GALLOON. A braid, lace or ribbon woven from silver, gold or silk threads, used for trimming upholstery, liveries and sometimes dress.

GINGHAM. Originally an Indian fabric made from cotton and tussar silk. Its distinguishing mark was that it was woven of dyed yarn in checks and stripes. The technique was soon copied in England and later in America, since when ginghams have been among the most serviceable fabrics for dress and household use. In the eighteenth century they were frequently used for case covers and upholstered furniture.

GROSGRAM (Grosgrain). A fabric which could be made of silk only, or of silk and mohair or silk and wool. It was thick and made a strong fabric, suitable for upholstery as well as dress. It was sometimes watered and was classed with the New Draperies of the late sixteenth century. A swatch of 'figured Grograms' illustrated in *Textiles in America* shows small lozenges, chevrons and stylized flowers. This particular swatch is of silk and worsted and is from a pattern book of about 1750 in the Nordiska Museet in Stockholm. In 1643, Worcester House had, in the gallery, '1 Elbow Chaire and 8 stools of silver figured grograine'.

HARDEN. A coarse cloth made from tow and used for sheets in poor families. It seems to have been not unlike hessian.

HARRATEEN. A worsted fabric, hot-pressed, used for furnishings in the eighteenth century. Ann Buck in 1748 sold harrateens, and they are listed in many trade cards of this period. Like so many fabrics of the eighteenth century, it is not always easy to find a piece in use, but at Hatfield House a lining to a bed canopy has been identified as harrateen from the list of fabrics used. The Blickling inventory of 1793 lists harrateen window curtains in a closet.

HOLLAND. A linen cloth originally imported from Holland, but later made in England. Holland was always of fine quality and is mentioned in countless inventories and accounts, being used for clothes, especially for accessories such as smocks and caps, but also for dresses. It was used for sheets and pillowcases, and also for bed hangings; in the Felbrigg inventory of 1771 is, in a chest, 'Enough Blue and white striped Holland for a Bed'. It is a fabric which has been used at least from the fifteenth century to the present day.

IMAGERY. A word used in connection with the designs on some tapestries and painted cloths. It implies a design which has figures in it, and the term can also be used when referring to embroidery.

INDIAN GOODS (Indian fabrics). A general term indicating any fabrics from the east imported into England. In the seventeenth and eighteenth centuries most people were extremely hazy as to the whereabouts of eastern countries, and because the East India Company was based in India, goods from China as well as India were spoken of as 'India goods', so it is not always easy to decide exactly where the goods did come from.

A receipt signed by the Duke of Bedford states: 'Received Jan 6 1752 of Samuel Davis nine pounds, nine shillings being what I paid for a piece of India silk for Woburn Abbey.' Mrs Delany in 1756 writes, 'Lady Lincolns private apartment ... was furnished with beautiful Indian painted taffets ...' The 1771 inventory of Felbrigg includes: 'Enough striped India muslin for the lining of a bed'. There was also India damask, India satin, and in the Duchess of Ormonde's closet in 1684 eight white India Damask curtains went with blue damask cushions and bed.

IRISH-STITCH. Both a stitch and a pattern, which can be muddling. Basically, it is a straight, plain stitch, one of the names for long-and-short stitch which is worked freely on cloth. However, when long-and-short stitch is worked on canvas, it becomes Florentine, bargello, flame, cushion, Hungary or Irish-stitch, and it also becomes the type of design. This stitch/technique has been popular for centuries and Lady Anne Clifford in her diary (1619) tells of the 'Irish stitch cushion' she worked when left alone at Knole. Dyrham Park in 1703 had four chairs and seven cushions in Irish-stitch, and there were and are bed hangings in the same technique. The design is always shaded, and moves up and down in a way that resembles flames.

KERSEY. A fabric which has varied in price and style according to where it was made. It was a coarse, twilled cloth made in many parts of England. It was known as Hampshire kersey, Suffolk kersey, Devon kersey and so on, and they all varied. There were also kersey 'dozens', which meant that a piece was twelve yards long, and 'straits', which meant that it was narrow. Kersey was used for stockings before knitted ones became fashionable, for heavy jerkins and as a covering for stools and chairs. Inventories and accounts give many different prices and descriptions. In 1533 white 'carsey' was 2s. 4d., in 1560 Hampshire kersey was 2s. 10d. per yard, and yellow and red kersey 4s. 7d. per ell. In 1692 Joseph Clarke of Roxwell was selling kersey at 2s. and 'kersey halfe thick' at 21d.

KIDDERMINSTER. A town in Worcestershire famous for its carpet manufacture. The carpets bearing this name were flat and reversible, made in strips which were sewn together, and were inexpensive. They were also known as Scotch carpets and Ingrain carpets.

LANCASHIRE CLOTH. There is an entry in the 1575 accounts of Sir Henry Sydney which merely states: 'A note of all such damask and Lancashire cloth which came from Penshurst'. It is not clear what is meant by 'Lancashire' cloth, though from the context it would appear to be some form of diaper used for table-linen.

LENO (Gauze). Originally a silk fabric from Gaza, but it can also be made from cotton or other yarn. The word leno refers to the method of weaving where the warp threads are twisted round each other and the weft is shot through to bind them. This makes a very light, open fabric. In the nineteenth century it was extensively used for shawls and other light accessories, and seldom for furnishings, but in 1827 Richard Flack, upholster and cabinet-maker of Shepherd's Market in London, made 'Leno Curtains for three Windows' for Crix at Hatfield Peverel. These must have been sun-blinds, but it is surprising that such an open-weave fabric should have been used.

LINSEY WOLSEY. A fabric with a delightful name which implies that it is made from a mixture of wool and linen. The *Oxford English Dictionary* defines it as originally a mixed fabric of wool and flax, later woven with a cotton warp and inferior wool weft. It was always a cheap fabric used mainly for dress, but at Dyrham Park in 1703 the hangings in 'Misses Closet' were of red linsey wolsey.

LUSTRING (Lutestring). A light silk, tabby woven like a taffeta, but stretched and gummed, giving a glossy, crisp look. It was a very fashionable fabric for dresses in the eighteenth century, and was also used for upholstery. Mrs Lybbe Powys in 1780 describes the drawing room at Hedsor as having a 'white flock paper; the chairs and curtains lute-string, white ground, a faint stripe and fringed'.

MANCHESTER. In the eighteenth century, Manchester became the centre for the English cotton industry, specializing in dress fabrics and, more particularly, household linen. Even today the department selling sheets, towels etc. in a store is sometimes known as the Manchester department. Apart from the general use of the word, there was a specific fabric called Manchester, and Mrs Papendiek describes one of her trousseau dresses as 'a Manchester cotton ... a stripe of cotton and wool mixed and a narrower one of satin'.[57] The Felbrigg inventory of 1771 includes '2 White Counterpanes, Manchester', but what exactly they were like is unknown. Blickling in 1793 had many curtains of 'stript Manchester' in the bedrooms and drawing room, which seems to resemble Mrs Papendiek's description.

MARCELLA. The Felbrigg inventory of 1771 lists, '1 counterpane Marcella quilting, scarlet silk lined with green silk'. There has been much discussion regarding marcella or Marseilles quilting, whether it was hand- or machine-made. This is due to the fact that in the nineteenth and early twentieth centuries, many loom-woven counterpanes were known as marcella quilts. But, like so much else, marcella quilting has changed its style over the centuries. Writing in 1770 Saint-Aubin says that Marseilles embroidery was made in quilting: small stitches outlined motifs, working through two thicknesses of fabric, and cotton roving was then inserted into each motif so that it was slightly padded, after which the unpadded ground was completely covered with fine French knots. He went on to say that quilts and quilted clothes were made in a slightly different way, by working the whole design through the three thicknesses of material: top, padding and lining. He ends by saying ominously that, 'Tapestry Makers have bestowed upon themselves the right to embroider bed coverings in this manner, an action that has led to some lawsuits.'[179]

This type of quilt had been made, mainly in Provence, for many years, and was very popular in England, particularly when made into petticoats, though there were problems, as Henry Purefoy explains when he writes in 1739 that he had had to return the 'Marseilles Quilt petticoat', which he had ordered for his very small mother, 'because of its weight'. In 1763 a patent was granted to Robert Elder for 'a new method of weaving and quilting in the loom ... as of India, French or Marseilles quilting'. This 'quilting in the loom' flourished, and from the fact that it was mainly made at Bolton in Lancashire it became known as Bolton quilting. The word 'Marseilles' became corrupted into 'marcella'. The last use of the fabric, made without the wadded interlining, was for men's waistcoats and evening-dress shirt-fronts.

MILLPUFF. This was the cheapest form of filling for mattresses, used by the very poor, and it consisted largely of dust, plus some ends of wool from the mills. It was cheaper and nastier than flock, and cost 2d. or $2\frac{1}{2}$d. per pound. It took fifty pounds of millpuff to make a mattress for a double bed.

MOCKADO. An imitation velvet, not unlike – but coarser than – Utrecht velvet, and the forerunner of the present-day moquette. Woven with a linen warp and a wool weft it could be plain, or stamped with a pattern. It was used for dress and for upholstery and curtains; 'two curtyns for the windowe of greene and white striped moccadoe' (1603). It was one of the New Draperies of Elizabeth I's reign. In the Bacon accounts it is listed as bought for clothing, and cost 22d. per yard. **Tuft moccadoe** seems to have been the same fabric, but with the pile standing up here and there in tufts, perhaps in a small spot pattern. It, too, was used for both dress and upholstery.

MOHAIR. A fabric made from the hair of the angora goat, but often mixed with other yarns such as silk or worsted. It was woven as a form of camlet, and was finished in different ways: plain, watered or figured, for example. In its various forms it was used for all types of furnishing: in 1715, Lady Grisell Baillie had a yellow mohair bed. At Dyrham Park in 1703, in the First New Nursery there was a mohair silk bed with matching cushions and mohair stuff wall hangings. It could be that the designs, if any, were similar, but obviously the wool was considered suitable for the walls while the silk was lighter and therefore more attractive on the bed.

MOREEN. A worsted fabric with a stamped or watered finish, very popular for all furnishing uses in the eighteenth and early nineteenth centuries. It was used for curtains in the Drinking Room at Blickling in 1773.

NEW DRAPERY. A difficult and ambiguous phrase denoting the fabrics made in England after *c.* 1550, especially in East Anglia, which were not indigenous in that particular form. Weaving in England from the time of Edward III and his wife, Philippa of Hainault, benefited from influxes of foreign craftsmen, generally known as 'Strangers'. These men arrived in England in waves, often due to religious troubles in their own countries, and frequently settled permanently in their adopted country. In 1554 Queen Mary licensed Strangers to teach Norwich weavers to make 'Sattens, Sattens Reverse, and Fustian of Naples'. In 1565 Dutchmen arrived to teach the making of 'bayes, arras, says, mockadoes, stamen and carsey'. In 1594 the fabrics were defined as:

divers sortes of wollen clothes and other commodityes commonly cauled duble, midle and single bays, rashe, stamelles of Florence, serge of French sorte, sayes of Flanders sorte, narrow worsteds, narrow grogranes, moccadoes of every sorte, Plumetes, fusades, carrells, Fustian of Naples, blankets cauled Spanishe rugges, knitt hose of worsted yarne and all sortes of nue draperies and other nue stuffs and commodities now made of woll only or most parte of woll have ben of late yeares chiefly devised and made within England by straungers.

This list shows that great care needs to be taken in deciding where a particular fabric was made. A Spanish rugg, for example, was probably not made in Spain, but may have been made in East Anglia either from the excellent wool from Spanish sheep, or after the style as rugg made in Spain, from Lincolnshire wool.

PALAMPORE. A coverlet made in India, composed of a single chintz panel. This is where it differs from a pintadoe (q.v.), which is a length of fabric. Palampores were first imported into England in the early seventeenth century, and were used on beds as single pieces rather than made into quilts. They became more popular than the 'pintado quilt' after about 1680, and their popularity can be gauged by figures quoted by Irwin for the year 1695–6, when the East India Company imported 20,000 large, 10,000 middling and 10,000 small palampores.

PANED. Widths of fabric made from joining narrow pieces of different coloured cloths, often red and green. A popular style of wall and bed hangings in the sixteenth and seventeenth centuries.

PARAGON. A coarse worsted fabric resembling a double camlet, used for hangings and seat furniture in the seventeenth and eighteenth centuries. The fabric still in the King's Closet at Knole is said to be paragon. In the 1684 inventory of Dublin Castle 'his Grace's dressing room' had curtains of yellow paragon, and squab cushions for cane-bottomed chairs of yellow damask with paragon covers, implying that the paragon was not nearly as valuable or vulnerable as the damask. In 1663, Mary Verney writes to Lady Elwes: 'I have yet my closet to furnish and I beg your assistance in it. I think to hang it with paragon, but the colour and whether it shall be watered or no I leave to you.'

However, although it is always assumed that paragon is made from worsted only, in the Dyrham inventory of 1703 the striped velvet bed has curtains of 'worsted Paragon'. Surely this must imply that paragon could have other yarns mixed with it on occasion. In 1674 Sarah Fell bought a yard and a nail of black paragon, 'for an Apron for myself'. This seems an unlikely article to be made from a coarse black worsted, unless it was very much a working apron.

PERPETUANA. A woollen fabric which, as its name suggests, is durable and akin to everlasting. Used for the lining of men's coats and for upholstery. In 1643 Worcester House had a bed with curtains and valance of blue perpetuana with lace edging, and in 1638 there was a 'redd perpetuana bed' in an upper nursery at Gosfield Hall, as well as a French bed of green perpetuana with curtain, valance and counterpoint 'laced with green and yellow lace and silk fringe, ye counterpoint lyned with bayes'. It seems to have been one of the many woollen and worsted fabrics which, in the seventeenth century especially, were changing their names for little reason and were being classed as New Draperies often for less.

PHILIP AND CHINA (cheyney). A fabric with a strange name. The derivation is not known, but it appears in various forms in many accounts and inventories in the seventeenth and eighteenth centuries. From the various contexts, it seems that it was a worsted cloth like a camlet (q.v.), brightly coloured and sometimes watered, and could be used for children's coats as well as upholstery. James Ayres quotes from John Wood's *A Description of Bath*, discussing the lodging houses, 'With Kidderminster Stuff, or at best with Cheyne, the Woollen Furniture of the principle Rooms was made.' In 1627, twelve yards of Philip and cheyney 'for a coate' cost 29s. 8d., but in 1712 an upholder's bill included '36 yds of fine norridge [Norwich] cheney 14s. 0d. per yard.'

Dyrham Park in 1703 had red cheyney hangings in some of the lesser bedrooms and in Castle Rising in 1742 there were both hangings and chair coverings of red china. Again, it must have been one of the fabrics which had variations which made it differ in value for in 1619 in the 'rich wearing apparell' of Richard Sackville, 3rd Earl of Dorset, are three entries of garments made of 'Phillipp and Cheyney': a green cloak, embroidered with two borders of gold twist, as well as a doublet and a pair of hose, both embroidered with gold twist.

On the interesting but inconclusive evidence of the stock of a Norwich weaver who chiefly made cheyney, Ursula Priestley has deduced that one type was made of a mixture of wool and worsted.

PIECE. The word 'piece', or, as it is more often spelt, 'pece', is found in old accounts and can give rise to confusion. It has two meanings: the first and more usual is what would now be called a bolt or roll, referring to a complete length of cloth. Lengths, then as now, varied according to different weavers and different cloths and could be anything from about twelve yards to thirty or forty. It was seldom that anything so specific was written as in the Bacon accounts of 1573, where the entry reads: 'Item a pece of Norwitch brod saie of 12 yardes 36s.' More often, one has to guess by context whether it is the specific meaning of the word or the second, more general meaning: an odd length, a piece or a small amount.

PILLOW BERE. A covering for a pillow. These coverings have had different names at different times, according to which part of the country they came from. While pillow bere was the most usual sixteenth- and seventeenth-century term, in Somerset they were called pillow ties and the modern term is pillowcase or pillowslip.

PINTADO. A Portuguese word meaning a spot or fleck, used to describe the stained cloths they found in India and brought back to Europe. John Irwin has pointed out that a pintado could be either painted or printed, and in some cases was both. Where the cloth was painted, it was done freehand, using dyes and painted mordants, and so was of a higher quality than those where the cloth was block printed. In the first half of the seventeenth century it was the expensive, painted cloths which were fashionable, being used for hangings for beds and walls. Pintadoes were sold as lengths of fabric measuring thirteen yards, and were meant to be cut up to fit the walls. The 'pintado quilt' was a real stuffed quilt, but was becoming unfashionable by the 1680s. In the next century all Indian fabrics were prohibited in England though, as usual, the prohibition did not stop them being sold and used. In 1641 Tart Hall had a 'suite of Hangings consisting of Foure Peeces of Indian Pantadoes, and Curtaynes of the same suite ... And foure little Pantadoe Carpetts for the same Roome'.

PLAID. A fabric made in Scotland, and presumably striped and checked like the modern tartan. The tartan rooms at Balmoral (with their tartan carpets), decorated by Queen Victoria and Prince Albert, are well-known, but they were following an older tradition. Dyrham Park in 1703 had a 'Plod Room', which contained: '5 pieces of Scots Plod Hangings, 2 Window Curtains and Vallens of the same, 4 Chairs and two Stools, a Couch and 3 Cushions all covered with Plod.' Where plaid was used in furnishing, it does seem that the whole room was covered in it. In 1641 at Tart Hall Mr Arden's Room 'Is hanged with Scotch Plad'. This room had a wooden couch-bed with a canopy, two long cushions and two little cushions, all covered with the fabric, as were an armed wooden chair, 'back and seat covered with Plad', and two 'little backe Chayres' and a table carpet.

Is plaid the same as Scottish or Scots cloth? There seems to be no firm answer. Two more examples show the possible confusion: in 1533 the L'Estranges of

Hunstanton bought thirteen score, or 260 yards, of Scottish cloth, a very large quantity, which surely must have been used for upholstery; in 1629 Lord Howard of Naworth bought thirteen yards of 'Scotts' for aprons for his two daughters.

PLUSH. Fabric woven from silk, wool, cotton or combination, with a pile rather longer than that of velvet. It was used for livery breeches, especially those of footmen, as well as for upholstery. Wool plush is very hard-wearing and for at least three hundred years has been used for coverings for seat furniture, in the nineteenth century in particular for table coverings and curtains. In 1696, Lady Grisell Baillie bought fifty-four ells of hair plush for hangings, at £3 8s. 6d. (Scots) the ell (roughly 5s. 6d. English money), and then bought fringe for the hangings and to edge the cover of a Japan table. The couch-bed of Anne, Viscountess Dorchester, was gilt and had '1 bed to lye on it of purple plush ... with a canapie, the outward vallance of purple plush laced with silver lace and silver fringe'. The curtains and inner valance were of damask and it was so opulent a bed that the plush must surely have been of silk rather than of wool. At Dyrham Park in 1703 there were ten elbow chairs covered 'with stript plush', and there are many other references to plush being striped.

RAYON. This is the trade name for artificial silk, which first came into use in 1924.

REP. A strong upholstery fabric, the reverse of cretonne (q.v.) in that it has a fine warp and a thick weft. It can be woven from cotton, wool or silk and was used for hangings, curtains and furniture upholstery, especially in the nineteenth century. It was approved of by Charles Eastlake as suitable for curtains.

RESEAU. A lace-maker's term, signifying a plain, netted groundwork. This could be used by itself for bed curtains, or could be darned, forming lacis or filet.

SARCENET. A plain, tabby-weave thin silk, which could also be twilled, and was always soft and supple, and therefore used for fine bed hangings among other things. When it was twilled this was generally stated. Beck thinks that it replaced the older fabric, 'Cendal', in the fifteenth century. Katharine of Aragon had bed hangings of embroidered sarcenet at Baynards Castle in 1535, and the Ham House inventory of 1654 lists sarcenet used for window curtains, case covers, etc. It could also be used to line curtains as well as for dress and was one of the most versatile fabrics in any century. In 1522 five yards of red sarcenet bought by the L'Estranges for the curtain of a bed cost 18s. 4d.

SATIN. Satin is a weave rather than a fabric, though the word is applied also to fabric. The weave is an uneven twill with floating wefts on the surface making a smooth unbroken texture. In the eighteenth century satins were often made of worsted and could be brocaded or damasked. They can also be made of silk or cotton. When they are silk they are generally left plain as their beauty depends on the light catching the smooth surface. Originally, satin was made in China, but by the sixteenth century at the latest it was made in Europe, and Bruges satin –

sometimes called Bridge satin – often appears on lists, generally at a cheaper price. A draper's bill of 1538 lists satin at 5s. 6d., 7s. 6d. and 8s. per yard, and Bruges satin at 2s. In 1519 the L'Estrange family bought black satin at 7s., crimson satin at 13s. and 'popenjaye grene satten of brydys' [Bruges] at 2s. 2d.; in 1591 the Bacons paid, per yard, 12s. for black satin, 14s. for white satin and 22s. for figured satin.

SAY. A very ancient English fabric of twill weave, originally woven from worsted, but could also be made of silk. It was manufactured mostly in Norfolk, Suffolk and Essex, and is found in the majority of sixteenth-century inventories, used for bed and wall hangings, table carpets and, later, window curtains. In 1514 John Borel of Great Yarmouth had two bed cloths of say, one green and one black, a say hanging in the hall, green say bed curtains in the Green Chamber, and red say hangings in the Red Chamber; all these would be woollen. In 1511 the L'Estranges paid 1s. per yard for black say and in 1573 the Bacons bought a piece of 'Norwitch brod saie of 12 yards 36s.', and paid £5 0s. 6d. for three pieces of green say.

SERGE. One of the New Draperies and, until the nineteenth century, a mixture of wool and worsted. Later it became all worsted, used for men's suitings rather than upholstery. It could also be made of silk. Serge was lighter than broadcloth and of good quality. It had many names, and was generally called after the town where it was made. Celia Fiennes in 1698 described the Exeter serges: 'the whole town and country is employ'd for at least 20 mile round in spinning, weaving, dressing and scouring, fulling and drying of the serges, it turns the most money in a weeke of anything in England ... the weavers bring in their serges and must have their money which they employ to provide them yarne to goe to work again.'[48] In upholstery, serge was used for case covers for beds and chairs, and in Ireland in 1684 the Duke of Ormonde had bed case curtains of grey serge, covers for silk brocade chairs of red serge and window curtains of both white and yellow serge.

SHAG. A fabric usually made of worsted, but sometimes of waste silk, with a long pile. Generally used for the lining of mantles, or for coats or bed coverings, but also used for upholstery. Dyrham Park (1703) had red shag hangings in a back closet, and a cushion of red silk and shag. Though in the seventeenth century it could be of good quality, it later became coarse and cheap.

SHALLOON. One of the New Draperies; a cheap, twilled worsted used for dress, linings and upholstery. Also known as 'rashes'. At Kilkenny Castle in 1684 bed and chair cases were of red shalloon and at Dyrham Park in 1703 there was a set of case covers in blue shalloon.

SHAWLING. The fabric from which the first English shawls to imitate the Indian were made in the late eighteenth century. It was also used for upholstery, dresses and waistcoats. It had a silk warp and a fine, worsted weft.

SOUTHEGE (Sultige, Soulwitch). A fabric unknown today, which was a coarsely woven linen used for linings. The Great Chamber at Hengrave in 1603 had curtains of southege for the great window and a portiere at 'ye Gt. Chamber doore' was lined with it. Peter Thornton suggests that at the windows it must have acted as sun-blinds. It was used for linings at Ingatestone in 1600 and in the Bacon accounts in 1588 it appears as sultige, at 6d. a yard.

STUFF. The *Oxford English Dictionary* defines it as any woven material, but referring more particularly to a woollen fabric. The phrase 'Norwich stuffs' refers to worsteds with or without the addition of silk, made as part of the New Draperies, and includes the many varieties of camlets, calamancoes, shalloons, tobines, etc. At Gosfield Hall in Essex in 1638 there were many yards of 'Stripte stuff' used for bed hangings, wall hangings and curtains, and in a trunk there were '60 peces of stripte stuff of light colours, some for hanging, others for window curtains and a paire of vallance of the same'. It would seem that this stuff is likely to have been one of the forms of camlet. In 1692 Joseph Clarke of Roxwell was selling seventy yards of stuff at 9d. a yard. The items in the inventory of the Rev. Richard Day in 1818: 'Stuff window curtains', and 'yellow stuff bed hangings', can only mean plain woollen fabric.

SURBASE. A border of moulding immediately above the base or lower panelling of a wainscoted room. Also a chair rail.

TEAR. The best fibres of hemp, which can be spun and woven into sheeting of excellent quality. These are sometimes called 'hemp tear' or 'tear' or 'tearinge' sheets.

TICKING. A linen twill, often woven in herring-bone pattern, strong and, before the manufacture of down-proof fabric, the most impervious to feathers. It was used in a number of ways: for aprons, corsets and gaiters, but its more general use was, and is, as a covering for pillows, bolsters, feather-beds and mattresses. When used this way it was known as a tick. In 1520 'a fetherbedde tick' cost 6s. 8d., and in 1573 nine yards of 'tike for a fetherbedde' cost 37s.

TISSUE. A rich, expensive fabric used when something showy and eye-catching was required. Often woven with either gold or silver threads, it was used for rich clothes as well as royal bed hangings and church furnishings. A draper's bill of 1538 lists crimson tissue at £3 a yard.

TOW. These are flax and hemp fibres which have been discarded. Tow could be spun and woven; it made soft but coarse sheeting. 'Towen sheets' are found in many inventories.

TWILL. A type of weave which produces a diagonal line in the fabric. In each row of weft a different series of warp threads are covered, which can be 2 × 1, (over two threads and under one), 3 × 1, 2 × 2 or any other permutation, but each row starts one thread further on, to produce the diagonal line.

UNION. Fabric made with a mixture of fibres, one of them being cotton. The most usual combination is cotton and linen, but the word can also refer to cotton/wool or cotton/silk.

VELVET. A rich, pile fabric, generally of silk but sometimes of cotton or wool. It was made in many weights, from fine for dress to heavy for upholstery. In Europe, Italy originally made the best velvets and they were often called by the name of the town which made them: Lukes velvet (from Lucca), or Genoese velvet. The latter had a design with pile and a flat ground, and was much used for rich bed hangings as well as upholstered furniture, while Utrecht velvet was one of the hardest-wearing, made from linen with goat hair pile and used for stout upholstery. A draper's bill of 1538 suggests that velvet from Lucca at 15s., 15s. 6d. or 16s. 6d. per yard was of finer quality than 'velvet' at 11s., 12s., 13s. or 13s. 4d. per yard.

VERMILION. Generally accepted to be a cotton cloth made in Manchester and dyed red, but the 1654 inventory of Ham House has, in Mrs Henderson's chamber and closet, 'Hangings, bed, window carpets, all in white vermilion all wrought in colours'. Peter Thornton considers this vermilion to be a type of worsted cloth. A book dated 1641, describing the cotton industry in Manchester, classes vermilion with fustian and dimity.

WADMAL. A coarse woollen cloth, used to line horse-collars and for rough types of clothing.

WARP. The strong, hard-twisted threads which are fastened lengthwise in the loom and form the basis of the fabric.

WEFT. The threads which cross from selvage to selvage in a fabric, interlacing with the warp.

WORSTED. Long-staple wool; also the fabric made from it which is fine, smooth and generally patterned.

WROUGHT. A word much used in inventories, and often seen on samplers, meaning worked, in the sense of embroidered.

LIST OF NATIONAL TRUST
PROPERTIES MENTIONED

Anglesey Abbey, Lode, Cambridge CB5 9EJ
Arlington Court, Arlington, Nr Barnstaple, Devon EX31 4LP
Basildon Park, Lower Basildon, Reading, Berkshire RG8 9NR
Belton House, Grantham, Lincolnshire NG32 2LS
Beningborough Hall, Shipton-by-Beningborough, Yorkshire YO6 1DD
Blickling Hall, Blickling, Norwich, Norfolk NR11 6NF
Canons Ashby House, Canons Ashby, Daventry, Northamptonshire NN11 6SD
Castle Coole, Enniskillen, Co. Fermanagh, Northern Ireland.
Clandon Park, West Clandon, Guildford, Surrey GU4 7RQ
Claydon House, Middle Claydon, nr Buckingham, Buckinghamshire MK18 2EY
Cotehele, St Dominic, nr Saltash, Devon PL12 6TA
Cragside House, Rothbury, Morpeth, Northumberland NE65 7PX
Dunham Massey, Altrincham, Cheshire WA14 4SJ
Dunster Castle, Dunster, nr Minehead, Somerset TA24 6SL
Dyrham Park, Chippenham, Wiltshire SN14 8ER
Erddig, nr Wrexham, Clwyd LL13 0YT
Felbrigg Hall, Felbrigg, Norwich NR11 8PR
Fenton House, Windmill Hill, Hampstead, London NW3 6RT
Ham House, Ham, Richmond, Surrey TW10 7RS
Hardwick Hall, Doe Lea, Chesterfield, Derbyshire S44 5QJ
Ickworth, The Rotunda, Horringer, Bury St Edmunds, Suffolk IP29 5QE
Kingston Lacy House, Wimborne Minster, Dorset BH21 4EA
Knole, Sevenoaks, Kent TN15 0RP
Lanhydrock, Bodmin, Cornwall PL30 5AD
Montacute House, Montacute, Somerset TA15 6XP
Osterley Park, Isleworth, London TW10 7RS
Oxburgh Hall, Oxburgh, nr King's Lynn, Norfolk PE33 9PS
Packwood House, Lapworth, Solihull, West Midlands B94 6AT
Peckover House, North Brink, Wisbech, Cambridgeshire PE13 1JR
Petworth House, Petworth, West Sussex GU28 0AE
Polesden Lacey, nr Dorking, Surrey RH5 6BD
Saltram, Plympton, Plymouth, Devon PL7 3UH

Shugborough, Milford, nr Stafford, Staffordshire ST17 0XB
Smallhythe Place, Smallhythe, Tenterden, Kent TN30 7NG
Standen, East Grinstead, West Sussex RH19 4NE
Tatton Park, Knutsford, Cheshire WA16 6QN
Uppark, South Harting, Petersfield, Hampshire GU31 5QR
Upton House, nr Banbury, Oxfordshire OX15 6HT
Waddesdon Manor, Waddesdon, nr Aylesbury, Bucks HP18 0JH
Wallington, Cambo, Morpeth, Northumberland NE61 4AR
Wightwick Manor, Wightwick Bank, Wolverhampton, Salop WV6 8EE
Wimpole Hall, Arrington, Royston, Hertfordshire SG8 0BW

BIBLIOGRAPHY

ACCOUNTS

1. Bacon, Nathaniel, MS Steward's Account 1587–97. Computer index and analysis, Centre for East Anglian Studies, University of East Anglia, with financial assistance from Economic and Social Research Council. Raynham Hall Box 33, Nathaniel Bacon Papers.
2. The Household Book of Lady Grisell Baillie, 1692–1733, ed. Robert Scott-Moncrieff, WS, Edinburgh, 1911
3. *The Household Account book of Sarah Fell of Swarthmoor Hall,* Cambridge University Press, 1920

Historical Manuscripts Commission

4. —— Ancaster
5. —— Bath
6. —— Hastings
7. —— de L'Isle and Dudley
8. —— Le Fleming
9. —— Middleton
10. —— Ormonde
11. —— Rutland
12. *Selections from the Household Books of the Lord William Howard of Naworth Castle,* Surtees Society, 1878
13. 'Household and Privy Purse Accounts of the L'Estranges of Hunstanton from AD 1519 to AD 1578', *Archaeologia,* Vol. XXV, 1834
14. 'Expense Book of James Master', ed. Canon Scott-Robertson, *Archaeologia Cantiana,* Vols. XV, XVL, XVIII, 1883, 1886, 1889
15. 'Extracts from "The Booke of the Howshold Charges and other Paiments laid out by the L. North and his commandement; beginning the first day of January 1575 and the 18 yere of Queen Elizabeth"', ed. Wm Stevenson, *Archaeologia,* Vol. XIX, 1819
16. *Strawberry Hill Accounts, Kept by Horace Walpole, 1747 to 1795,* ed. Paget Toynbee, Clarendon Press, 1927

GENERAL

17. Adburgham, Alison, *Liberty's: A Biography of a Shop*, George Allen and Unwin, 1973

18. Agius, Pauline, *Ackermann's Regency Furniture and Interiors*, Crowood Press, 1984

19. Arnold, Janet, 'Jane Lambarde's Mantle', *Costume* 14, 1980

20. Aspin, Chris, *The Cotton Industry*, Shire Publications, 1981

21. ——*The Woollen Industry*, Shire Publications, 1982

22. Aspinall-Oglander, C., *Admiral's Wife*, Longmans Green, 1940

23. —— *Admiral's Widow*, The Hogarth Press, 1942.

24. Ayres, James, *The Shell Book of the Home in Britain*, Faber and Faber, 1981

25. Baines, Patricia, *Flax and Linen*, Shire Publications, 1985

26. Baker, Collins and M. I., *The Life and Circumstances of James Brydges, 1st Duke of Chandos*, Oxford, 1949

27. Beck, S. William, *The Draper's Dictionary*, London, 1882

28. Beer, Alice Baldwin, *Trade Goods, A Story of Indian Chintz*, Smithsonian Museum Press, 1970

29. Benson, Anna F., *Textile Machines*, Shire Publications, 1983

30. Campbell, R., *The London Tradesman* (1747), David and Charles Reprints, 1969

31. Catling, Harold, *The Spinning Mule*, David and Charles, 1970

32. Chippendale, Thomas, *The Gentleman and Cabinet-Maker's Director*, reprint of third (1762) edition, Dover Publications, 1966

33. Clark, Hazel, *Textile Printing*, Shire Publications, 1985

34. Cornforth, J. and Fowler, J., *English Decoration in the Eighteenth Century*, Barrie and Jenkins, 1974

35. The Crystal Palace Exhibition, illustrated catalogue, 1851. An unabridged re-publication of the *Art Journal* special issue, Dover Publications, 1970

36. Davidson, Caroline, *The World of Mary Ellen Best*, Chatto and Windus, The Hogarth Press, 1985

37. Deloney, Thomas, 'The most pleasant and delectable history of John Winchcombe, otherwise called Jack of Newbury', *Elizabethan Fiction*, eds. R. Ashley and E. M. Moseley, Holt, Rinehart and Winston, 1953

38. Denvir, Bernard, *The Eighteenth Century. Art, Design and Society, 1689–1789*, Longmans, 1983

39. ——*The Early Nineteenth Century. Art, Design and Society, 1789–1852*, Longmans, 1984

DIARIES,
LETTERS AND JOURNALS

40. *The Ames Correspondence – Letters to Mary, 1837–47*, ed. J. A. Robinson, Norfolk Record Society, 1962

41. 'The Papers of Nathaniel Bacon of Stiffkey', eds. A. Hassell Smith, Gillian Baker and R. W. Kenny, Centre of East Anglian Studies, University of East Anglia, 1979

42. *The Blecheley Diary of the Rev. William Cole, 1765–7*, ed. F. G. Stokes, Constable, 1931

43. *Blundell's Diary and Letter Book, 1702–28*, ed. Margaret Blundell, Liverpool at the University Press, 1952

44. *The Diary of the Lady Anne Clifford, 1619–20*, William Heinemann, 1923

45. *The Letters and Journals of Lady Mary Coke*, Bath Kingsmead Reprints, 1970

46. *The Autobiography and Correspondence of Mary Granville, Mrs Delany*, ed. Lady Llanover, Richard Bentley, 1861

47. Edgeworth, Maria, *Letters from England, 1813–44*, ed. Christine Colvin, Oxford, 1971

48. *The Journeys of Celia Fiennes*, ed. C. Morris, Cresset Press, 1947

49. *The Journal of Mary Frampton, 1779–1846*, ed. Harriot Georgianna Mundy, 1885

50. 'Extracts from the Journal of Walter Gale, Schoolmaster at Mayfield, 1750', ed. R. W. Blencowe, *Sussex Archaeological Collection*, Vol. IX

51. Letter from Gillows of Lancaster to Thomas Leigh of Stow Hall, 1790, Norfolk Record Office, Hare 223X6 5552

52. Letter from Haig and Chippendale to Mr Andrews at Lord Walsingham's, Merton, 1786, Norfolk Record Office, WLS/L/9/427x2

53. *Reminiscences of a Gentlewoman of the last century. Letters of Catherine Hutton*, ed. Mrs Hutton-Beale, Cornish Bros, 1891

54. *The Lisle Letters* (abridged), ed. M. St Clare Byrne, Penguin Books, 1985

55. *Letters of a Grandmother, 1732–5. Being the correspondence of Sarah, Duchess of Marlborough with her grand-daughter Diana, Duchess of Bedford*, ed. Gladys Scott Thompson, Jonathan Cape, 1943

56. *John Norton & Sons, Merchants of London and Virginia*, ed. F. W. Mason, David and Charles, 1968

57. *Court and Private Life in the Time of Queen Charlotte: The Journals of Mrs Papendiek*, ed. Mrs Delves-Broughton, Richard Bentley and Son, 1887

58. *The Diary of Samuel Pepys*, ed. R. Latham and W. Matthew, Bell and Hyman, 1969–83

59. *Passages from the Diaries of Mrs Philip Lybbe Powys of Hardwick Hall, Oxon, 1756–1808*, ed. Emily J. Climenson, Longmans Green, 1899

60. *The Purefoy Letters, 1735–53*, ed. G. Eland, Sidgwick and Jackson, 1931

61. *A Foreign View of England in the Reigns of George I and George II. The Letters Home of M. César de Saussure*, John Murray, 1902
62. *Shardeloes Papers of the Seventeenth and Eighteenth Centuries*, ed. G. Eland, Oxford University Press, 1947
63. Southey, Robert, *Letters from England, 1807*, ed. J. Simmons, Alan Sutton Publishing, 1984
64. 'Stonor Letters and Papers', *Camden Miscellany*, Vol. XIII, 1924
65. *Lady Mary Wortley Montagu. Letters*, J. M. Dent, 1906

GENERAL (cont'd)

66. Dubois, M. J., *Curtain and Draperies*, trans. V. M. Macdonald, Batsford, 1967
67. Dutton, R., *The Victorian House*, Bracken Books, 1954
68. Early, R., *Master Weaver*, Routledge and Kegan Paul
69. Eastlake, Charles L., *Hints on Household Taste* (fourth ed., 1878, Longmans Green), republished by Dover Publications, 1969
70. Emmison, F. G., *Elizabethan Life: Home, Work and Land*, Essex Record Office, 1976
71. *English Furniture Upholstery, 1660–1840* (catalogue), ed. Karin-M. Walton, 1973
72. Evans, Nesta, *The East Anglian Linen Industry*, Gower, The Pasold Research Fund, 1985
73. Evelyn, Mary, *Mundus Muliebris or The Ladies Dressing-Room Unlock'd* (1690), ed. J. L. Nevinson, The Costume Society, 1977
74. Fairclough, O. and Leary, E., *Textiles by William Morris & Co., 1861–1910*, Thames and Hudson, 1981
75. Floud, P. and Morris, B., 'English Chintz', *CIBA Review*, Vol. I, 1961
76. Foskett, Daphne, *John Harden of Brathay Hall, 1772–1847*, Abbots Hall Art Gallery, 1974
77. Foster, Sir William, *John Company*, John Lane, The Bodley Head, 1926
78. —— *East India House*, John Lane, The Bodley Head
79. Gaskell, Elizabeth, *Cranford, A Tale*, J. M. Dent, 1900
80. Gilbert, Christopher, *Furniture at Temple Newsom House and Lotherton Hall*, National Art-Collections Fund and Leeds Art Collection Fund, 1978
81. Girouard, Mark, *Life in the English Country House*, Yale University Press, 1978
82. Grieg, John, *Diaries of a Duchess*, 1928
83. Hare, Augustus, *The Story of my Life*, George Allen, 1896
84. Harries, John, *Pugin*, Shire Publications, 1973
85. Harrison, William, *The Description of England, 1577*, ed. George Edelen, published for the Folger Shakespeare Library by Cornell University Press, 1968

86. Haweis, Mrs, *The Art of Decoration*, London, 1881

87. Heal, Sir Ambrose, *The London Furniture Makers*, Dover Publications, 1972

88. Hefford, Wendy, 'Bread, Brushes and Brooms', A paper read to the Tapestry Symposium, San Francisco, 1976

89. *Home Book: A Domestic Encyclopaedia*, Ward and Lock, nd

90. *Household Furniture and Interior Decoration Executed from Designs by Thomas Hope, 1807*, Dover Publications, 1971

91. Horner, J., *The Linen Trade of Europe*, McCaw, Stevenson and Orr, 1920

92. Hudson, W. I. and Tingey, J. C., eds., *The Records of the City of Norwich*, Jarrolds, 1906

INVENTORIES

93. Stephen Atkins, 1588, Norfolk Record Office, 4/168

94. Margery Balles, 1588, Norfolk Record Office, 4/73

95. Katherine Billingford, 1587, Norfolk Record Office, 4/28

96. Blickling Hall, 1793, Norfolk Record Office, Ref. MC 3/338 477x8

97. John Borel, 1514, Norfolk Record Office, NCC Wills, 125 Coppinger

98. Mansion and Hall at Castle Rising, Norfolk Record Office, How 495

99. *Arthur Coke of Bramfield, 1629*, Francis Steer, Suffolk Institute of Archaeology

100. Revd. Richard Day, 1818, Norfolk Record Office, INV 10/78

101. 'Anne, Viscountess Dorchester, 1639', Francis Steer, *Notes and Queries*, March, April, September, October, November, December, 1953

102. Richard, 3rd Earl of Dorset, 1619, in 'The Rich Wearing Apparel of Richard, 3rd Earl of Dorset', P. and A. Mactaggart, *Costume* 14, 1980

103. Sir Anthony Drury of Besthorpe, 1638, in Wymondham Inventories, Centre of East Anglian Studies, University of East Anglia

104. 'Edmund Dudley, 1509', *Archaeologia* Vol. LXXI, 1921

105. Dyrham House, 1703, Gloucester Record Office, 1799/E254

106. 'Sir William and Sir Thomas Fairfax, 1594 and 1624', *Archaeologia*, Vol. XLVIII, Part I, 1882

107. *Farm and Cottage Inventories of Mid-Essex 1635–1749*, Phillimore, 1969

108. 'Sir John Fastolfe, 1459', ed. Thomas Amyot, *Archaeologia*, Vol. XXI, 1825

109. Felbrigg Hall, 1771, Norfolk Record Office, WKC 6/463

110. 'Thomas of Gloucester', ed. Viscount Dillon and W. H. St J. Hope, *Archaeological Journal*, Vol. LIV, 1897

111. 'The Furnishing and Decorating of Ham House', Peter Thornton and Maurice Tomlin, *Furniture History* Vol. XVI, 1980

112. *The Hardwick Hall Inventories of 1601*, ed. Lindsay Boynton, Furniture History Society, 1971

113. *The History and Antiquities of Hengrave in Suffolk*, John Gage, 1822

114. 'The effects of Henry Howard, KG, Earl of Northampton, taken on his death in 1614', ed. E. P. Shirley, *Archaeologia,* Vol. XLII, 1869

115. 'Notes on the Collections formed by Thomas Howard, Earl of Arundel and Surrey, 1641', Lionel Cust, *Burlington Magazine,* Parts II and IV, 1911

116. 'The Goods of Dame Agnes Hungerford, attainted of murder 14Hen.VIII', *Archaeologia,* Vol. XXXVIII, 1859

117. Sir John Jernagham of Costessey, Norfolk Record Office, Jerningham Papers 55x3 (124)

118. 'View of the Wardrobe Stuff of Katharine of Aragon, 1535', *Camden Miscellany,* Vol. III, 1855

119. Kenilworth Castle, 1583, Historical Manuscripts Commission, de L'Isle and Dudley

120. Kilkenny Castle, 1684, Historical Manuscripts Commission, Ormonde

121. 'Leeds Castle', *Archaeologia Cantiana,* Vol. XV

122. Thomas Leman, 1534, Norfolk Record Office, NCC 30–42, Platfoots

123. William Money, Norfolk Record Office, Norwich, Arch. Inv. ANW/23/26/35

124. 'Will, Inventories and Funeral Expenses of James Montagu, Bishop of Winchester, 1618', ed. E. P. Shirley, *Archaeologia,* Vol. XLIV, Part II, 1862

125. 'Robert Morton, 1486–8', *Journal of the British Archaeological Association,* Vol. XXXIII, 1878

126. Margaret Peper, Norfolk Record Office, NCC 40–42, Robinson

127. *Probate Inventories and Manorial Excerpts,* ed. R. Machin, University of Bristol, 1976

128. Robert Raby, 1593, Norfolk Record Office, 10/384

129. 'Sir Thomas Ramsay, 1577', ed. F. W. Fairholt, *Archaeologia,* Vol. XL, Part II, 1862

130. 'George, Earl of Shrewsbury, at Sheffield Castle, 1582', *Journal of the British Archaeological Association,* Vol. XXX, 1875

131. John Skelton, 1611, Norfolk Record Office, 24/348

132. Sir J. Smyth, Bt, ed. J. S. Moore, *The Goods and Chattels of our Forefathers,* Phillimore, 1976

133. 'Standen Lordship, A Great Country House in 1623', Ambrose Heal, *Burlington Magazine,* May 1943

134. Stow Hall, 1627, Norfolk Record Office, Hare 223 x 6 5540

135. Stow Hall, 1709, Norfolk Record Office, Hare 223 x 6 5542

136. Stow Hall, 1721, Norfolk Record Office, Hare 223 x 6 5542

137. Stow Hall, sale catalogue, 1831, Norfolk Record Office, Hare 223 x 6 5562

138. 'Wills and Inventories of Suffolk', ed. S. Tymms, *Camden Society,* Vol. XLIX, 1850

139. John Sylver, 1603, Norfolk Record Office, 19/76

140. John West, 'Two Elizabethan Inventories', ed. L. G. Bolinbroke, *Norfolk Archaeology,* Vol. XV, 1904

141. Sir Roger Wodehouse, 'Two Elizabethan Inventories', ed. L. G. Bolinbroke, *Norfolk Archaeology*, Vol. XV, 1904

142. Lord Walsingham of Merton, 1785, Norfolk Record Office, WLS/L/8/427x2

143. Wollaton New Hall, 1550 and 1609, Historical Manuscripts Commission, Middleton

144. 'Worcester House, 1643', *Archaeologia*, Vol. XCI

145. 'Charles Wyndham of Stokesby', 1688, ed. Revd. J. Bulwer, *Norfolk Archaeology*, Vol. V

146. 'John de Veer, 13th Earl of Oxford, 1513', *Archaeologia*, Vol. LXVL, 1915

GENERAL (cont'd)

147. Irwin, J. and Brett, K. B., *Origins of Chintz*, HMSO, 1970

148. —— and Hall, M., *Indian Painted and Printed Fabrics*, Calico Museum of Textiles, Ahmedabad, 1970

149. —— and Schwartz, P. R., *Studies in Indo-European Textile History*, Calico Museum of Textiles, Ahmedabad, 1966

150. Jacobs, Bertram, *Axminster Carpets, 1755–1957*, F. Lewis, 1970

151. Jarry, M., *The Carpets of the 'Manufacture de la Savonnerie'*, F. Lewis, 1966

152. Jourdain, M., *English Interior Decoration, 1500–1830*, Batsford, 1950

153. Lasdun, Susan, *Making Victorians: The Drummond Children's World, 1827–32*, Victor Gollancz, 1983

154. —— *Victorians at Home*, Weidenfeld and Nicolson 1981

155. Leadbetter, Eliza, *Spinning and Spinning Wheels*, Shire Publications, 1979

156. Linthicum, M. Channing, *Costume in the Drama of Shakespeare and His Contempories*, Clarendon Press, 1936

157. Loudon, J. C., *An Encyclopaedia of Cottage, Farm and Villa Architecture and Furniture*, London, 1833

158. Markham, Sarah, *John Loveday of Caversham, 1711–1789*, Michael Dussell, 1984

159. Mauchline, Mary, *Harewood House*, David and Charles, 1974

160. Mayorcas, M. J., *English Needlework Carpets*, F. Lewis, 1963

161. Montgomery, Florence M., *Textiles in America 1650–1870*, W. W. Norton, 1983

162. —— *John Holker's Mid-Eighteenth-Century 'Livres d'Echantillons'*, Royal Ontario Museum, 1977

163. —— *Printed Textiles, 1700–1850*, Thames and Hudson, 1970

164. Naylor, G., *Arts and Crafts Movement*, Studio Vista, 1971

165. Newman, Aubrey, *The Stanhopes of Chevening*, Macmillan, 1969

166. North, Roger, *The Lives of the Norths* (ed. A. Jessopp, 1890), ed. Gregg, International Publishers, 1972

167. Origo, Iris, *The Merchant of Prato*, Penguin Books, 1963

168. Panton, J. E., *Nooks and Corners*, Ward and Downey, 1889

169. Parry, Linda, *William Morris Textiles*, Weidenfeld and Nicolson, 1983

170. Peel, Mrs C. S., *The Stream of Time*, John Lane, The Bodley Head, 1931

171. Percival, MacIver, *The Chintz Book*, Frederick A. Stokes, nd

172. Plummer, Alfred and Early, Richard, *The Blanket Makers, 1669–1969*, Routledge and Kegan Paul, 1969

173. Praz, Mario, *Interior Decoration*, Thames and Hudson, 1964

174. Riley, Noel, (ed.) *World Furniture*, Octopus, 1980

175. Robinson, George, *Carpets*, Pitman, 1966

176. Robinson, Stuart, *A History of Printed Textiles*, Studio Vista, 1969

177. La Roche, Sophie von, *Sophie in London, 1786*, Cape, 1933

178. Rosenstiel, Helene von, *American Rugs and Carpets*, Barrie and Jackson, 1978

179. Saint-Aubin, C. G. de, *L'Art du Brodeur, 1770*. trans. Nikki Schuer, Los Angeles County Museum of Art and David R. Godric, 1983

180. Sheraton, Thomas, *The Cabinet-Maker and Upholsterer's Drawing Book, 1793–1802*, Dover, 1972

181. Sperling, Diana, *Mrs Hurst Dancing, and other Scenes from Regency Life, 1812–23*, Victor Gollancz, 1981

182. Spufford, H. M., *The Great Reclothing of Rural England*, Hambledon Press, 1984

183. Standen, Edith A., 'English Washing Furnitures', *Bulletin*, Vol. XXIII, Metropolitan Museum of Art, 1964.

184. Stow, John, *The Survey of London*, Dent, 1912

185. Swain, M., *The Needlework of Mary, Queen of Scots*, Van Nostrand Reinhold Company, 1973

186. Tattersell, C. and Reed, S., *A History of British Carpets*, 1966

187. Thomson, Gladys Scott, *The Russells in Bloomsbury 1669–1771*, Jonathan Cape, 1940

188. Thornton, Peter, *Seventeenth-Century Decoration in England, France and Holland*, published for the Paul Mellon Centre for Studies in British Art by the Yale University Press, 1978

189. —— *Authentic Decor*, Weidenfeld and Nicolson, 1985

190. Troubridge, Laura, *Life among the Troubridges*, ed. Hope-Nicholson, John Murray, 1966

191. Walton, Karin-M., 'Upholstery from 1660–1900', *World Furniture* (cf. no. 174)

192. Waterson, Merlin, *The Servants' Hall*, Routledge and Kegan Paul, 1980

193. Webster, T., *Encyclopaedia of Domestic Economy*, Longman Brown Green and Longmans, 1847

194. Winchester, Barbara, *Tudor Family Portrait*, Jonathan Cape, 1955

195. Wood, J. A., *Description of Bath*, 1765

196. *Workwoman's Guide* (second ed, 1840), reprinted and restored by Bloomfield Books and Publications, 1975

197. Wright, L., *Warm and Snug*, Routledge, 1962

INDEX

References to illustrations are in bold type